Abduction

Definition: The unlawful carrying away
of a person.

What the men said in their defence:

Hank Shoeman: "Mistaken identity."
Burr Covington: "I was just doing my job."
Rafer Starr: "It wasn't safe for her to be
out alone."

Are these men guilty?

Seduction

Definition: The act of tempting into sin.

What the women said in their defence:

Poppy O'Neal: "He was gorgeous!"
Lindsey Major: "His slow Southern drawl
left me breathless."
Hayley Harper: "Men are stronger, so we have
to rely on our feminine wiles."

Now who is guilty?

DIANA PALMER

got her start in writing as a newspaper reporter and published her first romance novel for Silhouette Books in 1982. In 1993, she celebrated the publication of her fiftieth novel for Silhouette Books. She is listed as one of the top ten romance authors in the U.S.A. Beloved by fans worldwide, Diana Palmer is the winner of many awards.

JOAN JOHNSTON

is the bestselling author of over twenty historical and contemporary romances, whose books continually top bestseller lists. Joan started reading romances to escape the stress of being an attorney with a major national firm, and soon discovered that writing romances was a lot more fun than writing legal bond indentures. In addition to being an author, Joan is the mother of two children.

REBECCA BRANDEWYNE

is a bestselling author of historical novels. Her stories consistently place her on the bestseller lists, including the *New York Times* and *Publishers Weekly*. This is her first contemporary romance and her first novella for Silhouette.

Abduction & SEDUCTION

Diana Palmer
Joan Johnston
Rebecca Brandewyne

SILHOUETTE

*All the characters in this book have no existence outside the imagination
of the author, and have no relation whatsoever to anyone bearing the
same name or names. They are not even distantly inspired by any
individual known or unknown to the author, and all the incidents are pure
invention.*

*All rights reserved including the right of reproduction in whole or in part
in any form. This edition is published by arrangement with Harlequin
Enterprises II B.V. The text of this publication or any part thereof may not
be reproduced or transmitted in any form or by any means, electronic or
mechanical, including photocopying, recording, storage in an
information retrieval system, or otherwise, without the written permission
of the publisher.*

*This book is sold subject to the condition that it shall not, by way of trade
or otherwise, be lent, resold, hired out or otherwise circulated without the
prior consent of the publisher in any form of binding or cover other than
that in which it is published and without a similar condition including this
condition being imposed on the subsequent purchaser.*

*First published in Great Britain 1996
by Silhouette Books, Eton House, 18-24 Paradise Road,
Richmond, Surrey TW9 1SR*

Abduction and Seduction © Harlequin Enterprises II B.V. 1995

The publisher acknowledges the copyright holders
of the individual works as follows:

Redbird © Diana Palmer 1995
The Bluest Eyes in Texas © Joan Mertens Johnston 1995
The Bounty © Rebecca Brandewyne 1995

*Silhouette and Colophon are Trade Marks of
Harlequin Enterprises II B.V.*

ISBN 0 373 48286 8

69-9605

*Printed in Great Britain by
BPC Paperbacks Ltd*

CONTENTS

CONTENTS

REDBIRD
Diana
Palmer

Chapter One

She was there again. Hank Shoeman glared out the window at the figure on the balcony of the ski lodge below. His cabin was on a ridge overlooking the facility, just far enough away to give him the privacy he needed when he was composing. But it wasn't far enough away from the binoculars the slender young woman at the ski lodge was directing toward his living room window.

He shoved his hands into his jeans pockets and glowered at the distant figure. He was used to attention. Leader of the rock group Desperado, and a former linebacker for the Dallas Cowboys, Hank had had his share of adulation from women. In the old days, before his marriage and divorce, it had been flattering and heady to a Texas ranch boy. Now, it was nothing more than a nuisance. He'd had all he wanted of love. And he'd had more than he wanted of star-struck young girls looking for it.

He sighed, the action pulling his silk shirt taut over a hard, impressively muscular chest, and tautening the jeans that outlined powerful long legs and narrow hips. He was thirty-eight, but physically he looked no more than thirty. He had a good body, still fit and athletic. It was his face that frightened people.

He wore a thick beard and a mustache and his dark hair, while scrupulously clean, was unruly and thick around his collar. He wasn't bad-looking, but it was impossible to see that. He liked the camouflage, because it kept all but the most enthusiastic young groupies at bay.

None of the rock group looked much better than Hank with his growth of beard, except for Amanda, of course. The other three male members of the band—Deke and Jack and Johnson—looked as disreputable as Hank did. But Desperado's music won awards, and they were much in demand for public appearances.

The problem with that right now was that Amanda was pregnant. It would be the first child for Amanda and her husband, Quinn Sutton, who lived in Wyoming with his son Elliot. The whole family was anxious because Amanda's pregnancy had been fraught with problems and she'd been forced to take to her bed to prevent a miscarriage. That meant canceled public appearances and vicious rumors that the band was about to break up. It was let people think that, or admit that Amanda was in fierce difficulties with her pregnancy. No one wanted that tidbit of information to get out, and have reporters hounding her. For the moment, they didn't know exactly where in Wyoming she lived. And Hank was here in Colorado, far away from the group's studios—both the one down the hill from Quinn Sutton's ranch in the Tetons, and the one in New York City.

Reporters had hounded him so much that he'd had to escape from the New York studio where the group did some of their recording. It had been impossible to go near Amanda's house, for fear of leading reporters right to her doorstep.

So, this cabin in Colorado was Hank's last resort. He'd come here to work on a new song which he hoped might be a contender for another award. The music had been written, now it was up to Hank to complete the lyrics, but it was slow going. Worrying about Amanda and the future of the group was not conducive to creative effort.

Perhaps he was working too hard, he thought. He needed a break. That woman at the ski lodge was getting on his nerves. If she was a reporter spying on him, he wanted to know it. There had to be some way to get her off his trail and spare Amanda any further media blitz.

He shrugged into his parka and drove to the ski lodge in his white Bronco. The chains made a metallic rhythm on the thick-packed snow covering the road that led to the lodge. Bad weather had plagued the area this January, and there had just been a long period of subzero temperatures and blinding snow, which had made it impossible to ski for the past several days.

When he got to the lodge, it wasn't crowded at all. People who could get out had already gone. Only a handful of hearty, optimistic souls were left in residence, hoping for slightly less arctic temperatures and better skiing when conditions improved.

He walked into the lodge, towering over everyone and attracting a lot of unwanted attention. He went straight to the owner's office.

Mark Jennings got up from his desk and walked around it to shake hands with the visitor.

"What brings you down here, Hank?" he asked with a grin. "Lonesome, are you?"

"I should be so lucky," Hank murmured dryly. "I came down to see which one of your guests is auditioning for the KGB."

Mark's smile faded. "What?"

"You've got a guest with binoculars who spends a lot of time looking in through my living room window," he replied. "I want to know who she is and what she's looking for."

Mark whistled. "I had no idea."

"It's not your job to watch the guests," the other man said, clapping him on the shoulder with a big hand. "Maybe she's a groupie. I'd like to know, in case she's trying to gather material for the wire services. I've had enough publicity just lately."

"I understand. What can I do to help?"

"I thought I'd hang out in the café for a while and see if she turns up for lunch. I'd recognize her. She's wearing a bright blue parka and a matching cap."

Mark frowned. "Doesn't sound familiar, but I don't get out of this office much lately. We don't have a lot of people staying here, though, so she shouldn't be too hard to spot."

"If you don't mind, I'll have a look around."

Mark nodded. "Help yourself. Any chance that you and the group might sign on next season for entertainment?" he added hopefully.

Hank chuckled. "Ask me again in a few months."

"Don't think I won't!"

Hank shook hands with him and went on into the café, shucking his parka as he walked. It was a bad time to have to hunt down a spy. He was already upset enough about Amanda and the relentless press. Lately his career was playing a bad second to complications of every sort.

He glanced around as he walked into the small café. There were only three women in it. Two of them were drinking coffee at a table overlooking the ski lift. The other was clearing tables. She saw Hank and grinned.

"Hi, Hank," she greeted him, tossing back her blond hair. "Long time no see!"

"I've been busy, Carol," he said with an affectionate smile. She'd been a waitress at Mark's place for several years. There was nothing romantic between them; she was just a friend.

She moved closer, so that they wouldn't be overheard. "Better watch your step down here today," she said confidentially. "One of the women at the side table is a reporter for *Rolling Stone.* I heard her telling the other woman that she'd gotten some juicy gossip about Amanda and that you were in hiding up here. She said she was going to file a really big story with her magazine over her computer modem tonight."

He caught his breath in muted anger and stared at the table intently. One of the women was very petite with short dark hair. The other was a redhead, attractive and full figured. He scowled. "Which is which?" he asked impatiently.

She grimaced. "That's the thing, I couldn't tell. I dropped a plate and I wasn't looking at them when I overheard her. Sorry, Hank. You know most of their reporters, don't you?"

He nodded. "But I don't recognize either of those women. She could be a stringer or even a free-lancer, hoping to find something worth selling to them on a tentative go-ahead."

"I'll bet it's the redhead," she whispered. "She looks like a reporter."

"And I'd bet on the brunette," he remarked as he suddenly registered the color of her jacket. Royal blue. She was the one who'd been spying on him with the binoculars.

"Could be," Carol replied. "I wish I could be more help. Heard from the rest of the group?"

He shook his head. "We're all taking a rest from public appearances."

"I guess you need one! Give everyone my best, won't you?"

"Sure."

He watched the women from the next room, staying out of sight for a minute, before leaving the lodge. He was easily recognizable these days, with all the media attention, and he couldn't afford to give that reporter a shot at him.

He was going to have to do something, but what? If she filed that story, reporters were going to swarm Amanda like ducks on bugs. He couldn't have that. Her pregnancy had been one big secret so far, ever since she started to show and the band cut short their tour. They were still recording, but no one knew why they'd left the road so quickly. Where Amanda was, on Quinn Sutton's ranch, no one was likely to be able to get near her. Quinn was a formidable bodyguard, and he loved his pretty blond wife to distraction even if they'd gotten off to one of the world's worst starts.

He leaned against the hood of the Bronco, ignoring the sudden snow flurries and folded his arms over his chest while he tried to decide on a course of action. How was he going to prevent the reporter from filing her story? All sorts of wild ideas occurred to him, the first being that he could cut the telephone wires.

"Great solution," he murmured to himself. "You should try writing fiction."

As he turned over possible solutions to his problem, lo and behold, the brunette came walking out the front door of the ski lodge with a camera and binoculars around her neck and a backpack over one shoulder. She came down the steps and started around the Bronco and Hank when the perfect solution presented itself to him on a silver platter.

Without thinking about consequences, jail terms or FBI intervention, he suddenly walked behind her, picked her up bodily and slid her into the Bronco past the steering wheel. Before she could get over the shock, he had the vehicle headed up the mountain.

Poppy O'Brien stared at him with wide dark eyes full of shock. "Either I'm still asleep and dreaming or I'm being kidnapped by a grizzly bear," she said suddenly.

"I'm not a grizzly bear."

"You look like a grizzly bear."

He didn't look at her. "Insults won't do you any good."

"Listen, I have terrible diseases . . ." she began, using a ploy she'd heard on a television talk show.

"Don't flatter yourself," he remarked with a speaking glance. "I don't seduce midgets."

"Midgets?" Her dark eyes widened. "I'm five foot five!"

He shrugged. "Okay. So you're a tall midget. You're still too small for a man my size."

She looked at him fully then. His head almost touched the roof of the Bronco. He was huge; not fat, but well built and powerful looking. "Are you one of those wild-eyed mountain men who kidnap hikers?"

He shook his head.

"Hopelessly lonely and desperate for companionship?"

He smiled reluctantly. "Not a chance."

"Then would you like to tell me why you've kidnapped me?"

"No."

She leaned back against the seat. He looked sane, but one could never tell. She studied him with curiosity and just a little apprehension. "What are you going to do with me?" she asked again.

"I don't know."

"That's reassuring."

"I won't hurt you."

"That's even more reassuring." She frowned as she studied him. "You look familiar."

"Everyone says that."

"Have you ever worn a wide-brimmed hat and asked people not to start forest fires?"

He did chuckle then. "Not lately."

"I'm on my way to look for a lost dog. I promised."

"He'll come home."

She glared at him. "After I've found the dog, I have to pack. I'm leaving tomorrow," she informed him.

"Fat chance."

She took in a sharp breath. "Now you listen here, Tarzan of the Snow Country, what you're doing is a federal offense. You could be arrested. You could go to jail."

"Why?"

"Because you're kidnapping me!"

"I'm doing no such thing," he returned, pulling up into the driveway of the cabin. "I'm extending my hospitality to a ski lodge guest who was lost in the mountains."

"I am not lost!" she stormed. "I was at the ski lodge, right in front of the ski lodge . . . !"

"You looked lost to me. It's snowing. Very hard, too," he remarked as he got out of the truck. In fact, it was worse than snow. It looked like the beginnings of a blizzard. "Come on. Let's get inside."

She folded her arms. "I am not leaving the truck," she informed him bluntly.

"It isn't a truck. It's a four-wheel-drive vehicle."

She lifted her chin. "Oh, details, details! I am not . . . ohh!"

In the middle of her impassioned resistance, he picked her up and carried her to the cabin.

She was too shocked to resist. She'd been independent most of her life, and at twenty-six she was used to being on her own. She was attractive, and she knew it, but she was also intelligent and studious, traits that didn't endear her to suitors. Her choice of career had made it impossible for her to carry on any sort of affair. She'd spent years in school with midterms and final exams always hanging over her head, with lab after lab eating up her free time. The only people she spent time with were fellow students. The curriculum required for a science degree was so much more difficult than that required for a liberal arts degree that it often seemed she did nothing but study.

And then after graduation, there was the apprenticeship, and that required all sorts of odd hours that none of the other partners wanted. She was the one who spent weekends and holidays and nights at work. Two boyfriends had quickly given her up for women who had nine-to-five day jobs and were geared to nights on the town.

None of that had prepared her for being swept off her feet, literally, by a blue-eyed grizzly bear.

The sheer power and size of his body had her as spellbound as a young girl. She lay in his huge arms like a statue, gaping up at him as he balanced her easily on one knee while he unlocked the cabin door.

He caught that rapt stare and laughed mirthlessly. He was used to the look. His ex-wife had found him fascinating at first. Afterward, it was his best friend and the man's bank account that fascinated her. The divorce was inevitable, with all the time Hank spent on the road. His best friend had probably been inevitable, too. Hank was powerful and talented, but he wasn't handsome. His best friend was. He'd given in to the divorce without a protest, and the parting had been amicable—on the surface, at least. He'd settled a nice amount of money on her. She was grateful. He was alone, as usual. He'd gone home afterward to the Texas ranch that his father and five brothers still owned. It had been comforting there, but he never had fit in. The only horse big enough for him to ride was a Percheron and he'd never been able to spin a rope. He often thought that his brothers despaired of him.

He put the woman down and closed the door, locking it and pocketing the key. Then he took a good, long look at her. She was attractive, pert and pretty and a little irritated. Her dark eyes glared up at him fearlessly.

"You can't keep me here," she informed him.

"Why not?"

"Because I have responsibilities. I have a job. I need a telephone right now, as a matter of fact, so that I can tell someone I'm not looking for that dog."

"Dream on," he said pleasantly. "Can you cook?"

Her eyebrows lifted. "Cook what?"

"Anything."

He was stripping off his parka as he spoke. Her eyes drifted over a magnificent body in jeans and a well-fitting, long-sleeved red shirt. He could have graced a magazine cover. He was perfectly proportioned and huge. He made her feel like a child as he towered over her.

"I can cook toast," she said absently. "How tall are you?"

"Six foot five," he said.

"You must eat like a horse."

He shrugged. "I use up a lot of calories."

She was still staring at him, fascinated. "Who are you?"

He laughed without humor and his blue eyes began to glitter. "Pull the other one."

"I beg your pardon?"

"You might as well get comfortable," he informed her. "You're going to be here for several days."

"I am not. I'll walk back to the lodge."

"Not in that you won't," he said, gesturing toward the window, where snow was coming down outside at a frightening rate.

She gnawed on her lower lip, a nervous habit that often resulted in a sore mouth. "Oh dear," she said uneasily, more worried about the possibility of losing her job than of being sequestered here with a madman.

"You'll be perfectly safe here," he said, mistaking her apprehension. "I won't attack you."

"Oh dear, oh dear," she repeated again. "They'll think I'm having too good a time to come back. They'll think I'm not serious about my job. They didn't really want me in the beginning because they thought I was too young. They'll use this as an excuse to find someone to replace me.''

"No doubt," he said irritably. "But what does it matter? You'll find another job."

She glared at him. "Not like this one, I won't!"

"Pays good, does it?" he asked, thinking that reporters always seemed to get a high rate of pay for selling out people's private lives for public consumption.

"Very good," she retorted, "with excellent chances for advancement."

"Too bad."

"You have no right to keep me here," she informed him.

"You had no right to spy on me," he returned.

Her face stiffened. "I beg your pardon?"

"You've had those damned binoculars trained up here for the past few days," he said shortly. "Spying on me."

"Spying…and why, pray tell, would I want to spy on you? Do you think I'm so desperate for a man that I have to peek through windows to get a glimpse of one?"

"You don't need to play games with me," he said coolly. "I'm not likely to be taken in by you. I'm an old hand at fending off groupies."

"This is unreal," she snapped. "Things like this don't happen except in books and movies! Men don't go around kidnapping women unless it's a desert and they're wearing long sheets!"

"Sorry," he said. "I didn't have a sheet handy."

"And what do you mean, calling me a groupie?" She put her hands on her slim hips and glowered up at him with flashing dark eyes.

"Why were you spying on me?"

"Spying...!" She threw up her hands. "I was watching a bald eagle," she said shortly. "They've just released a pair of them ten miles north of the ski lodge, as part of a federal repopulation program. I'd come to see them."

"Oh, my God, tell me you're not one of those animal-loving fanatics!"

"If there were more of us in the world, it wouldn't be in such a mess."

He looked angry as he studied her. "They tried repopulating wolves up north. The damned things are eating lambs and calves all over the mountains, and the people who released them went back home to their apartment buildings."

He said it with such sarcasm and contempt that she almost took a step backward. But she was made of sterner stuff. "Nature exists largely on a system of checks and balances. You've overlooked the fact that without predators, prey multiplies. If you don't believe that, look at Australia where the rabbits hadn't enough natural enemies and overran the country."

"Well then, why don't we ship them some of our leftover wolves?" he asked smugly.

"Show me a wolf who can survive in the desert and it might be a good idea."

"You hotshot animal lovers might consider crossbreeding a wolf with a camel. I hear they're doing some fantastic genetic experiments in labs all over the country."

"To produce healthier animals and disease-resistant strains of plants."

"Hybrids," he scoffed. "Hybrids are sterile, aren't they?"

"I don't deal in experiments," she informed him hotly. "I wouldn't know."

"They turned loose two eagles. Isn't that an experiment?"

She was losing ground. "Why have you brought me here?" She tried again for an answer.

"I'm a lonely man," he said sarcastically. "I don't have any company up here, and I can't get girls. So periodically, I stake out the ski lodge and appropriate their overflow." He lifted an expressive hand. "Think of it as repopulating my bachelor environment with healthy new specimens. That should appeal to someone like you. And think of all the juicy material you can use later."

"Material? Use? For what?"

"Cut it out," he said carelessly. "We both know what you do for a living. I heard it all from Carol at the lodge."

"Carol? Oh, the blond waitress." She sighed. "Well, I guess it doesn't matter if you know, does it? I mean, I wasn't exactly hiding it from anyone."

"Just as I thought. Now. How about something to eat?" He indicated the window. "It's highly doubtful that you could go anywhere right now even if I was willing to let you leave. Which I'm not."

She pursed her full lips and stared up at him curiously. "When the snow clears, I'm heading out," she informed him sweetly. "Or you'll find yourself in jail the minute I can get to a telephone."

"Threats are only useful when you can enforce them."

"And you think I can't?"

"I think that by the time you leave, you won't need any." He was hopeful that he could convince her not to bother Amanda. He was persuasive when he tried to be, and if she liked animals, she had to have a soft center. Knowing the enemy was half the battle. He didn't think he was in for any surprises with her.

Chapter Two

"What's your name?" he asked as he fried bacon.

"Poppy O'Brien," she replied. "And yours?"

He chuckled. She was a game player, all right. "Call me Hank."

"Hank what?"

He glanced toward her with an insolent smile. "Just Hank," he said with faint challenge.

She joined him in the kitchen. "Have it your way. I suppose if I'd kidnapped someone I wouldn't want to give them my real name, either." She started opening cabinets.

"What are you doing?" he demanded. It irritated him that she felt free to rifle through his kitchen.

"I'm going to make biscuits. Unless you think you can."

"I can make biscuits," he said defensively.

"A lot of people can. But can you eat them?" she asked.

He hesitated. After a minute, he paused in his own chore and produced vegetable shortening, flour, milk and a big bowl. "Go for it."

She rolled up the sleeves of her blue sweater and proceeded to make drop biscuits. He'd finished with the bacon and was working on beating eggs in a bowl.

"They'll be cold by the time the biscuits get done if you cook them now," she said pointedly.

He didn't argue. He finished beating the eggs, covered the bowl and put them in the refrigerator. Then he perched himself on the edge of the big table and watched her pat the biscuits into a pan and dab milk onto the tops.

"You do that as if it's a regular thing with you," he commented.

"It is," she said. "I've been feeding myself for a long time. Eating out is expensive. I cook a lot."

"Do you cook for someone?" he probed.

She smiled as she put the biscuits into the oven she'd already had him preheat. "Yes. For myself."

He stuck his hands into his pockets and stared her down.

She lifted a shoulder. "I don't have time for that sort of thing," she said. "I work nights and week-ends and holidays. Before I got this job, I was in school."

High school, he figured, by the look of her. She seemed very young. She wasn't hard on the eyes at all, with that trim figure and her big dark eyes and soft oval face. She had a vulnerable manner that appealed to his masculinity. His wife had been a take-charge sort of woman, very businesslike and intelligent, but with hard edges that he could never smooth. She liked being a real estate executive and she had no thoughts of being a housewife and mother. She didn't like children. She did enjoy pretty clothes and parties, though. His best friend was taking her to a lot of those, he heard.

Poppy glanced at him and saw the expression that narrowed his deep blue eyes. "Do you have someone to cook for?" she asked bluntly. If he could ask questions, so could she.

"I was married," he said flatly. "She took up with my best friend and divorced me. I wasn't home enough to suit her."

"I'm sorry."

"Don't be. It was a friendly divorce. We weren't compatible." He looked down at his hand-tooled leather boots. "I wanted kids. I have a bunch of brothers back home."

She leaned back against the pine counter and folded her arms across her chest. "I don't have any family left. My mother died when I was born and my father was killed in an airplane crash four years ago."

"Are you an only child?"

She nodded. "It's a good thing I was goal-oriented and self-sufficient, I guess," she confessed. "I threw myself into studying and got over it in time."

"How did you manage to support yourself while you got through high school?" he asked curiously.

"High school?" Her eyes widened. "I was in college." She laughed. "How old do you think I am?"

"Eighteen. Maybe nineteen."

She grinned. "Thanks. I'm twenty-six."

His heavy brows drew together. "Hell!"

"I am. I have a degree."

"In what—"

The thunderous, crashing sound outside cut him off. He rushed to the window and looked out. Snow had come off the mountain above the lodge in a small avalanche, taking down telephone lines and power lines.

"Good thing Mark's got emergency generators," he murmured. "So have I. But those telephone lines are well and truly out until this weather clears a little."

"Do you have a phone?" she asked from beside him.

He looked at her. "No. I've been using the phone at the lodge. I hate telephones. Unlisted numbers are a farce—there's no such thing. You ought to know that."

She wondered how he did know that her private line was flooded with calls from people at two in the morning whose problems couldn't wait until the office opened.

She laughed. "Well, yes, I do know."

He glanced back out the window. "The lodge is okay, at least. I met a guy in the ski patrol this morning when I went out for supplies. He said they'd checked the slopes earlier and there was no threat. I wonder what caused the avalanche?"

"People skiing outside the safe boundary, a gunshot from an irresponsible hunter, God knows." She grimaced. "I hope that poor dog got found."

"Marshmallow heart," he accused. "The only dog I know of around here is a stray who hangs around the lodge for handouts. He belongs to a retired Austrian skier who lives about a half mile over the hill. That dog knows these mountains better than any human being, and he doesn't get lost. Somebody was pulling your leg." One eye narrowed. "Who sent you out?"

She frowned. "It was one of the younger ski instructors, the one they call Eric. He said that he'd start from the other end of the trail and we'd meet in the middle at some little cabin..." She stopped. "Why are you laughing?"

"Eric Bayer," he said, nodding. "They call him St. Bernard, because he's pulled that lost-dog stunt so many times with pretty young tourists. That cabin is almost a shrine to his prowess as a lover."

She flushed to her hairline. He watched, smiling.

"Where do you come from?" he asked lazily.

"Sioux City, Iowa," she said. "Why?"

"It figures." He moved back into the kitchen just in time to remove the biscuits before they burned. They looked light and fluffy and they were just tanned enough to be tempting. "Nice," he pronounced.

"Thanks." She got butter from the refrigerator while he scrambled the eggs. She made coffee and when the eggs were ready, she poured it into two thick mugs and put them on the small, square kitchen table.

"Forks," he said, handing her one. "I don't fuss with table settings when I'm alone here."

"Ah," she said. "So you're not usually alone?"

"Only when I'm working." He raised his fork and took a mouthful of scrambled egg. "And you should know," he added mockingly, "because *Rolling Stone* prints something about every visit I make here."

Her eyebrows arched. "Rolling Stone? They're a rock group, aren't they? I thought they were in England. Do they have a newsletter?"

"You do that amazingly well," he remarked.

"Do what?"

"The innocent look," he replied, finishing his eggs before he started on the biscuits. "I wish I had some jam. I ate the last of it yesterday and forgot to get more."

"Too bad. What was that about looking innocent?"

"Eat your lunch before it gets cold. These are great biscuits!"

They must have been, he was on his fourth one. She smiled. "Breakfast for lunch," she remarked. "I can't wait to see what you eat for the evening meal."

"Cereal, usually," he remarked. "Or sandwiches. I don't cook much when I'm working. If I get a yen for breakfast in the middle of the day, I have it," he added firmly.

She smiled. "I wasn't complaining. I love breakfast."

Her easy acceptance of the odd meal put him at ease. He finished eating and sat back with the coffee mug in one huge hand and looked at her. She was small. Not tiny, but small, and beautifully proportioned. He liked her soft complexion and those big brown eyes. She had a pretty mouth, too, very full and sweet-looking.

"I feel I should tell you that I know karate."

His eyebrows lifted. "Do you, really?"

She nodded.

He smiled lazily. "Do you really think it would do you any good against someone my size?" he asked gently.

She looked him over. "You ruined it."

"Ruined what?"

"I was going to tell you that I knew karate and several *other* Japanese words."

It took a minute to sink in. When it did, he began to laugh.

She smiled, too. "And to answer that, no, I don't think it would do me a bit of good against someone your size. Even if I knew how to use it." She finished her coffee and put the mug down. "Why did you think I was spying on you?"

"You kept looking in my living room window."

"The eagle was sitting on the top limb of one of those aspen trees behind your house."

He let out a soft whistle. "There really was an eagle?"

"Two of them," she amended. "Beautiful eagles. They're huge birds. I'd never seen any up close before. I thought they were small, but they aren't, and they have pale golden eyes."

"I've seen eagles," he replied. "I spend a lot of time here and in Wyoming."

"I'd love to see Wyoming," she remarked. "I've always wanted to go to Cheyenne during the rodeo season."

"Don't you animal lovers consider rodeo a cruel sport?" he taunted.

"I'm not a fanatic," she said pointedly. "And I know better than some people how well treated most rodeo stock is. My dad used to handle bulls for the bull-riding events, back in Oklahoma."

"I thought you said you were from Sioux City."

"I live there now. I grew up outside Oklahoma City." She touched the rim of the coffee cup. "Where are you from?"

She was laying it on thick, but he was too tired to question her. He'd been up late for the better part of a week trying to write lyrics that just wouldn't come. "I'm from Texas, up near Dallas."

"Around the cross-timbers country?" She smiled at his surprise. "I've been through there a time or two with Dad, when he went to rodeos."

"It's pretty country. So is this."

The portable generator made a noise and he glared toward the back of the house. "Damn that thing," he muttered. "I knew I should have replaced it. If it goes out, we'll freeze and starve to death in here."

"Hardly," she said. "There's plenty of cut wood out front and you have a fireplace. I know how to cook on a fireplace."

"Good thing," he muttered. "I sure as hell don't."

"I gather that there's no way out of here except down the mountain we just came up?"

He nodded.

She looked out at the blinding snow and rubbed her arms. "You still haven't told me why you brought me up here."

"Does it matter now?" he asked. "You can't leave, anyway. From the looks of that snow, we're going to be cabin-bound for a few days until they can get the snowplows in."

"Well, yes, I think it does matter," she replied. "After all, nobody's ever tried to kidnap me before. I'd like to know what I've done."

"Why do you insist on playing games with me?" he muttered. "I know who you are!"

"Yes, you've already said so."

"Then you know what you've done," he said. "You threatened to call in a story that would damage several careers and possibly cost a woman her child."

"Call in a story." She repeated it again, staring blankly at him. "Call it in to whom? And how would

I, since the only things I know how to fill out are medical reports?''

"Medical reports?"

She glowered at him. "Yes, medical reports, prescriptions, medicines, that sort of thing. I have a degree. I'm in practice. That's why I need to be back home, before I lose the partnership I've worked so hard to get!"

"You're a doctor?" he bellowed.

"Yes. Dr. O'Brien!"

He slapped his hand over his forehead. "Oh, God, I got the wrong one!"

"Wrong one. Am I to gather that you meant to kidnap some other poor woman?"

"Yes!" he said impatiently. He ran his hand through his bushy, thick hair. "Damn! Damn, damn, damn, she's probably halfway to New York by now with a heaving bosom full of unsubstantiated facts!"

"She, who?" Poppy demanded.

"That damn reporter!"

"The girl I was sitting with when you came in? But she isn't due to leave for two more days. She's meeting her fiancé in Salt Lake City and then they're going on to Los Angeles."

"She is?"

"That's what she said."

He leaned forward. "This is important. Did she say anything to you about Amanda Sutton?"

"I don't remember any names," she said. "She was talking about a singer who'd vanished from sight and the breakup of a big rock group."

"Which rock group?" he asked.

She grimaced. "Sorry," she said apologetically. "I don't keep up with pop music. I like classical and opera."

He stared at her, long and hard.

"You needn't look like that," she muttered, sweeping back the fall of hair that dropped onto her brow. "There isn't one thing wrong with symphonies and opera!"

"I didn't know that anyone in the world still listened to them." From his perspective, rock music was all that existed. He spent all his time with people who composed it or played it.

"I see," she returned. "You're one of those MTV fanatics who think that music without a volcanic beat isn't worth listening to."

"I didn't say that."

"I am so *tired* of skeletal men in sprayed-on leather pants wearing guitars for jockey shorts, with their hairy chests hanging out!"

He couldn't hold back the laughter. It overflowed like the avalanche that had brought half a ridge down a few minutes before. "You're priceless."

"Well, aren't you tired of it, really?" she persisted. "Don't you think that there's a place in the world for historical music, beautiful music?"

He sobered quickly. He didn't know how to answer that. It had been a long time since he'd listened to anything classical, and he'd certainly never thought of it in that way. "Historical music?" he asked.

"Yes." She began to smile. "It's like talking to someone who lived a century, two centuries ago. You play the notes they wrote and hear them, just as they heard them. History comes alive in that moment, when you reproduce sounds that were heard in another time."

His heart leapt in his chest. He thought about the history she'd mentioned. Then her wording came back to him.

"You said you play the notes... do you play?"

"Piano," she said. "A little. I only had lessons for five years, and I'm not gifted. But I do love music."

His face softened under its thick covering of hair. "But not rock music," he persisted.

"So much of it is noise," she said. "After you listen to it for a while, it all blurs into steel guitars. But, once in a while, another sort of song sticks its head out and a few people find magic in it." She mentioned one of his songs, one of Desperado's songs. "There were a lot of flutes in it," she recalled, closing her eyes and smiling as she remembered it. "Beyond it was a high, sweet voice that enunciated every word. And the words were poetry." Her eyes opened, dark and soft with memory. "It was exceptional. But it wasn't their usual sort of music, either. The announcer said so. He said the composer did the song on a dare and didn't even want it included on the album, but the other members of the group insisted."

That was true. Hank had been certain that no one would like the soft, folksy song he'd written. And to his amazement, it had won a Grammy. He'd let Amanda accept it for him, he recalled, because he was too embarrassed to take credit for it publicly. "Did you see the video?"

She shook her head. "I've never had time to watch videos. I just listen to the radio when I'm driving."

Incredible. She loved his music and she didn't even know who he was. He wasn't sure if he was insulted or amused. It was the only song of that sort that he'd ever written and he'd sworn that he'd never do another one. A lot of the music critics hadn't liked it. He was trying to break out of the mold and they didn't want to let him. It was a kind of musical typecasting.

"Do you remember the group the reporter was talking about?" he asked, returning to his earlier question.

"She told me, but I was watching the eagle out the window," she confessed sheepishly, and with a grin. "I'm afraid I wasn't listening. She was alone and wanted to talk, and I was the only other person handy when she came in. She was friendly and I didn't mind sharing the table. It was just that the eagle came pretty close to the window..."

"You really do like animals." He chuckled.

"I guess so. I was forever bringing home birds with broken wings and once I found a little snake with its tail cut off by a lawnmower. I couldn't stand to watch things suffer and not try to help."

His blue eyes searched her dark ones for longer than he meant to. She stared back, and he saw the color flood her cheeks. That amused him deep inside and he began to smile.

Poppy felt her heart race. He didn't seem to be dangerous or a threat to her in any physical way, but that smile made her feel warm all over. She hadn't been at a disadvantage, except when he'd carried her inside the cabin. Now she wondered if she shouldn't have fought a little harder for her freedom. He was very big and powerful, and if he wanted to, he could...

"You're amazingly easy to read," he remarked gently. "There's nothing to be nervous about. I don't force women. It's the other way around."

She didn't quite believe him. He had a fantastic physique, but he looked like a grizzly bear. She couldn't imagine him being beset by women.

"Are you rich?" she asked.

His eyes narrowed and the smile faded. "Meaning that I'd have to be rich to attract a woman?" he drawled with muted anger.

He hadn't moved or threatened, but the look in his eyes made her uncomfortable. "I didn't say that."

"Yes, you did."

"I didn't mean to insult you. It's just that you're, well, you're . . . bushy."

His lips compressed. "Bushy?"

"You look like a grizzly bear!"

"A lot of men wear beards and mustaches!"

"Most of them have some skin on their faces that shows, too!"

He moved away from the window and took a step toward her. She took a step back.

"There's no need to start stalking me," she protested, looking him right in the eye. She stopped. "I won't run. You can't make me run. I'm not afraid of you."

She acted like a woman confronting an attack dog. It would have amused him if he'd been a little less insulted.

"I haven't had to chase women in ten years," he said through his teeth, and kept coming. "They chase me. They hound me. I can't even check into a hotel without having someone search the room. I could have a woman twice a day if I felt like it, and I wouldn't have to pay them for it. I turn down more proposals in a week than you've probably had in your lifetime. But you think I look like a grizzly bear and no woman would want me unless I was rich."

She held up a hand, nervous of him now. "I didn't say that at all," she began soothingly. She came up against something hard, and realized that he'd edged her back against a wall. "Now, see here," she said firmly, "this isn't any way to win an argument, with sheer brute force."

"Isn't that what you think I'd need to get a woman?"

"I didn't mean it," she assured him. She tried to edge past him, but he put an arm that was like a small tree trunk past her on one side and another on the other side and trapped her.

"What makes you think you're qualified to judge?" he continued irritably. "You're almost thin. There's nothing to you. You act as if you've spent your life buried in books. What do you know about men?"

"I date," she said shortly. "In fact, I can go out anytime I like!" And she could, with one of her partner's sons, who seemed to have six hands and used every one of them the time she'd been crazy enough to go to a movie with him. He'd have taken her out again if she liked, but she wouldn't go to the front door with him!

"How much do you have to pay him?" he mocked.

When that sank in, she drew in an angry breath, forgot her embarrassment and fear and raised her hand sharply toward his hairy cheek.

He caught it with depressing ease and pressed it against the side of his face. The hair that grew on it was surprisingly soft, when it looked like steel wool.

"You don't know much about men's egos, do you?" he asked, bending. "If you don't learn one other thing, you'd better learn right now that insults have consequences. And I'm just the man to show you how many!"

She started to defend herself, and before she could get a single word out, his lips had opened and fitted themselves exactly to the shape of her soft, shocked mouth.

Chapter Three

It hadn't occurred to her that a human grizzly bear would be so good at kissing. He wasn't clumsy or brutal. He was slow and almost tender. Even the huge hands that slid around her waist and brought her lazily against him were all but comforting.

He nibbled at her upper lip where it clung stubbornly to her lower one. "It won't hurt," he breathed softly. "Give in."

"I won't..."

The parting of her lips gave him the advantage he'd been looking for. He eased them open under his with a pressure that was so slow and arousing that she stood, stunned, in his embrace.

He towered over her. At close range, he was even larger than he'd seemed at first. His big hands spread over her back, almost covering both her shoulder blades, and he smiled against her shocked gasp. His teeth gently worried her lower lip while his tongue trailed over it, and she thought dizzily that she'd never known such an experienced caress from the few, the *very* few, men she'd dated.

He felt her stiffen and lifted his head. The blue eyes that searched her dark ones were wise and perceptive. His hand came up and traced the soft color that overlaid one high cheekbone.

"You taste of coffee," he murmured.

It was beginning to dawn on her that he might not be lying about his success with women. And she didn't think it was because he was rich. Not anymore.

He didn't see fear in her face, or experience. He saw a charming lack of it. His big thumb smoothed over her lips and her body seemed to leap into his at the sensation he produced.

"Nothing to say, Poppy?" he asked.

She shook her head, her eyes unblinking as they sought his for reassurance.

"You're perfectly safe," he replied, answering the look. "I'm not a rake, even if I do fit the picture of a kidnapper. But I had noble motives."

"You're . . . very big, aren't you?" she faltered.

"Compared to you," he agreed. His eyes narrowed as he studied her. She did look very small in his arms. He looked down to her breasts, pressed against his shirt. She barely came up to his chin and she had a fragile build. If he made love to her, it would be touch and go, because she was so much smaller. He scowled.

"What's wrong?" she asked curiously.

He met her eyes. "I was thinking about how careful I'd have to be with you in bed," he said absently.

She flushed and pushed at him. "You'd be lucky!" she raged.

He smiled at her ruffled fury and let her go. "Wouldn't I, though?" he agreed lazily. Her red face told him things she wouldn't. "You're very delicately built. I've deliberately limited myself to tall, buxom women because I'm so big. Do you know, I can't even let myself get into fistfights unless I can find another man my size?"

She studied him, under the spell of a hateful attraction. Her heart was still racing. His shirt was open at the neck and there was a dark, thick nest of hair in it. She wondered what he looked like under his clothes and could have choked on her own curiosity.

"You never told me what you do," she said, diverting her eyes to his face.

"I used to play professional football," he volunteered.

She frowned, searching his features. "I'm sorry. I don't watch it. I'm not much of a sports fan."

"It figures. It was a long time ago."

That explained how he could afford this nice cabin in such a luxury area of the state. He'd probably made a fortune in professional sports and saved a lot of it. It would explain the women, too. All at once, it bothered her to think of him with women.

She wrapped her arms over her breasts. "How long will that last, do you think?" she asked, nodding toward the snowstorm.

"A couple of days," he said. "I'll get you back to the lodge as soon as I can, I promise." He sighed heavily, wondering where that reporter was, and if she'd managed to get out. "I fouled this up really good," he muttered. "Poor Amanda. She'll never forgive me if they get to her."

Amanda? She frowned. "Have I missed something?"

"Probably." He turned away. "I'll check on that generator. I don't have a television here, but there's a piano and plenty of books. You ought to be able to amuse yourself."

"Thanks."

He paused as he shouldered into his parka and looked at her. "If you don't get back to your job, they won't really fire you, will they?"

"I don't know." It worried her. She interpreted his expression and smiled ruefully. "Don't worry. I'd be stuck at the lodge anyway, even if you hadn't kidnapped me, wouldn't I?"

That seemed to lessen the guilt she read on his face. "Maybe. Maybe not. I'm sorry. I'll make it up to you, if I can. I should have made sure before I acted."

"What were you going to do with that reporter?" she asked.

"I was going to keep her here until I could warn Amanda," he said. "She's not having an easy time of it and all the wire services are after the story. I thought I was safe here, but they can track you down anywhere."

Amanda must be his girlfriend, because he was trying so hard to protect her from the press. She wondered why. "Is she married?" she asked involuntarily.

"Yes," he said solemnly. "I'll be back in a minute."

So that was it, she thought as he left the cabin. He was in love with a married woman and the newspapers were after him. He must be somebody very famous in sports to attract so much media attention even if he didn't play football anymore. She wished she'd paid more attention to sports. He was probably very famous and she'd go home without even knowing his name. She thought whimsically of selling her story to the tabloids—"I was kidnapped by a football star..." But of course she couldn't do that, because she didn't even know his full name.

She wandered out of the huge living room and down the hall. There were two bedrooms, one with a huge, king-size bed and the other with a normal bed. They were nicely decorated and furnished, and each had its own bathroom. Farther down was a room with all sorts of electronic equipment, including speakers and recorders and wires and microphones, a huge keyboard, an electric guitar and a piano. She stood in the doorway, fascinated.

After a minute, she approached the piano, drawn by the name on it. She knew that name very well; it was the sort of instrument even a minor pianist dreamed of being able to afford. It must be his hobby, playing, and he must be very rich to be able to buy something so astronomically expensive to indulge that hobby on.

Her fingers touched the keys and trembled. It was in perfect tune. She sat down on the bench, remembering when she was a child how she'd dreamed night after night of owning a piano. But there had been no money for that sort of luxury. She'd played on other people's pianos when she was invited, and along the way she'd picked up some instruction. Eventually, when her father died, she was left with a huge insurance policy that she hadn't even wanted; she'd wanted her parent back. But the money had put her through college, bought her a small, inexpensive piano and lessons to go with it. And it had made it possible for her to make her own way in the world. She didn't earn a lot just now, but if she could continue in the partnership—if they didn't fire her—she had prospects.

She put her trembling hands on the keyboard, thinking that if she'd had the opportunity to study as a child, she might have made music her life.

She closed her eyes and began to play the *Moonlight Sonata,* softly at first, and then with more power and pleasure and emotion than she'd ever felt before. This magnificent instrument was all hers to enjoy, and enjoy it she did. When the last chord died into the stillness, she came back to her surroundings with a jolt as she realized that she wasn't alone in the room.

She turned around. Hank was there, leaning against the doorway, something in his eyes that she couldn't grasp. He wasn't smiling. His face was somber and oddly drawn.

"I'm sorry!" she stammered, rising quickly to her feet. "I didn't mean to presume..."

"Why aren't you playing professionally?" he asked surprisingly.

She stared at him blankly. "I chose medicine instead of music."

"A noble choice, but you have a gift. Didn't you know?"

She looked around her, embarrassed. "You play, too, I guess? Is it a hobby?"

He smiled to himself. "You might say that."

"I've never thought of a football player as a musician," she said quietly. "It's . . . surprising."

"Some people think so. I'm too damned big for most hobbies. At least music fits me."

She smiled gently and turned her attention back to the piano. She touched it with loving fingers. "She's lovely, isn't she?" The wonder in her voice was evident. "A real lady."

He was touched and delighted by her unconscious reverence. "That's what I call her," he remarked. "Odd that you'd think the same way, isn't it?"

"I guess a lot of people love music."

"Yes. Even football players."

She laughed self-consciously, because he sounded bitter. "Did that sting? I'm sorry. I didn't mean to sound disparaging. I've never known anybody in sports before. I know a little about baseball, and once I met a minor-league baseball player."

"The thrill of your life?"

"Oh, no, getting my degree was that." She glanced at him uneasily. Some people were immediately hostile when she mentioned her extensive education.

He lifted a bushy eyebrow. "Fitting me for a mold?" he mused. "Will you faint if I tell you that I have a degree of my own?"

Her eyes brightened. "Really?"

"I'm a music major," he said.

"I'll bet that gave the sports announcers something to talk about during games—" She stopped dead. Things she'd read and heard on television, bits and pieces were coming back to her. She didn't follow sports, but there was one sports figure who'd confounded the critics and the fans when he suddenly dropped out of professional football to found of all things a rock group. He'd only had a mustache then, not a full beard and long hair besides. She'd seen his photograph in the paper, and she'd seen an interview on television.

"Oh, my God," she said in a whisper.

"Put it together, did we?" he mused, smiling. "Go ahead."

"Desperado," she said. "You played for the Dallas Cowboys and quit after the best season you'd ever had to go into music. Everybody thought you were crazy. Then you won a Grammy..."

"Several Grammies," he said, correcting her.

"Several. Amanda is your lead singer," she added, remembering that tidbit. "She's beautiful. But... didn't she marry?"

He chuckled. "Yes. She married a poor Wyoming rancher and she's very, very pregnant and Quinn Sutton is beside himself with worry. She's not having an easy time. We're trying to protect her from the press and it hasn't been easy. We're all afraid that word is going to get out about her problems with the pregnancy and she's going to be covered up by the press."

"We?"

"The group," he said. "She's very special to all of us, although she and Quinn are deeply in love."

"Are you in love with her?" she asked bluntly.

"I was, in the old days," he said easily. "We all were. She's beautiful and talented. But now she's kind of like a kid sister that we try to take care of. I'd do anything to protect her. Even," he added ruefully, "kidnap a reporter."

"That would have been terribly intelligent," she said sarcastically. "What a story it would make!"

"I didn't say I was thinking clearly," he muttered darkly. "I had to act fast, before she could file that story. And look what a great job I did!"

"Anybody can make a mistake. But she doesn't know about Amanda, you know," she added. "She knew that you were here and she was going to tell her office that a man at the lodge said you were about to get engaged to someone you met here. *That's* the hot scoop she had."

He leaned back against the door and laughed delightedly. "Good God!"

"So it doesn't really matter if she gets to a phone, does it?"

"No." He groaned and ran a hand through his thick hair. "Hell, I could have saved myself all this trouble!"

"Not to mention saving me a little," she said irritably.

He looked surprised. "I saved you from St. Bernard."

Her lips protruded. "I don't need saving from a man like that. He had lips like a lizard."

He chuckled. "Did he?"

She closed the lid on the piano. "He wasn't my type at all."

He moved closer and raised the lid. "What is your type?" he asked as he ran his elegant fingers over the keyboard.

"I'll know the minute I find him," she assured him.

He lifted his head and looked into her dark eyes. "You don't like rock music, you said."

"I don't listen to it," she confessed. "Except that one song that I told you about."

"Yes. This one."

He sat down at the piano and began to play it, softly, smoothly, his eyes seeking hers.

"It was you," she said slowly.

He nodded. "Amanda sang it. I don't have a lead voice, only one good enough to second the rest of them. But I can write music. None of them can."

She came to stand just behind him, with a soft hand on his shoulder as he increased the tempo.

"I meant it to be a rock song. Amanda made me slow it down. They ganged up on me and made me put it on the album. I didn't want to."

"Why?"

"Because it's intimate," he said shortly. "It's part of me, when I do something like this. There are things I don't want to share with the world."

"You should share music like this, though," she replied. "It's exquisite."

He smiled at her. "But you like opera. And historical music."

Her fingers became unconsciously caressing on his shoulder. "Yes. But this is beautiful."

He finished the piece and lifted his hands from the keyboard. She hadn't moved.

He reached up and smoothed his fingers over her hand before he lifted it to his mouth.

He swiveled around and caught her by the hips, his eyes darkening, narrowing as they looked up at her.

She felt him move before she saw him. He drew her to him and eased her to her knees between his outstretched legs. Then he framed her face in his big hands and bent to kiss her with slow, tender hunger. She started to protest, but he stayed the instinctive backward movement of her head and kept kissing her, until she gave in to him and slid her arms around his neck.

It wasn't until his hand trespassed onto her soft breast that she stiffened and caught his fingers.

He lifted his head and looked at her flushed face as she fought with his invading hand. There was something very calculating about his expression.

"You're . . . analyzing me," she accused.

"You aren't used to a man's hand on your breast," he commented, watching her gasp. "You're twenty-six, right? Then why haven't you had a man, Poppy?"

"For heaven's sake!" She pushed at him and he let her go. She scrambled to her feet, pushing back her hair, and stared unseeing out the window while she fought for composure.

He joined her at the window, leaning idly against the window frame with his big hands in his pockets.

"Are you physically or emotionally scarred in some way?"

She shook her head.

"Then, why?"

She frowned. "What do you mean, why?"

"Why haven't you slept with anyone yet?"

He seemed to think it was a matter of course, that women had the same freedom that men did and should enjoy it.

"Well, I don't respect men who sleep around just because they want to satisfy a fleeting physical hunger. Why should I want to be that way myself?"

He frowned. "Everyone sleeps around."

"Bull," she said, raising her hand when he started to speak. "And don't quote me statistics. Statistics depend on whom you interview. If you ask two hundred people in New York City what they think of a free sexual life-style, and then you ask the same question of two hundred people in a small town in Iowa, you're going to get a heck of a different set of statistics!"

His big shoulders moved. "I hadn't thought about it that way. But the times are changing."

She only smiled.

"Don't tell me," he chided gently. "You're going to save yourself for the man you marry."

"Of course I am," she said matter-of-factly.

He threw up his hands. "Lunacy," he muttered. "You don't know what you're missing."

"Sure I do. I'm missing all those exciting risks, including the one that can kill you." She pursed her lips as she studied him. "And if we're going to get so personal, how much of a swinger are you?"

"I'm not," he replied, shocked. "Only an idiot sleeps around these days!"

She burst out laughing.

He liked the way she laughed, even the way she lost her temper. "Want to draw straws to see who gets to cook supper?"

She traced his face with soft eyes. "I'll do it, if you'll tell me what you like. Not cereal," she added.

"Steak and baked potatoes and salad, then," he said.

"I like steak, too."

"Two of each for me," he added. "I have to get enough protein."

"I'll bet you're expensive to feed," she remarked.

"Yes. But I'm rich," he added with a meaningful glance.

"I take it all back, what I said about buying women for yourself," she told him pertly.

"Oh?"

The expression on his face was only faintly threatening, but she left him with the piano, just the same.

* * *

They shared meals and conversation for two days. He didn't come near her in any sexual way, although she caught his gaze on her. He wasn't feeling well. His skin was flushed and he had a terrible cough. He'd been out working on that generator her first day at the cabin, and he hadn't really been dressed properly for the cold and the vicious snow. He'd caught a cold and it had gone into his chest. She was worried now, because he was obviously feverish and there was no telephone, no way to get him to a hospital. When he went to bed, he refused to take even an aspirin.

She went to bed in the guest room, reluctantly, hoping that he'd be better the next day even when she knew in her gut that he wouldn't.

The third morning, he didn't get up. If only she had access to her supplies back at the clinic in Sioux City, she could have used enough antibiotic to do him some good. As it was, she could only hope that he had a virus or the flu and not pneumonia. If it was a bacterial pneumonia, he could die if help didn't come in time.

She went into his bedroom to check on him, and had to force her legs to carry her the rest of the way. He'd thrashed his way out of the covers and he was lying there totally nude on top of the sheet and blanket. Her embarrassed eyes couldn't leave him. She'd never seen a man in such a condition before. He was beautiful without his clothing, tanned all over, with just enough body hair to make him attractive to the sight and not enough to make him repulsive. It was all on his chest and flat stomach, black and curling hair that ran over his broad chest in a wedge and down over the ripple of powerful muscles to his flat stomach and powerful thighs. Her eyes lingered there with curiosity and fascination and a little fear. She didn't need anyone to tell her that this man was physically exceptional.

He groaned and his eyes opened. He was flushed with fever, his lips dry, his body lifting as he coughed and grimaced from the pain.

"I've picked up that damned bug my band had," he said hoarsely. "Getting chilled working on the generator must have pushed me over the edge." He sat up, realized his condition and with a rueful smile, jerked the sheet over his hips. "Sorry. I must have kicked off the covers. But then, you're a doctor. I don't suppose you're easily shocked by a man's body."

She wasn't about to answer that.

He lay back and coughed again. She moved a little closer, grimacing. "We're going to have a problem if you get worse. Your medicine cabinet is inadequate and I don't have my bag. I don't even have the right medicines or enough of them. The best I'm going to be able to do is mix up a folk remedy for cough and give you aspirin for fever.''

''I don't need nursing,'' he told her.

''Of course not,'' she agreed. ''Oh dear, oh dear.''

He closed his eyes, too weary to talk anymore, and fell asleep. She spent the rest of the day sitting by his bedside in a chair, trying to keep his fever down with aspirin and his cough at bay with a mixture of honey, lemon and whiskey. Amazingly the cough remedy seemed to do some good. But the fever didn't go down, despite the aspirin.

The generator was holding, thank God, so it was warm in the cabin. She had to get that fever down. He did at least have a thermometer, but what it registered was hardly reassuring. A high fever could burn up the very cells of the body. She had to stop it.

She got a basin of warm water and a washcloth and towel. With a deep breath as she gathered her nerve, she turned the covers back.

He lay quietly until she began to bathe him, then he groaned harshly and opened his eyes. ''What are you doing?'' he asked in a weak, raspy tone.

''Trying to get the fever down,'' she said. ''I'm sorry, really I am. But this is the only way I know. The aspirin is only holding it at bay. It's very high. I'll try not to let you get chilled in the process.''

"Stroke of luck, kidnapping you," he said with wan humor. "And they say you can't find a doctor when you need one."

She winced, but his eyes had closed again and he didn't see it. She kept on sponging him down, drying him with the towel as she went and feeling his skin slowly begin to cool.

It wouldn't have been so complicated if his body hadn't started reacting to the motion of the washcloth against areas that were normally hidden to the eyes.

He groaned again when she reached his flat stomach and his eyes opened as his powerful body suddenly reacted helplessly—and visibly—to her touch.

She drew her hand back at once and blushed to the roots of her hair. The terrible thing was that she couldn't drag her eyes away. She was paralyzed by the forbidden sight, fascinated and shocked.

"It's all right, Poppy," he said huskily. "Don't be embarrassed. It's a natural reaction, even if it seems shocking to you."

Her wide eyes sought his for reassurance.

"Go ahead," he said gently. "Don't worry about it. We'll both ignore it. Okay?"

She hesitated for a minute, but as the shock wore off, she began to weigh her embarrassment against his state of health. "Sorry," she said as she continued, working her way down his powerful legs.

"You're a doctor," he murmured, but he was watching her narrowly. "Aren't you?"

"Well, yes. Sort of."

His eyebrows lifted. "Sort of?"

She cleared her throat as she finished sponging him down and gently pulled the cover up to his waist, averting her eyes as she did so. "Yes. I am a doctor. I have a degree and a diploma to prove it. But..."

"But?"

"Well...I'm not exactly the sort of doctor you think I am." She put the basin and cloth on the floor by the bed.

"What sort are you?" he persisted.

She bit her lower lip and looked at him guiltily. "I'm a veterinarian," she confessed.

Chapter Four

"You're a what!"

"Please lie down, and don't get excited," she pleaded, pushing him gently back against the pillows. "And it's all right, really, I did have two years of premed, so I'm not a dunce about human anatomy."

"I don't believe this," he groaned, throwing a big arm across his eyes. "My God, I'm being treated by a vet!"

"I'm a good vet," she muttered. "I haven't lost a patient yet. And you shouldn't complain about being treated by a vet, if you insist on looking like a grizzly bear!"

She got up from the bed and walked out with the basin and cloth and towel, fuming. He acted as if she were guilty of malpractice, and she'd been nursing him all night long!

He must have thought about that, because when she went back into the bedroom, he was more subdued.

"I'm sorry," he said shortly. "It was a shock, that's all. I don't guess you slept all night, did you?"

"I slept in the chair there," she said. "I was nervous about leaving you with such a high fever."

"Thanks."

"I'd have done the same for any sick animal," she replied.

"Rub it in," he said with a wan smile.

She smiled at him. "I'd love to."

He was barely strong enough to glower at her. "What if you catch this stuff?"

"Then I guess you'll have to look after me, if the blizzard doesn't stop," she informed him.

He lifted an eyebrow and let his eyes work their way up and down her slender body with a speaking glance. "I'd get to sponge you down, then, huh?" He smiled wickedly. "What a thrill."

She flushed. "You stop that! I didn't enjoy it!"

"Didn't you? I thought you were familiar with a man's anatomy until I saw that scarlet blush. I wondered if you were going to faint." His blue eyes narrowed. "You haven't seen a naked male like this before, have you?"

She moved restlessly. "I've seen lots of naked male dogs," she said defiantly.

He chuckled, stifling a cough. "It's not quite the same thing."

She could have agreed wholeheartedly with that, but she wasn't going to. She pushed back her hair with a weary hand. "If you'll be all right for a few minutes, I'll heat up some soup."

"You're tired. Why don't we both sleep for a little while, and then you can worry about food."

"Are you sure?"

"I'm sure. I don't feel half as bad as I did last night. Go on. Grab a couple of hours' sleep. I'll wake you if I need you."

"How will I hear you?" she asked worriedly. "The guest room is down the hall...."

"Curl up beside me, if you're concerned about that. It's a big bed."

She wasn't sure, and it showed.

"Don't be silly," he said gently. "I'm too sick to be a threat."

He was. She gave in, smiling shyly as she went around to the other side of the bed and lay down, all too aware of the expanse of his hair-roughened chest, the length of his powerful body. He was really huge this close and she'd never been more aware of her lack of stature. Of course, beside him, a six-foot woman would seem small. She curled up under the covers and stifled a yawn.

"Don't you want to put on something less constraining?" he said. "I won't look."

She smiled. "I'm too tired even to do that. I could sleep for...a week...." Her voice trailed off. She was out like a light.

It was dark when she woke up. A night-light was on and Hank was snoring gently beside her. He'd knocked the covers off again, but it was chilly now. She got up and went around the bed to replace them, pulling them up over his chest and tucking them over him. He looked younger when he was asleep, relaxed and unstressed. She wondered what he was like when he wasn't upset or sick. She'd probably never have the chance to find out, because he was famous and she was a nobody in the veterinary practice back home. It would be something to remember, though, that she'd known someone like him, even briefly. Under normal circumstances, she was certain that they'd never have met at all.

She went into the kitchen and heated some soup. He must be hungry. He was a huge man. He needed nourishment.

She carried the bowl of soup back into the bedroom and put it on the bedside table before she shook him awake.

"Let me take your temperature first, then I'll feed you," she said, sitting beside him on the bed. She put the thermometer under his tongue and he watched her while she timed it. It beeped just as she'd counted off a minute.

"It's down!" she said, delighted.

"Of course it's down, it was only a virus," he muttered.

"How can you be so sure?"

"Damned if I know. I'm not a vet," he said, drawling out the word.

"I still know more about medicine than you do," she said curtly, reaching for the soup.

"The hell you do. I've had more operations and been in more emergency rooms than you'll ever see over the years."

With all sorts of football injuries, no doubt, she thought, but she didn't argue. He was obviously feeling better and spoiling for a fight.

"Eat," she demanded, holding a spoon of chicken noodle soup to his firm lips.

"I hate chicken soup."

"It's made with real chickens," she said coaxingly.

"Prove it."

She put the spoonful back into the bowl and searched until she found a tiny cube and produced it for him to see. "There!"

"Right. A square chicken. A microscopic square chicken."

"You really must feel better," she said pointedly. "You're being very unpleasant."

"I have a reputation for being very unpleasant," he informed her. "Ask the group."

"You're one of them. They wouldn't admit it. They'd lie for you. They wouldn't want your adoring public to know what a bad man you really were."

"Point taken." He laid back against the propped pillows with a sigh. "Okay. Go ahead. Feed me."

She did, liking the power it gave her. She smiled, enjoying herself. She'd never had anyone to take care of, because her father had never been sick. She took care of animals but it really wasn't the same.

He was enjoying her tender ministrations, too, and hating to admit it. "I'll be back on my feet by tomorrow," he said. "So don't get too fond of this routine."

"God forbid," she agreed.

But he let her feed him the entire bowl of soup, and the warm feeling it gave him wasn't just from the temperature of the liquid. Afterward, he stretched and then relaxed with a long sigh. "God, I'm weak. I feel as if I don't have enough strength to get up." He smiled grimly. "But I've got to, for a minute." He threw back the cover, ignoring her flush, and got to his feet. He staggered a little, and she forgot her discomfort in the rush of concern she felt.

She got under his powerful arm and helped support him.

"Thanks," he said, starting toward the bathroom. "I feel like I've been clotheslined."

"I guess you do. I'm sorry you're sick."

His arm tightened. "You'd better be glad of it," he said grimly as he noticed her shyly appreciative eyes on his body. "I like having you look at me like this. I like it too damn much."

She felt pulsing heat run through her body, and quickly averted her eyes. "I'm not looking," she said at once.

"Of course you're looking. You can't help it. I fascinate you, don't I?"

She glared up at him. "I'll find you some shorts."

"I won't wear them," he returned with a cool smile. "I'm not changing the habit of a lifetime to satisfy some prudish animal doctor."

"I am not a prude!"

"Right."

She refused to notice his amused expression. She helped him to the bathroom door, waited until he called her and then helped him back to bed, averting her eyes while she tugged the sheet up to his waist.

He sighed, his chest rattling a little. He propped himself up on the pillows and coughed, reaching for a tissue.

"It's a productive cough, at least," she said to herself. "That's a blessing. And if the fever's dropping, hopefully, it's a viral bronchitis and not pneumonia."

He lifted an eyebrow. "Well, you sound professional enough."

"Medicine is medicine," she said pointedly. "Of course, the anatomical structure is a bit different and the pharmacology certainly is, but ways to treat illnesses are basically the same."

He didn't feel like arguing. He yawned widely. "I'm so tired," he said softly. "So tired. I feel as if I haven't had any rest in years."

"From what you've said, I wonder if you've had any rest at all," she remarked. "Perhaps being stuck up here is a godsend."

"I wouldn't say that," he murmured. "The only good thing about it is that reporter doesn't know about Amanda. God forbid that she should cause trouble. Most of that magazine's reporters are top-notch."

"She doesn't work for a magazine," she recalled. "She said she was trying to sell a story that would get her foot in the door. But she was also on the trail of some sports star who was supposed to be hiding out in the Tetons up in Wyoming."

"A hopeful," he said, relieved.

"She was pretty optimistic. And very ambitious."

He fingered the sheet. "Something you should know about."

"I only want to work in a partnership and not have to do all the rough jobs and odd hours," she said wistfully. "I was lucky to get the partnership at all. There are four of us in the practice, but I'm the junior one. So until I prove myself, I can't really expect much free time."

"It sounds to me as if they're the lucky ones," he muttered. "Are they all men?"

She nodded. "All older than me, too. I'm just out of college and full of new ideas, new theories and treatments and they think I'm a hotshot so they won't listen."

"You probably make them feel threatened," he said pointedly. "And as to who's the lucky one, I think it's the other partners, not you. They're getting all the benefits and none of the unpleasant work."

"I could hardly open my own practice fresh out of school," she began.

"Why not? Plenty of people do!"

"I'm not rich," she said. She went to the window and looked out. The snow was still coming down without a break in sight in the sky. "I barely had enough money in the bank to finish school, and part of it was done on government student loans. I have a lot to pay back. That doesn't leave much over for furnishing an office.''

"I see.''

She shrugged and turned back with a smile. "I don't mind working my way up from the bottom. Everybody has to start somewhere. You did.''

It was a nicely disguised question. He adjusted the pillows and leaned back again. "I started as a second guitarist for a group that got lost at the bottom of the pop charts. Eventually I worked up to helping do backup work for some of the better musicians. That's how I met Amanda Sutton—she was Amanda Corrie Callaway back then,'' he added with a smile. "She and I started working together on a project, along with another guy in the band, and we discovered that Amanda had a voice like an angel. It didn't take us long to put an act together, add a drummer and a second guitarist, and audition for a record company.'' He shook his head remembering. "We made it on the first try. Amazing, that, when some people take years just to get a record company executive to listen to them.''

"Didn't it help that you'd been a football star?''

"Not in music,'' he replied with a rueful smile. "I was a nobody like the rest of the group until our first hit.''

"Why the name Desperado?" she asked.

"You've never seen a group shot of us, I gather?"

She smiled apologetically. "Sorry."

"Look in the top drawer of the desk over there against the wall." He pointed toward it.

She opened it and there was a photograph of four men and a woman.

"Now do you need to ask why?" He chuckled.

"Not really." They were a frightening bunch, the men, all heavily bearded and mustached with unruly hair and they looked really tough. Amanda was a striking contrast, with her long blond hair and dark eyes and beautiful face.

"We've been lucky. Now, of course, we may really have to stop performing. It all depends on how Amanda is doing." He looked briefly worried. "I hope she's all right. I can't even telephone to ask how she is. At least I know Quinn won't let anything happen to her. He's a wild man where Amanda is concerned."

She thought about having someone that concerned for her welfare and wondered how it would feel. Her father had cared about her, but no one else had since he died. She'd been very much alone in the world.

She picked up the soup bowl, but her mind not at all on what she was doing.

He didn't understand the sadness in her face. He reached out and caught her wrist. "What's wrong?" he asked softly.

She shrugged. "I was wondering what it would be like to have someone worry that much about me," she said, and then laughed.

He let go of her wrist. He'd been wondering the same thing. His lean hand smoothed over the bed-cover. "I want a bath. Do you suppose you could run some water for me?"

"You're very weak," she cautioned. "And what if you get chilled?"

"It's warm in here. Come on. I can't stand being grungy."

"Grungy?"

He chuckled. "Maybe there's a better word for it somewhere."

"If you get stuck in the tub, how will I ever get you out?" she asked worriedly, measuring him with her eyes. "Heavens, I couldn't begin to lift you!"

"That's a fact. But I wouldn't risk it if I didn't think I could cope. Humor me."

"All right. But if you drown," she advised, "I'm not taking the rap for it."

She went into the bathroom and filled the tub with warm water. It was a Jacuzzi, luxurious and spotless, and she envied him. Her guest bedroom had a nice shower, which she'd used the night before, but nothing like this. She put soap and lotions and towels close to hand and went to help him out of bed and across the tub.

"It's big," he declared as he lowered himself into it. "Why don't you strip off and come in with me?"

She chuckled, trying not to let her faint, remaining embarrassment show. She'd grown used to the sight of his body, although it still intimidated her a bit. "I might fall and break my leg. Where would we be then?"

He stretched his big arms over the sides. "Just as well, I suppose." He sighed, letting his gaze wash over her like warm water. "You aren't the type, are you?"

"What type?"

"For brief interludes," he said seriously. "You're a forever-after girl, despite the fact that forever-after doesn't exist anymore."

"It could, if two people loved each other enough," she said.

"My wife and I loved each other, when we married," he said. "We thought it would last forever." He smiled cynically. "It lasted for a while, then we burned out."

She chewed on her lower lip and frowned a little. "Oh."

"I learned one thing from it. Marriage requires more than a mutual fever. You need common interests, backgrounds, and you need to be friends as well as lovers. That's trite, but it's true."

"It's a hard combination to find," she said.

"People don't have time to look for it anymore." He picked up the cloth and soap and lathered his arms and chest slowly.

"I'd better go . . ."

"Don't be silly. Sit down."

She perched herself on a chair by the bench that contained a hair blower and electric razor, along with a rack of lotions and powders. She folded her hands together on her jean-clad legs and tried not to look uncomfortable.

"In the old days, people lived in small communities and everyone knew everyone," he said while he bathed. "Now we're all so busy trying to support ourselves that we move around like migrating birds. We don't stay in one place long enough to get to know people."

"Your singer, Amanda. How did she meet her husband?"

He chuckled. "They got snowbound together up in Wyoming," he said. "And he was the ultimate misogynist. He hated Amanda on sight. But she's feisty and she has a kind heart. It was only a matter of time until they fell in love. Unfortunately that happened before he found out who she really was. He went all noble, because he was poor and she was famous. So for her own good, he threw her out. She left and her plane crashed on the way to L.A.''

She caught her breath. ''He must have been devastated.''

''Half out of his mind,'' Hank replied, remembering the band's nightmare trip back to Wyoming. They'd all left on the bus because Hank and the boys didn't like airplanes. But Amanda had insisted on flying. Hank had felt responsible because he hadn't pushed harder to get her to come with them. ''Quinn skied down an unpatrolled ridge into the valley to get her—only a handful of men in the country could have made that run, but he was an Olympic contender in downhill in his younger days. Hell of a trip it was. He found her badly concussed, damn near dead, and he had to have another man ski down to help tow her out of the valley on a litter to a waiting helicopter. There was too much wind for the chopper to land where the crash occurred. As it was, they barely made it in time. Three days after the doctor pronounced her on the mend, they got married, right there in the hospital.''

''My goodness!''

''They'd been married for two years when she got pregnant,'' he recalled. ''They were both over the moon about it, but she's a lot more fragile than she looks. It's been a rough pregnancy and she's had to have constant medical care. We'd more or less given up touring when she first married, but we had one commitment we couldn't break, for a charity in New York. She barely got through it and Quinn put his foot down, hard. He's kept her home since then. He won't even let her do recording sessions now. The rumor is that we're breaking up the group."

"Are you?"

He finished bathing his legs. "I don't know." He looked at her. "The band wouldn't be the same without Amanda. No singer could replace her."

"I don't suppose so," she agreed gently. "But I'm sure the baby is the most important thing to her right now."

He nodded. There was a bitter look on his face that she didn't miss.

"Why didn't your wife want a child?"

He glared at her. "That's none of your business."

He sounded fierce, but she overlooked the bad temper because of the sadness in his blue eyes. "I'm sorry. I didn't mean to pry."

He paused long enough to wash his hair and rinse it before he said anything else. "She said that I wasn't cut out to be a parent," he said shortly. "That I wasn't home enough or patient enough. And besides that, she didn't want a child who might grow up to look like me."

Her eyes lingered on his broad shoulders and chest, on the power and strength of his tanned, hair-roughed skin. "What's wrong with you?" she asked dreamily.

He caught his breath as the surge of desire shot through him like a bolt of lightning.

She saw the tautness of his face and grimaced. "I keep putting my foot in it, don't I?" she said miserably. "Honestly, you make me feel like a babbling adolescent!"

"That isn't how you make me feel," he said with grim humor. "What she meant," he explained, "was that I've got a thick neck and an oversize body and a face that only a mother could love. She said with her luck, she'd have a little girl with a big nose and feet like a duck."

"What a cruel thing to say," she replied, wounded for him. "I expect you'd have a very pretty little girl with blue eyes and brown hair. Except that if you have four brothers, it's a lot more likely that you'd have a little boy."

"So I've heard." He let his narrowed eyes sweep over her. "You're very delicately built," he said quietly. "Slender hips, small breasts, almost a foot shorter than I am. We'd have a hard time just making love, much less having a child together."

She couldn't believe he'd said that. She just looked at him, flustered.

"You know everything there is to know about me, physically." He continued in that same quiet, gentle voice. "But it's one thing to look, and another to consider the problem of intimacy." His eyes narrowed more. "I'll bet you're as small as I am big," he said insinuatingly.

She jumped up from the chair, red faced and shocked. "How dare you!"

"Tell me you haven't thought about how we'd fit together in my bed," he challenged, and he wasn't smiling.

Her fists clenched at her sides. "You can't talk to me like this!"

He searched her outraged eyes with curiosity and faint tenderness. "Another first, hmm?" he mused. "And you're a vet. How did you survive labs?"

"Half the people in my class were women," she informed him. "We forced the men to respect us enough not to make sexist remarks."

"I'm not making sexist remarks," he argued. "I'm indulging in a little sexual logic." He pursed his lips and held her eyes relentlessly. "If I'm very careful, we might try," he said gently.

"Try what?"

"And I can use something. There won't be any risk."

She clenched both fists tighter. "You can stop right there. I'm not sleeping with you!"

He smiled without malice. "You will," he replied. "Eventually."

"I won't be here eventually. The minute the snow lets up and the snowplow clears the roads, I'm getting out of here!"

"I've never been to Sioux City," he remarked conversationally. "But you're an old-fashioned girl, so I guess I'll have to chase you for a while, won't I?"

"You don't need to start thinking that you'll wear me down. You won't. I have no inclination whatsoever, at all, to...to..."

He stood up slowly in the middle of her tirade, turned off the Jacuzzi and stepped out onto the mat. She couldn't take her eyes off him. It must be some deep-seated weakness, she decided, some character flaw that made her into a blatant Peeping Tom.

And it was worse than ever when he reacted to her appreciative eyes and laughed about it.

She groaned as she pulled a huge bath sheet from the heated towel bar and handed it to him.

He ignored the bath sheet. His hand shot around her wrist and jerked, pulling her completely against his wet body. Even in his weakened condition, he was alarmingly strong.

She started to struggle, the sheet dropping to the floor, but he clamped a big hand around her waist and held her firmly to him, groaning in pleasure as her hips moved sharply in her efforts to escape.

She subsided at once, made breathless by the huge body so intimately close to her. He was so tall that she felt the insistent pressure of him, not against her hips but against her midriff. She caught onto him to keep from reeling, and the feel of that thick mat of hair under her hands paralyzed her with curious pleasure.

"Shrimp," he accused at her temple.

"Giant," she taunted.

His hands swept over her back, burning hot through her thin cotton blouse, flattening her breasts against his diaphragm.

"We don't even fit together like a normal man and woman," he remarked as he looked down at her. "We're like Mutt and Jeff."

But it felt right. It felt as natural as breathing to stand close against his aroused body and be at home. She laid her cheek against his damp chest and just stood there, letting him hold her close, while she tried to deal with the unfamiliar feelings that were overwhelming her. It felt like more than physical attraction. It felt like . . . love.

Chapter Five

"I'm out of my mind," he said pleasantly. "I must be, even to consider such a thing with a midget like you. We'd be totally incompatible in bed."

She closed her eyes and relaxed against him, feeling him tauten in response. "No, we wouldn't. I studied anatomy. I'd have to be a foot shorter than I am to be worried. A woman's body is very elastic."

"Is yours elastic enough to accommodate mine?" he asked quietly.

She lifted her head and looked up into his blue, blue eyes. She felt the hunger all through her, burning and hot. "I think so," she said involuntarily.

His jaw clenched as he searched her face. "Then, let me."

She swallowed. Her fingers went up to touch his hair-roughened face. His lips were the only bit of skin visible below his cheekbones and his blue eyes. "I can't."

He scowled. "Those damned old-fashioned ideas again! This is the nineties, for God's sake!"

"I know." She traced his hard mouth and wanted so much to lie in his arms and learn what it was to love. But it wasn't what she wanted. "I'm not emotionally strong enough for brief affairs. That's why I don't have them. I really do want a home and children, Hank. I want my husband to be the first. If that's outdated, I'm sorry. I don't feel inferior or out of step just because I put a high value on my chastity. I hope the man I marry will feel the same way about his body."

His hands loosened. "In other words, you don't want a permissive man for a husband."

She lowered her eyes to his broad chest. "I suppose a lot of women think a man like that can reform, that he can be faithful. But if he's had a hundred women, he's already proven that he can't. He sees sex as an itch to scratch. He'll probably always consider it that casual, so he'll feel free to sleep around after he marries. And it will probably surprise him if his wife objects."

His big hands smoothed up and down her arms. "I guess I've given you the impression that I'm that way with women."

She looked up. "Yes."

He took a slow breath and smiled tenderly. "You don't think I might one day value a woman enough to become faithful rather than risk losing her?"

"I don't know you," she said solemnly.

"No. You really don't." He hesitated for another minute, but then he let her go and bent to pick up the bath sheet she'd dropped.

She moved away while he dried himself, finding a robe hanging behind the door that she handed to him when he was through. He put it on without a protest and let her help him back to the bedroom.

"Your hair is still damp," she said.

"It dries fast. Don't bother about the blower." He started toward the bed, but she diverted him into the chair.

"I want to change the sheets first. You'll be more comfortable."

He smiled. "Thanks."

"Where are they?"

He told her where to look and sat like a lamb while she remade the bed and then helped him out of his robe and into the bed.

"Are you all right?" she asked, because he looked so tired.

"I'm just weak. I think I may sleep for a while."

"That would be the best thing for you. Do you need anything?"

He shook his head. He studied her blouse for a long time, and she wondered why until she looked down and flushed. It had gotten so damp while she was standing against him that it had become see-through, and she wasn't wearing anything under it because her bra and the clothes she'd put on yesterday were in the load of laundry she'd started earlier.

Her arms came up over her body and she looked at him defensively.

"They're very pretty," he said with quiet reverence, and no mockery.

"Marshmallows," she muttered with self-contempt.

"Stop that," he said sharply. "I don't like big women."

Her eyebrows lifted. "All men do..."

"Not me," he repeated. "You're perfect just the way you are."

He eased her inferiority complex quite a lot, because he obviously wasn't lying about the way he felt. She managed a self-conscious smile. "Thanks."

He arched his arms behind his head and shifted with an oddly sensuous movement of his body. His eyes cut into hers, faintly glittering. "Open your blouse and come down beside me. I'll put my mouth on them and show you ten different ways to moan."

She flushed, jumping to her feet. "No doubt you could. I'm grass green that way. But I wouldn't thank you for reducing me to that condition, even if a dozen other women have."

She walked toward the door and heard him mutter under his breath.

"I haven't had a hundred women," he said angrily.

"Oh, sure." She laughed as she put her hand on the doorknob.

"I've had one. My wife. And she left me impotent."

The shock that tore through her spun her around to face him. He wasn't joking. It was all there, in his drawn face, his bitter eyes, even in the taut line of his mouth.

"But you're not impotent!" she blurted.

"Not with you," he said, chuckling softly. "You can't imagine what a shock it was to find out. I've been putting off women for years because I was sure that I couldn't perform in bed."

She leaned back against the door. Her legs felt weak. "You weren't married for very long, though, were you?"

"Six years," he told her. "Before that, I gave everything in me to football. I lived in the gym. I had no interest in seducing scores of women, however prudish that sounds. I was like you, bristling with idealism and romance. I saved myself for the right woman. Except she wasn't the right woman," he said shortly.

"We burned each other up in bed, but we had nothing to talk about in broad daylight."

"Did she . . . know?"

"No," he replied. "Because by the time we decided to get married, I discovered that I was one in a line. She'd had one lover after another until I came along, and never wanted to marry any of them. She said that she didn't think she could ever be faithful to one man, but I was certain that she could. More fool me," he added bitterly. "Amusing, isn't it, that you know already that permissive people find it difficult to be faithful, and I had to learn it the hard way."

"I wasn't in love," she reminded him. "You were."

"I should have known. Permissive people don't seem to make faithful lovers."

"But if she was like that," she began, moving closer to the bed, "experienced, I mean . . . how did you become impotent?"

"I stopped being able to want her after she had her third extramarital affair," he said honestly. "And without a lifetime of experience behind me, I thought that meant that I was permanently demanned. So I didn't try."

She saw him quite suddenly in a different light. Not as a playboy of the music world, but as an intense, deeply emotional man who felt things right down to his soul.

"Feeling sorry for me, Poppy?" he taunted as she paused by the bed.

"Oh, no. I'm feeling sorry for her," she said. "How sad to have someone love you so much and to be able to feel nothing in return."

"She's happy. She has a husband who doesn't require faithfulness, and plenty of money to spend."

"That wouldn't make me happy."

He smiled. "What would?"

"Being loved. Having a home. Having children. I'd still practice, of course. I guess I'd have to marry a man who was willing to sacrifice a little so that I could, but I'd make sure he never regretted it."

"Do you have hang-ups about sex?" he asked curiously.

"Just about having it before I get married," she replied, and grinned at him. "Deep-seated principles aren't easily uprooted."

"People shouldn't try to uproot them," he replied. "I'm sorry about that. It was a delicious surprise to find myself so quickly capable with you. I wanted to explore it." He shrugged. "But I shouldn't have put pressure on you."

"I want to," she said sincerely. "I'll bet you're a wonderful lover. But I want it all, the white wedding gown, the wedding night, the honeymoon...I'm greedy."

He smiled. "Don't sound as if you're apologizing for it. You're a breath of fresh air to a cynic like me." He frowned quizzically at her. "Has it occurred to you that in a few days we've become as intimate as a married couple except in one respect?"

"We still don't know each other."

"You'd be surprised at what I know about you," he remarked gently. "You like to go barefoot on the carpet. You're neat, but not fanatical about it. You like to cook, but you don't like to clean up. You're intellectual so no situation comedies for you. You like nature specials and news and politics and music. You have a kind heart and you like animals and children, but underneath all that is a passionate nature held under very tight control." His eyes narrowed on her body. "You'll be a demanding lover, little Poppy, and some lucky man will probably find you next to insatiable in bed."

She lifted both eyebrows. "Stop that."

"I wish it was going to be me," he replied. "But I've already messed up one marriage by leaping in with my eyes closed after a one-week courtship. I'm not going to do it twice in one lifetime."

"Neither would I, although you didn't ask."

"Sit down." He pulled her down on the bed and drew her hand to his chest, holding it there. "I'm on the road six months out of the year, recording and making business deals, doing interviews and talk shows and working with underprivileged inner-city kids. It's a project of mine, finding volunteers to work with them once a week to help keep them out of trouble," he added with a grin. "When I'm home, and home is Texas, I compose to the exclusion of everything else. Sometimes I go for a whole day without eating, because I'm so wrapped up in my work that I forget to cook." He smoothed his thumb over the back of her hand. "I'd make a lousy husband. In fact, I did. I can't really blame her—"

"I can." She interrupted him. "If you love someone, you accept it all, the separations, the good times, the bad times, the illnesses. It's all part of marriage."

"You've already had the illness part," he mused.

"I'd have done that for anyone," she protested.

"You did it for me, though," he replied. "Blushing all the way. You don't do it so much anymore, though," he added amusedly. "You're getting used to me, aren't you?"

"You're very nice, when you forget to grumble."

"I have my faults. A quick temper is the worst of them. But I don't drink or gamble, and when I'm not working, I'm fairly easy to get along with." He searched her eyes. "Why are you called Poppy?"

"My father told me that my mother loved flowers," she recalled. "But he added that when I was born, the first thing she thought of was a poem about poppies growing in Flanders Fields where the veterans of World War I were buried. She went into the hospital to have me on Veterans Day and they were selling Buddy Poppies...." She smiled.

"Muddled, but I get the idea," he said. "My name is Henry, but everyone called me Hank from the time I was in grammar school."

"It's a nice name."

"So is yours." He drew her hand to his lips and kissed it softly. "Thank you for taking care of me."

The gentle caress was thrilling. She smiled. "It was very educational."

One blue eye narrowed. "Just don't start experimenting with men who aren't sick," he said.

Her eyebrows went up.

He laughed and let go of her hand. "Now I know I must be delirious with fever."

"I guess so," she murmured dryly. "I'll finish the wash then clean up the kitchen while you nap."

"You don't have to do that," he said gently.

"We both need some clean clothes. It's no trouble."

"Thanks, then."

She shrugged, smiled and went back to her chores. All the while she was thinking about Hank and how easily they seemed to fall into living together. Not that it was the normal sort of living together, she reminded herself.

But it was exciting all the same, and there was a closeness here that she'd never known. She liked just being with Hank, listening to his deep voice as he talked. He was intelligent and kind, and not at all the unprincipled rounder she'd thought he was. She thought of him in a totally different light now, and she knew that she was going to miss him terribly when the weather broke enough to let them out of this cabin.

She tried to put it out of her mind while she did the chores. She was beginning to feel very much at home here. The views were spectacular and she enjoyed the solitude. It would have been the ideal place to live, with the right man.

It occurred to her that Hank was the right man, the one she'd been looking for all her life. But it was impossible. You couldn't fall in love in four days, not the sort of love you needed to get married. Besides, Hank had a failed marriage behind him and he didn't want to risk a second. All that would have been left for them was an affair, which she couldn't accept.

She finished the washing and put the clothes into the dryer, wondering how it was going to be when she got back home. Probably she'd put this adventure into perspective and forget about it in a few months. Of course she would.

Hank slept for the rest of the afternoon, while Poppy amused herself with the piano, lowering the volume to keep from disturbing the man in the master bedroom. The song he was working on was lying on the table beside the piano. She glanced over the tune and began to pick it out, slowly, smiling as the beautiful melody met her ears.

He didn't have more than a few words on paper, rhyming words mostly and not in any sort of order. Love, he'd written, when the feeling stirred fluttered like a . . . and he'd crossed out two words that didn't quite rhyme with it.

"A bright redbird," she mumbled, "playing in the snow."

"That's it!"

She jumped and caught her breath. Hank was leaning against the doorframe in his bathrobe. His blue eyes were glimmering, and he was laughing.

"I couldn't get the rhyme or any sort of reason to go with those words," he explained. "But that's it, that's exactly it . . . !"

He moved to the piano and slid onto the bench beside her. He played the song with a deep bass beat that emphasized the sweetness of the high melody.

"Love when the feeling stirred, fluttered like a redbird, playing in the snow," he sang in his deep, soft voice, looking at her and grinning. "Flew like an arrow through the sky, higher than a redbird flies, left me all aglow."

Only words, she thought, but when the music was put with them, major and minor chords intermixing, when he sang the words, when the deep, throbbing counterrhythm caught her up—it was going to be a hit. She knew it and felt goose bumps rise on her arms at the power and beauty of it.

"You feel it, too, don't you?" he asked, stopping. "It's good, isn't it? Really good."

"The best yet," she had to agree. "Who did the music?"

One corner of his mouth tugged up just a fraction of an inch and she laughed. "Silly question," she murmured. "Sorry."

"It will take some more work, but that's the melody." He chuckled. "Imagine that, I'd been sitting in here for a solid week trying to come up with something, anything...and all I needed was a veterinarian to point me in the right direction." He grinned at her. "I suppose you treat birds, too, don't you?"

She nodded. "Parrots and canaries and parakeets, for lung infections. Birds are mostly lung, you know." She searched his face. "You shouldn't be up. It's too soon."

"I heard you playing my song," he explained. "I had to come and see what you thought of it."

"I think it's great."

He smiled. "Thanks." She was slowly touching the keys again and some soft sadness in her face touched him. "What's wrong?" he asked.

She looked up. "The snow's stopped."

He looked out the window. He hadn't noticed. He got up from the bench and walked to stare out the other window down at the road. It had stopped, and the sun had come out. "Great skiing weather now," he murmured. "The snowplows will dig us out by tomorrow." He stuck his hands into the pockets of his robe. "You'll be free."

What an odd way to put it. "I don't plan to rush out and file kidnapping charges against you," she said pointedly.

He turned. "That wasn't how I meant it, although I will apologize handsomely for kidnapping you by mistake." His eyes swept over her very slowly, almost possessively. "I suppose you'll be rushing back to your practice."

"I need to."

"What if you don't have a job to go back to?" he persisted seriously.

She blew out a soft breath. "Well, I suppose they'll repossess my car and my apartment first..."

"Is there somewhere else you could work, if you had to?"

"Of course!" she said, laughing. "Sioux City isn't that small. There are other practices. I could find something, but it wouldn't be as a partner. I'd have to start at the bottom again."

"Honey, I don't think you've realized that you're at the bottom right now."

The endearment made her heart race. She dropped her eyes before he could read the pleasure it gave her.

"Sorry. That slipped out," he said, teasing.

"Oh, I liked it," she replied. "Nobody ever called me honey except the mailman, and he was seventy."

He burst out laughing. "I'll have to make up for that. You can't leave until morning, anyway, not unless they get those roads cleared early."

"I wouldn't leave until you were well, regardless," she said, surprised at his assumption that she couldn't wait to get out.

His face smoothed. All expression went out of it. "I see."

"You needn't look shocked," she said. "You'd do it for me."

"Yes, I would." He began to realize how much he'd do for her. Under different circumstances, they might have had a real beginning. But it was the wrong time, the wrong place, and he was still afraid of the risk.

"It's been an experience I'll never forget," she said absently. "I'll listen to your tapes from now on. I suppose I was a bit of a musical snob."

"Maybe I was, too. I think I'll buy an opera tape or two."

She smiled. "That's nice. You might try Puccini."

"Is he that Italian singer?" he asked.

"He's the composer. He's dead. But Domingo and Pavorotti sing the operas he wrote. My favorite opera is *Turandot.*"

"*Turandot.*" He smiled back. "I'll remember."

She got up from the piano. "How about something to eat?"

"You took the words right out of my mouth!"

She went into the kitchen and made potato pancakes and steak and biscuits with a side salad. When she went to call Hank, he was out of bed and dressed in jeans and a green pullover shirt. Despite that overshadowing growth of hair that covered his face, concealing its shape, he looked wonderful to Poppy.

"Are you sure you feel like eating at the table?" she asked worriedly.

"Yes. I'm still a little weak, but I'm on the mend."
He smiled. "Doesn't it show?"

She nodded. "I guess it does."

They ate at the small table in the kitchen. His appetite was much better, and he was only coughing occasionally now. He ate heartily. Considering the speed of his recovery, it didn't take much guesswork to tell that overall, he was in great shape.

"How did you learn to cook like this?" he asked.

"From my dad. He was a chef. He really was good at it, too. He taught me how to make pastries and sauces. I enjoy cooking."

"It shows. This is delicious."

"Thank you!"

They were silent until they finished eating. They drank their second cup of coffee at the kitchen table, and Hank stared into his mug pensively.

"You're brooding, aren't you?" she asked.

He nodded. He looked up into her eyes and held them for a long, static moment. "I haven't had anyone around me, close like this, for a long time. You've grown on me, Poppy," he mused half-humorously. "I'm going to miss you."

She smiled back, a little sadly. "I'm going to miss you, too. I haven't had anyone to look after or care about since my dad died. It's been lonely for me."

He turned the coffee mug idly on the table's glossy surface. "Then suppose we keep in touch," he suggested without looking at her.

Her heart leapt. "Oh, that would..." She calmed her tone. "That would be nice. I'd like that."

He smiled at her. "So would I. I'll give you the address here and in Texas. Write to me when you get back."

"Are you terrible about answering letters?" she asked.

He shook his head. "I'm very good about it, in fact. I answer most of my own fan mail with the help of a secretary."

"I see."

"No, you don't." He corrected her, interpreting her expression accurately. "I don't leave her to do the answering, I dictate the replies. And I won't let anyone answer your letters. I'll do it myself."

Her stiff posture relaxed. "Then I'll write."

"And don't assume that if you don't hear back immediately that I've forgotten you or that I'm ignoring you," he added. "I'm on the road a lot, I told you. It may take a week or two, sometimes longer, for my mail to catch up with me."

"I'll remember," she promised.

He reached out and covered her soft hand with his big one. "One more thing," he said gently, coaxing her eyes up to meet his. "Find another job."

She gaped at him. "My job is my business."

"Your job is a joke," he returned. "They're using you, sweetheart, dangling the idea of a partnership so that they can get someone to take over the jobs they don't want. There won't be any partnership. One day they'll find someone more useful and you'll be out on your ear, perhaps at the most inconvenient time."

"You're very cynical," she remarked.

He nodded. "I'm an expert on people who use other people," he told her. "I've been used a time or two myself."

She wiggled her eyebrows. "Can I have three guesses about how they did it?"

He glowered at her. "I'm serious."

She finished her coffee. "Okay. I'll think about it."

"You do that."

She got up and put the dishes in the dishwasher. "Is there anything else that needs doing?"

"Yes." He came up behind her and slipped his lean arms around her, hugging her back against him. "I need to be ravished."

She laughed with pure delight. "I'm not up to your weight," she reminded him, looking up over her shoulder with sparkling dark eyes. "And besides, I'd never be able to overpower you."

"I'll help."

She shook her head. "No. I expect that you're as addictive as caffeine. One taste of you wouldn't be enough. I'd get withdrawal symptoms."

He chuckled and hugged her closer for a minute. "So would I. And I'm probably still a little contagious," he added with a sheepish grin as he let her go. "No matter," he mused, watching her. "When I'm well and truly back on my feet, I'll come calling. Then, look out."

The soft warning kept her going, all through the rest of the day, and through the anguish of the parting the next morning, when he had to take her to the ski lodge and leave her with barely more than an affectionate hug.

She worried about him all the way to the airport on the lodge's shuttle bus, because even though the snowplows had been along, the roads were still treacherous. But as the shuttle passed the road to his cabin, she saw that his Bronco was safely parked at the door and smoke was coming out of the fireplace. He'd made it home, and hopefully, he'd be fine. She settled back into her seat, trying not to cry. It was amazing, she thought, how five days in Colorado had altered the rest of her life. Her last thought as they left the snow-covered valley behind was how would she survive until she saw Hank again?

amazing, she thought, how five days in Colorado had altered the rest of her life. Her last thought as they left the snow-covered cabin behind was how would she survive until she saw Hank again.

Chapter Six

Poppy began to realize very quickly after her return to Sioux City, Iowa, that Hank had been right about her supposed partnership. The vets with whom she worked seemed to have plenty of free time and yet they made three times her salary. She was always the one to work nights and weekends and holidays, and whenever the weather was particularly bad, it was Poppy who had to go out on large-animal calls. That could be very difficult indeed when she was asked to deliver a calf or a foal, or treat a mean-tempered bull for a cut.

She had bruises all over her, a bad cold and there was no mention of an increased salary or a partnership two months later. She was getting fed up. And not only with the veterinary practice.

She'd written twice to Hank. So far, there hadn't been even a postcard in reply. On one of the music talk shows, which she'd started watching, there had been one tidbit about Amanda Sutton being in a hospital in Wyoming awaiting the birth of her first child and some more rumors about the breakup of her group, Desperado. But that was all the news there had been. Remembering how fond Hank was of Amanda, Poppy hoped she was all right and that her child had been born healthy.

She tried very hard to remember what Hank had said about not being upset if she didn't hear from him right away. But when two months rolled into three, she began to put the past in perspective. The time she'd spent with Hank had been a five-day interlude and nothing serious had really happened, except for a few kisses. He'd told her he wanted nothing less than another marriage, so what had she expected? Perhaps he'd decided that even friendship with her was too much of a risk, and he'd withdrawn.

She couldn't blame him. He hadn't had an easy time of it where women were concerned. But the last thing on her mind had been trapping him into a relationship he didn't want. When she thought about it, it seemed likely that he'd had his share of ambitious women stalking him because he was rich and famous. She wasn't like that, but he wouldn't know. He didn't know her at all. Apparently he didn't want to.

Poppy tried to put him out of her mind, but his new song, "Redbird," had just been released on an album along with several other newly recorded tracks. It meant that Amanda had to be working again, because her sweet, clear soprano could be heard above the deep bass voices of her group. The song that

Poppy had given him the inspiration for was as beautiful as it had sounded in the cabin, and it was a surprise to find that her first name was mentioned in the dedication of the album, jointly to Carlton Wayne Sutton—very obviously the new baby—and herself. She tingled all over at the thought that Hank had remembered her even that well. She was a nobody, after all, hardly his sort of woman. The terrible thing was that she had no close girlfriends, no one to share the thrill with. She mentioned it to a clerk in the nearby record shop, but he only smiled and agreed that it was a great honor. She was sure that he didn't believe her.

Her stamina was giving out. Despite her youth, the practice was really getting her down. Eventually she couldn't take it anymore and she went looking for another job.

She found it in a very small practice in a town twenty miles outside Sioux City, in a farming community. The elderly veterinarian there had one young partner but needed someone to take care of the office while the two of them were out on large animal calls. Poppy wasn't overly eager, but she was pleasant and had qualifications that they liked.

"What about experience?" Dr. Joiner, the elder partner, asked gently.

"I'm working for a group practice in Sioux City," she explained, "but I have to do all the large animal calls and work nights and holidays and weekends." She smiled sheepishly. "I'm sorry. I suppose that sounds as if I'm lazy. I'm not, and it is a great opportunity to learn how a practice works. But I'm so tired," she concluded helplessly.

Dr. Joiner exchanged a speaking glance with his young partner, Dr. Helman. "It isn't quite so busy here," he explained. "But we have enough work for three people. The thing is, I can't offer you a partnership. You'd be a salaried employee and nothing more."

"Oh, that's all right," Poppy said, relieved. "I don't think I've got enough stamina for another partnership."

Dr. Joiner chuckled. "Dr. O'Brien, you're a peach. I'll be happy to have you aboard. When can you start?"

She explained that she'd have to give two weeks' notice, and that she'd make sure she got a reference from her partners. She thanked Dr. Joiner again, smiled at Dr. Helman and set off to her office with a lighter heart.

The partners weren't surprised when she announced her resignation, and they gave her a good recommendation as well. They apparently expected that no junior partner was going to last very long with what was expected of her or him. But they were interviewing other new graduates the last few days Poppy worked for them. She couldn't even warn the excited prospective employees. They'd have to find out the truth the same harsh way she had. But it would teach them a good lesson. Heaven knew, she'd learned hers.

She kept her apartment. It was only a twenty-five-minute drive to the new office, and she'd have to have time to look for a new place to live that was closer, if her new job worked out.

The job itself, after the long, strenuous practice she'd left, was wonderfully uncomplicated and enjoyable. She didn't have to work every weekend. The other vets alternated with her. Each one was on call a different night, so she didn't have to work every night, either. Holidays were shared. It was heavenly and the odd thing was that she made just as much money as she'd made in the practice. She felt at home after just one week on the job. She decided that moving closer was a pretty safe bet, considering how well they all worked together.

She found a room in a nice, comfortable boarding house and paid a week's rent in advance. Then she went to pack up her things and have them moved to her new home.

It didn't take long, because she didn't have much. She made two trips in her car and was just packing it for the third time when the telephone rang inside. It was supposed to be disconnected already, so she ignored it. The last few calls had been salespeople doing promotions. She couldn't imagine who might be looking for her, short of her old partners. Certainly, she knew, it wouldn't be Hank Shoeman. It had been over four and a half months and he'd surely forgotten all about her by now. She'd faced that fact, without much enthusiasm, because her memories of him were sweet.

She settled in her new apartment in the boarding house and got more comfortable in her job over the next week. She'd just finished examining and inoculating a three-month-old poodle puppy when she heard the waiting-room door open. She was alone in the office, because it was just after hours and the receptionist had gone home. Drs. Joiner and Helman were out on calls.

"I'll only be a minute!" she called out. She finished with the poodle, assured the owner that he was in excellent health and that he'd be automatically notified when to bring the dog back for his next round of shots.

He thanked her and she smiled happily as she watched him leave. She finished writing up the chart and went out into the waiting room, hoping that it was going to be something uncomplicated so that she could go home and eat.

She opened the outer office door with her professional smile, and stopped there, frozen in place.

The man looked familiar, and not familiar. He was wearing a gray suit. His hair was conventionally cut. He had a mustache, nothing more. The rest of his lean, handsome face was clean-shaven, and except for a couple of thin scars and a crooked nose, it was an appealing face. Blue eyes twinkled out of it as he studied her in her neat white lab coat.

"Nice," he said pleasantly. "You haven't lost a pound, have you? And I gather that this new job doesn't require your life's blood."

"Hank?" she asked uncertainly.

He nodded.

"Your hair...your beard," she began.

"I'm changing my image," he explained. "I'm tired of looking like a refugee from a cave."

"You look very nice," she said.

"So do you. How about supper?"

"There aren't any restaurants around here," she told him. Her heart was beating madly. "You didn't answer my letters."

"It's a long story," he said. "I'll tell you everything you want to know. But for now, I'd enjoy a

good meal. I've spent two days tracking you down
and except for breakfast at the hotel and a couple of
sandwiches, I'm running on empty."

"There are lots of restaurants in Sioux City," she
said.

"Then we'll go there. Do you need to stop by your
apartment first?"

She shook her head, bemused by the sight of him.
He looked unspeakably elegant and sexy. She wanted
to throw herself into his arms and tell him to forget
about explanations, it was enough that he was here.
But she couldn't do it. He was probably on his way to
or from Texas and had only stopped in because he
wondered what had happened to her. It wasn't a proposal or a proposition; it was just a visit. She had to
remember that and not let her imagination run away
with her.

She took off her lab coat and slid her arms into the
deep pink cotton jacket she wore over her pale pink
blouse. She took time to run a brush through her hair
and refreshen her makeup before she rejoined Hank
in the outer office.

"I have to lock up," she explained, and took time
to do that, too. When the lock was secure and
checked, and the burglar alarm set, she walked with
Hank to his car. But she stopped short when she saw
it, and her uplifted face was wary and a little scared.

He reached down and took her hand, holding it tightly in his. "It's all right," he said gently.

The driver came around, smiling, and opened the door of the big white stretch limousine for them. Hank helped Poppy inside and slid in next to her. The driver closed them in and went around to get behind the wheel.

Hank had already told him where to go. He took off without a word, and Hank closed the curtains between front and back and turned on the interior light.

Poppy's expression fascinated him. She looked at everything, explored the CD deck, the television, the well-stocked bar, the telephone . . .

"Six people could ride in here," she remarked, smoothing her hand over the burgundy leather seat.

"Six people usually do," he replied, stretching out lazily to study her. "Like it?"

She grinned. "I love it. I only wish I had a friend that I could brag about it to."

"Surely you have one or two."

She shook her head. "I don't make long-lasting friends that easily. Only casual ones. My best friend married years ago, and we lost touch."

He crossed one long leg over the other. "Did you see the song on the charts?"

"Yes! It was great! Thank you for the dedication."

He waved her thanks away. "Thanks for the help. Everyone loved it, especially Amanda."

"How is she?"

"Blooming," he said with a smile. "She and Quinn and Eliott are all moonstruck over that baby. They take him everywhere, even to recording sessions with the group." His eyes were sad and faintly wistful. "I've always envied them that closeness. Now I envy them the baby."

"The album was dedicated to him, too," she recalled.

"He's a good-looking kid," he said. "Even cries with rhythm. We're all going to buy him a set of drums when he's two."

"Do they still hang people in Wyoming?" she asked meaningfully.

He got the joke at once and chuckled. "Quinn might just do that to me." He locked his hands behind his head, pulling his suit coat pleasantly taut over the powerful muscles of his chest and arms while he looked at her. "I've been tying up loose ends, settling business affairs, getting recording contracts and publicity tours finalized. I'm free for the next two months."

"You're not in town on business, then?" she asked conversationally.

His blue eyes narrowed. "You know why I'm in town, Poppy."

Her heart jumped but her face gave nothing away. "Actually I don't. I wrote you two letters, neither of which was ever answered. There wasn't a telephone call or any communication for months. You don't ignore people for almost half a year and then just drop by as if you saw them yesterday."

"You're mad." He sighed. "Yes, I was afraid you would be. I kept trying to put down what I felt on paper, and failing miserably. I couldn't boil it down to a telephone call, either. Just when I thought I'd fly out here, something kept coming up. It's been a long five months, honey. The longest five months of my life. But I'm here now, and you're going to have hell getting rid of me."

"Don't you have contractual obligations to fulfill?" she asked.

He shook his head, slowly. "That's why it took me so long to come after you. I didn't want any interruptions."

She shifted back against the leather seat. "I won't have an affair with you, so if that's why you came, I'll save you the time."

He began to smile. "Have you forgotten what a low boiling point you have with me?"

"Yes," she said uncomfortably. "And that should bother you. One more groupie might be more than you could take."

"Not if she was you," he said pointedly. "I'd love having you throw yourself at me and hang on for dear life."

"Why?"

"That's something we'll talk about for the next few days." He stretched again and yawned. "I haven't slept. You're a hard woman to track down. Eventually I phoned every single veterinarian's office in the city. Do you know how many there are?"

"I have a fairly good idea," she replied, shocked. "Couldn't you have had your secretary or someone do that for you?"

"Why, no," he said, surprised at the question. "It wouldn't have occurred to me to trust something so important to another person."

She flushed. "You'd forgotten all about me, surely? I've seen some of the photos on your other albums. You attract beautiful women."

"Beauty isn't everything," he replied. "And sometimes it isn't anything at all. You're beautiful to me, Poppy, because you have the kindest heart of any woman I've ever known. I've never had anyone want to take care of me when I was sick until you came along. And under those circumstances, too, when I'd practically kidnapped you. You'd have been perfectly justified in walking out and leaving me there to cough myself to death.''

''I couldn't have done that,'' she protested.

''Not even if you'd hated me. Yes, I know. But I don't think you hated me, Poppy,'' he mused, watching her like a hawk. ''In fact, I think you felt something quite different on that last day we spent together.''

''Compassion,'' she said abruptly.

''Compassion.'' He smiled. ''Is that all I get?''

''What do you want?''

He leaned forward with his hands clasped loosely over his long legs. ''I want you to love me, Poppy,'' he drawled deeply. ''I want you to become so obsessed with me that you grow pale if I'm out of your sight for an hour. I want you to hate women who look at me or touch me. I want you to ache for me in your bed at night, and go hungry for the feel of me in your arms.''

She already felt that way. She wasn't telling him so, however. She cleared her throat. ''Well!''

''And before you start raging at me about indecent proposals before dinner,'' he added slowly, ''I want a hell of a lot more than one night with you.''

Her eyebrows levered up. ''An affair is still...''

"I want a baby, Poppy," he said in a deep, soft whisper. "I want a son of my own, so that I don't have to stand over Amanda and Quinn and covet theirs."

Her body reacted to the statement in an unexpected way, so that she had to fold her arms over her breasts to keep him from noticing.

He noticed anyway, and his eyes gleamed with feeling. "You want it, too, don't you?" he said coaxingly. "A home, a husband, a family of your own. Maybe a few pets to look after, too."

"My job..."

"Whatever," he said easily. "If you want to keep on practicing, that's all right with me. It will give you and the kids something to do when I'm out of town."

Her heart was racing wildly in her chest. He looked sane. Perhaps he had a fever again.

"I'm not crazy," he explained. "I'm just lonely. So are you. So if we get married and make a family together, neither of us will ever have to be lonely again."

"There are plenty of women who would be willing..."

"I want you," he said simply. "You can't imagine how empty my cabin has been since you left." He laughed, but without mirth. "All my life I've been self-sufficient, independent. Women have chased me for years, before and after my marriage. But here you come, spend less than a week in residence, and you're living with me still, here and here." He touched his head and his heart. "I can't get rid of you. And believe me, I tried. I tried for five months."

She glared at him. "Maybe I had more success at it than you did," she taunted.

"Maybe you didn't."

He reached across the space that separated them and lifted her body right into his arms.

"Now, you see here...!"

His mouth hit hers while she was getting the last word out. He wasn't brutal or rough, but the action was amazingly effective. She went under without a protest. Her arms went around his neck and she lifted to the slow, soft caress of his hands even as her mouth opened to accept the deep, hard thrust of his tongue inside it.

Her legs trembled where they lay over his. He drew her closer and deepened the kiss even more, held it until he felt her begin to shudder. His hand smoothed up over her thighs, her flat stomach, her breasts. She moaned.

"You got over me, right?" he whispered against her mouth. "It's really noticeable, how completely you've gotten over me. Open your mouth again..."

She barely heard him above the wild throb of her heart. She clung to him while one kiss led to another, each more arousing than the one before. He turned her so that her hips pressed deeply into his own, so that his arousal was suddenly blatantly threatening. But she wasn't afraid.

"You're so small," he groaned as he let his mouth slide onto her throat. "Too small!"

She kissed his cheek, his temple, his closed eyelids with quick, warm lips. "I'll fit you," she promised. "I'll fit you like a glove."

"Poppy," he groaned again in anguish.

"Do stop worrying," she whispered as she found his mouth. "I love you."

"No more than I love you," he whispered back, holding her closer. "Are you going to marry me, complications and all?"

"I don't seem to have any choice. How else can I protect you from scores of sex-crazed beautiful women?"

He chuckled and kissed her again, murmuring his agreement against her soft, welcoming mouth.

And they were married, six months to the day after Hank had abducted Poppy to his mountain cabin. The whole group of Desperado was there as witnesses in the small Wyoming church where Amanda had married Quinn Sutton several years before. They spoke their vows and exchanged rings. The look Hank gave his new bride would have melted snow, but fortunately it was summer.

"Where are you going for your honeymoon?" Amanda asked them when they'd changed and were ready to get into the limousine.

"That's our secret." Hank chuckled. He kissed Amanda's cheek, and the baby's, and shook hands with Quinn Sutton and Elliot.

"Well, write when you get time," Quinn asked. "Let us know you're okay."

"I'll do that. Take care of each other. We'll be in touch."

The Suttons all stood close together, waving until Poppy and Hank were out of sight.

"They're a very special couple, aren't they?" Poppy asked, sliding as close to Hank as she could get.

"A very special family," he agreed. "We're going to be one, too. I'll prove that to you tonight," he said, his voice deepening, lowering. There had been nothing more than kisses all during the time they waited for their wedding day. Now the time had come for all the secrets to be unveiled for Poppy and she was as excited as she was apprehensive. She loved him. That had to be enough, she reminded herself. She slid her small hand into his big one and snuggled close.

* * *

But she was less comfortable after they ate a leisurely supper and cleared away the dishes. Her disquiet showed on her face, too.

He tossed aside the dishcloth and pulled her gently in front of him. "Weddings are traumatic at best," he said quietly. "We can wait until you're rested and feel more like a new experience."

She nibbled at the skin on her lower lip. "I'm not usually so cowardly," she began.

He took her face in his big hands and tilted it up to his tender eyes. "I don't have anything that you haven't already seen," he reminded her.

"But I do," she said miserably. She plucked at his shirt. "And I'm grass green and inhibited . . . !"

"And five minutes from now, you won't know your own name," he whispered as his mouth searched for her lips and opened on them.

Actually it took less time than that for him to reduce her to insensibility. Her desire for him matched his for her, and by the time he carried her into the bedroom, she was fighting her way to his bare chest through the confining shirts that separated them.

"Slowly," he whispered as he put her down and slid onto the bed beside her. "Slowly, darling, we have all the time in the world. Nice and easy, now. Let's not rush."

She was shivering with new sensations, new expectations, but he gentled her until she lay drowsily in his big arms and let him undress them. She didn't have the will to protest or the sense to be embarrassed as he studied her pink nudity with covetous, possessive eyes. His hands were slow and thorough, like his warm mouth. He aroused her and excited her, and when she was whimpering softly with the overwhelming pleasure of his ardor, he moved into total possession.

She stiffened a little and gasped, but his mouth savored hers, and pressed reassuring kisses over her closed eyelids as he coaxed her into accepting the raw intimacy of his body.

"You are...very much a virgin," he whispered against her trembling lips, and he smiled. "Is it all right? Am I hurting you?"

"No," she managed to say. Her nails dug into his shoulders as he moved again, very tenderly.

"It stings, doesn't it?"

"Yes."

"Only a little further," he said half to himself, and his mouth crushed down hard on hers, his tongue shooting deeply into her mouth. The action shocked her so much that she relaxed and allowed him complete and total access to the soft warmth of her body.

She cried out, surprised, because it was the most profound experience of her entire life. Her eyes opened wide and she looked straight into his.

"Yes," he whispered huskily. "It's a miracle, isn't it? Man and woman, fitting together so closely, so completely, that they form one person." He kissed her damp face gently as he began to move, each tender shift of his body bringing a sudden, sharp pleasure that lifted her to him in delight. "Feel the rhythm and move with me," he coaxed, smiling as she began to match him. "Think of it as composing a symphony, making music...that's it. Hard now, baby. Cut loose and move to the beat. Move hard. Real hard ... !"

She lost control of herself completely then and although she heard his urgent whispers, she seemed outside her body, watching it dance to his tune, contort and convulse with pleasure that seemed to feed on itself. Finally there was a hot burst of it that made her cry out against the unbearable sensations deep within her body. She buried her face against his throat and moaned endlessly as it went through her in waves. Somewhere in the heat of it, she heard him, felt him, as he joined her in that surreal existence with a hard shudder that arched his powerful body down roughly against hers.

Minutes later, the dazzling heat and color began to fade away and she found tears falling down her cheeks.

"It stopped," she whispered miserably.

He rolled onto his side and gathered her very close. "We'll get it back again when we've rested." He kissed her gently. "For a first time, it was fairly volcanic, wasn't it?" he mused. He laughed delightedly. "And we fit, don't we?"

"Oh, yes." She nuzzled closer, shivering with pleasure and love. "Hank..."

His mouth slid over hers. "We've just said all there is to say, and we never spoke a word," he whispered into her mouth. "I'm glad you waited for me, Poppy. I wish that I'd been able to wait for you, all my life."

She hugged him closer. "I'll settle for the rest of our lives," she said gently, "and everything that's ahead of us."

His big arms folded her close. "Love, then. Years and years of it."

She smiled against his chest. "And children to share it with."

"Yes." He tugged the cover over them, because it was chilly at night this high up in the mountains. "I'm glad I didn't apologize for abducting you," he murmured. "It was the only sensible thing I've done in the past few years."

"All the same, you can't abduct anyone else, ever."

"Oh, I'm reformed," he promised her with a grin. "The only thing I expect to abduct in the future is a piano now and again, so that I can compose an occasional song."

Her eyes fell to his mouth. "I particularly like the way you compose in bed. Would you like to try a new theme? Something on the order of a blues tune?"

He rolled over, smoothing her body against his in the growing darkness. "I think I can manage that." He chuckled. "How about you?"

She whispered that she had no doubts at all; about that, or about the future with him. It was going to be wonderful. And she told him that, too.

* * * * *

Dear Reader,

When Silhouette phoned and asked if I'd do a selection for their new *Abduction and Seduction* special collection, I immediately thought, "Oh, boy, now I can do my sheikh story!" But deserts and camels faded in my mind when I thought of Hank Shoeman from *Sutton's Way* (August 1996 Desire) and considered a request from a reader, asking nicely for Hank's story. This seemed the perfect opportunity to fulfill that request.

Let me emphasize that in real life, I do not support the idea of any woman being abducted by a strange man. This story is strictly a romantic fantasy and it has rules: (1) The hero must be decent and kind–hearted; (2) his motives must be noble; and (3) the heroine must not be forced to do anything against her will. Hank abducts our heroine because he wants to spare Amanda Corrie Sutton any scandalous publicity. And as the story turns out, *he* becomes the captive when he falls in love with his abductee.

I hope the reader who asked for this story—and she knows who she is—likes it!

All my best. All my love,

Diana Palmer

THE BLUEST EYES IN TEXAS

IN TEXAS

Joan
Johnston

Chapter One

Lindsey Major pressed her fingers against her temples to ease some of the awful pressure, then rolled onto her side, hoping that would relieve the pain in her head. As she did, her skirt wrapped around her legs. That was odd, because she slept in men's pajamas and had since she was a teenager and thought it was a cool thing to do. She reached a hand down to untangle the yards of material and realized it wasn't just any old skirt, it was ankle-length taffeta. She was still wearing her ballgown!

Lindsey sat up abruptly, which set her head to pounding ferociously and brought a wave of nausea. She fought the sick feeling, sliding her feet onto the floor and carefully pushing herself upright on the edge of the bed. Which was when she realized she wasn't in her own bed upstairs in the Texas governor's mansion. She was . . . somewhere else.

It wasn't a dream. I was kidnapped right off the front porch of the mansion. I've been drugged. That's why my head hurts.

Lindsey caught a glimpse of herself in the mirror across the room and was appalled at what she found.

Her tawny golden hair had fallen from its sleek French twist. The makeup she had sparingly applied to what the press had labeled "the bluest eyes in Texas" was so badly smudged that she looked like a raccoon on a binge. And her beautiful strapless taffeta dress—a glorious shade of lavender that rivaled the remarkable color of her eyes—was crumpled from having been slept in. Lindsey tried to remember what had happened after the struggle on the porch, but drew a blank.

There was no window in the room, no route of escape. She crossed to the only door and slowly, silently, tried the knob. It was locked. She pressed her ear against it, hoping to get some clue as to who had kidnapped her and what terms they were demanding for her release. She could actually make out voices in the next room. Two men were arguing. What they said sent a cold chill down her spine.

"I say we might as well enjoy her while we can. Hector ain't gonna let her go even if the governor commutes the Turk's sentence like he asked and the Turk goes free."

The Turk! Lindsey thought with despair. *I should have known!*

Turk Valerio, the man who had accidentally shot and killed her mother in his abortive assassination attempt on her father five years ago, had been sentenced to die for his crime. The Turk had boasted that he would never be executed, that the Texas Mafia, headed by Hector Martinez, would find a way to set him free. Lindsey had the sinking feeling that she had become a pawn in a very deadly game.

"I want to know what it feels like to do a lady," the man said. "And I sure as hell want to see them blue eyes when I'm pumping into her—before Hector does what he threatened, I mean." The kidnapper made a disgusted sound in his throat. "She's gonna be a mess after that."

"I can see the governor's face when he read that note," a second voice, one with a distinct Texas drawl, said. "'Commute Turk Valerio's sentence by noon tomorrow, or I'm gonna blind the bluest eyes in Texas.' Bet the man turned white as a ghost!" A high-pitched, almost girlish giggle followed.

"Hector won't like it if you touch the girl," a third voice said flatly.

"Well, Hector ain't here," the man with the deep Texas accent retorted. "I agree with Epifanio. I say we enjoy the girl now, while we can. Only, I want her first."

"I get her first, Tex," Epifanio countered. "It was my idea."

"You're too hard on women," Tex complained. "There won't be any left for me."

"I'm telling you both, leave the girl alone," the third voice said.

"Hell, Burr, you wouldn't spoil our fun, would you? Besides, me and Tex together, we're bigger 'n you. I don't think you could stop us all by your lonesome." That horrible, high-pitched laugh resounded again.

"Make a move toward that door and we'll see," the man called Burr replied in a steely voice.

Lindsey's heart was thumping loud and hard in response to the fight-or-flight instinct that had taken over when she realized her peril. They planned to blind her! But they were going to rape her first! Any minute she expected Epifanio and Tex to come bursting through the door—right past the man called Burr, who was all that stood between her and immediate disaster. And good old Burr hadn't said anything about protecting her from the man who wanted to blind her, only from the two men intent on rape.

Lindsey looked around for a weapon. Her eyes alighted on the lamp beside the bed, which had a porcelain base. It ought to make a good club. She quickly pulled the plug from the wall and stripped the lamp of its shade, then dragged a chair over to one side of the door and climbed onto it so the lamp could be wielded from above. She waited, terror stealing her breath and making her suck air in harsh gasps. How much time did she have? How long before she was fighting for her life?

Lindsey watched in breathless horror as the doorknob began to turn.

She brought the lamp down on the head of the first man through the door, who collapsed at her feet with a groan. She stared openmouthed at the second man who filled the doorway. He was huge.

"What the hell?"

She took advantage of the big man's confusion to give him a hard shove. As he fell back through the doorway, she leapt off the chair and darted past him. Unfortunately, he reached out at the last moment and caught her skirt. It tore at the waist but didn't pull free. He began to rein her in like a lassoed heifer.

"You did me a favor, *chiquita,* getting rid of Tex like that. Now I have you all to myself."

Lindsey clawed and kicked, but to no avail. He snagged an arm around her waist and pulled her tight against his chest.

"Let me go!" she cried.

He shook his shaggy-haired head. "Not so fast, *niña.* I like you right where you are."

She kicked him in the shin, which was when it dawned on her she was barefoot. She must have lost her high heels sometime during the kidnapping. The blow surely hurt her worse than her assailant, because she yelped in pain, while he just laughed.

She caught sight of the third man—the one who must be Burr—watching her, his fierce, hooded eyes filled with...loathing? She couldn't take her eyes off him, even as Epifanio pulled her body tight against his.

Burr's lips were pressed flat in disgust, distorting the shape of his mouth. His chin had a slight crease down the center of it and jutted as though seeking a confrontation. A diamond sparkled in one earlobe, and she saw a tattoo on his arm below the folded-up sleeve of a black T-shirt, although she couldn't make out what the tattoo was. He had a day's growth of black beard that did nothing to hide the angular planes of his face. His cheekbones were high and wide, and his nose was crooked from having been broken, from the look of it, more than once.

The pull of tearing fabric brought her attention back to the Mexican. She bucked violently to free herself from his grasp.

He ripped the bodice of her gown, exposing the white merry widow beneath it. "Fight me, bitch," he said in a low, rusty-hinge voice. "I like it when a woman fights."

Lindsey didn't disappoint him. Furious and frightened, her fingernails clawed down the side of Epifanio's face, leaving four distinct bloody scratches. She grasped his hair and yanked hard, then reeled when he slapped her across the face with his open hand, drawing blood where her teeth cut her lip.

Lindsey got a quick glance at what appeared to be a coiled black snake tattooed on Burr's arm as he grabbed Epifanio and spun him around. She felt herself pulled free of Epifanio's grasp and flung past him. She hit the wall hard and, momentarily stunned, slid down in a heap.

"I told you to leave her alone."

Dazed, she watched Burr confront Epifanio. He was easily as tall as the Mexican, but lean where the other man was barrel-shaped. His hair was as shiny black as a raven's wing and clubbed into a tail at his nape. He wore tight black jeans and black cowboy boots.

Burr was all sinew and bone. And clearly dangerous. His spread-legged stance was challenging, his balled fists intimidating. A muscle worked where his jaw was clenched. His eyes were a brown so deep it was almost black. There was no compassion in those beautiful dark eyes, just cold-blooded menace.

"Stay out of this, Burr," Epifanio warned. "The woman is mine."

"She belongs to Hector. He'll have your hide if you keep up with what you're doing. Let her be, Epifanio."

Epifanio's eyes narrowed. His lips flattened. "Get outta my way, Burr."

Burr didn't move an inch.

A switchblade appeared in Epifanio's hand. Lindsey flinched when she heard the *snick* as he flipped the blade from its sheath.

"Move outta my way, Burr."

Burr shook his head, a slight, almost imperceptible movement.

Epifanio lunged with the knife, intent on catching Burr by surprise. Burr caught the wrist of the hand that held the switchblade just as it reached his body, turning it aside so the knife skimmed across his chest instead of plunging into it. Lindsey gasped when she saw the streak of red left by the blade.

It dawned on Lindsey that she could escape while the two men were locked in mortal combat. She inched backward toward the door but found it impossible to take her eyes from the drama unfolding before her. It seemed unlikely that Burr would win. He was outmatched in size and strength by the other man. Given that scenario, it was imperative that she escape if she could.

She scrambled toward the door on her hands and knees, forcing herself to ignore the fact that Burr was probably going to die for coming to her rescue. He was a villain, just like the others. If Epifanio didn't kill him, he was going to spend the rest of his life in prison for kidnapping her.

Lindsey pulled herself upright using the doorknob. She had opened the door a mere inch when someone grabbed her, and a flat male palm forced the door shut.

She made a guttural sound deep in her throat that was part outrage, part fear. She turned with her fingers arched into claws aimed at her captor's face, then realized it was Burr who had hold of her. She searched quickly for Epifanio and saw him lying on the floor, the switchblade imbedded in his chest.

Her hand froze in midair, and her stomach revolted at the sight of the dead man. Her eyes shot to Burr's face, which gave no evidence of any feeling whatsoever—neither revulsion nor remorse—for what he had done.

She swallowed back the bile burning her throat. "Is he dead?"

"Yes."

"What are you going to do with me?"

"The hell if I know," he muttered viciously. "We'd damn well better get out of here. Keep your mouth shut when we're in the hall.'' He opened the door and started to drag her through it.

Lindsey was too terrified to cooperate with her savior—an unshaven man in a black T-shirt and jeans, a man with a pierced ear and a ponytail and a snake tattoo, simply didn't fit her image of a knight in shining armor. "Let me go,'' she pleaded. "I won't tell them anything about you.''

"Look, Blue Eyes—'' As Burr spoke, there was a shout from the other room.

It was Tex.

"Hey! Where the hell do you think you're going?'' Tex took one look at Epifanio's body, and a gun appeared in his hand from a holster that had apparently been hidden inside his denim jacket. He aimed it in Burr's—and therefore Lindsey's—direction.

"You sonofabitch!'' he hissed.

Lindsey squeezed her eyes shut against the sight of the deadly gun bore, waiting for the sound of shots. But there was only one deafening blast, close to her ear. Her eyes flashed open.

Tex lay in the doorway, a pool of blood spreading on the beige carpet around his body.

She turned to stare, horrified, at Burr, who was holding a .38 snub-nosed revolver in his hand. While she watched, he returned the small, deadly weapon to his boot.

Lindsey had been in such a constant state of terror for the past few minutes that her body quivered from excess adrenaline. She felt dizzy, and she wanted desperately to give in to the darkness that threatened to overwhelm her. She wanted even more to live. And she knew that if she fainted now, she might never see daylight again. Her eyes sought out Burr's, wondering what the chances were that he would let her go.

"You're in shock," he said matter-of-factly. He manhandled her over to the couch, forced her to sit, and shoved her head down between her knees. When she tried to rise, he ordered, "Stay there!"

He peered out into the hall, looking to see if anyone was curious or stupid enough to personally investigate the shot. "We don't have much time. Someone has probably called the authorities about that gunshot."

Lindsey closed her eyes to avoid seeing the two bodies and breathed deeply, trying to regain her equilibrium. She heard Burr pacing the carpet and muttering to himself. He picked up the phone receiver and dropped it back into the cradle.

"Damn! Damn it to hell!"

She sat up and stared at the furious man standing spread-legged across from her with his hands on his hips.

"I guess I don't have any choice," he said. "Come on, let's go."

"Go where?" Lindsey demanded in her most imperious voice.

"Look, Blue Eyes. When I say 'jump' you say 'how high?' Have you got that?" He grabbed a black leather jacket off one of the chairs and slipped his arms into it.

"If you let me go," Lindsey said, "I'll tell my father you saved me from those two men."

"Hell, if I let you go, Hector will just snatch you back up again. Or shoot you or your father or some other member of your family. He means business. You don't have any choice. You're coming with me."

"Where?"

"Damn it, just do what you're told!" He grabbed her arm and yanked her up off the couch.

Lindsey tried to jerk herself free, but ended up nearly wrenching her arm from the socket. She saw the direction Burr's eyes took as she slammed into him and looked down to see what he found so fascinating. Which was when she realized the extent of the damage to her bodice. The merry widow was far more concealing than many bathing suits she had worn, but it was an undergarment. It did its job well, forcing her generous breasts upward so that a great deal of flesh was mounded above the two white cups.

Burr swore. "You're not going anywhere like that without attracting more attention than I want." He pulled off his jacket and handed it to her. "Put that on."

She looked down the full-length taffeta skirt all the way to where her toes curled into the thick carpet. "I don't think your jacket is going to completely solve the problem." It was warm, though, and smelled, surprisingly, of a very male after-shave.

Burr pursed his lips as he observed her bare feet. "I suppose you're right. Guess we'll have to use the stairs down to the garage in the basement."

She started to take the jacket off, and he said curtly, "Keep it."

He didn't give her a chance to protest, just grabbed her hand and headed for the door. He stopped at the portal and turned to her. "If you scream, I'll have to knock you out. Do you understand?"

Lindsey nodded. She had no doubt he would do as he promised. Her mind was racing, trying to think of some way she could escape him. But no one appeared in the stairwell, and she knew he would catch her if she tried to flee. They had nearly reached the garage in the basement. Lindsey knew she was running out of time. She had to take the chance that someone would hear her and come to her rescue.

She took a deep breath and screamed.

"Damn you, lady! I warned you!"

Lindsey saw the fist coming, felt her teeth snap when flesh connected with flesh, felt her legs begin to crumple under her. She was stunned, but not unconscious, so she heard Burr swear again as he caught her in his arms, threw her over his shoulder in a fireman's carry, and moved stealthily into the garage.

Chapter Two

Burr was furious at the way things had turned out. This wasn't supposed to have happened. He had hoped to let the situation play out naturally. But Tex and Epifanio had gotten the bright idea to rape the governor's daughter. He couldn't let that happen, so he had interfered.

And blown eighteen months of undercover work as a member of the Texas Mafia.

He damned all spoiled little rich girls, like Miss Lindsey Major, who believed they were immune to the rules that applied to everybody else, who considered themselves too far above the vermin that roamed the dark alleys of the world to ever be threatened by them. She had been told that Hector Martinez was planning something. Burr had risked a great deal to make the anonymous phone call to the governor's mansion himself. She had answered the phone, so he knew she had been made aware of the danger. And damned if she hadn't ignored his warning and gone out to that charity ball after all!

She had cavalierly dismissed the security man at the end of the walk, instead of having him escort her to the front door of the mansion—where she had been snatched and dragged back into the concealing forsythia bushes before she could get inside.

But he had to admire her spunk. No tears from Miss Lindsey Major, just clawed fists and fight. Unfortunately, she had complicated things by screaming when he had warned her to be quiet. God only knew what repercussions there would be when word got out that he had hit her.

Hell, he hadn't wanted to take the job in the first place, but the captain of the Rangers had convinced him that someone had to do it. The last Texas Ranger they had sent undercover, Burr's best friend, Lieutenant Larry Williams, had been found dead in his car trunk. Burr was a natural to take Larry's place, the captain had said, because he had grown up in the gangs in Houston along with Larry, and he knew the rackets. He had the snake tattoo from his youth and understood the lingo. A pierced ear and long hair and a black leather jacket had completed his disguise. No one with the Texas Mafia had suspected Burr Covington was actually a lieutenant in the Texas Rangers.

He had been really close to nailing Hector Martinez for the murder of his friend, but all that effort was down the john now. It was some comfort to know he would be able to convict Hector of kidnapping the governor's daughter. But they would have to catch Hector first, and that was going to be more difficult than it sounded. Hector had more underground hiding places than a rattlesnake.

Burr wasn't sure what to do now. He had been hoping against hope that he could continue his role undercover. But after what he had done to Epifanio and Tex, and with the governor's daughter in his custody, there wasn't much chance of that. He needed to get in touch with Captain Rogers and find out what he was supposed to do with the woman. With any luck, it would be a simple matter of tucking her away somewhere safe until they either caught Hector or the Turk's death sentence was carried out.

Burr set the governor's daughter down on the passenger side of a black Jaguar with black leather seats. The car happened to be his own, but it fit the image he had been portraying, so he had used it. He saw the woman was regaining consciousness, so he gave her cheek a little slap.

"Wake up," he said. "We need to talk."

He might as well tell her who he was, Burr figured. That way she was more liable to cooperate. Although, even that wasn't a guarantee. A woman used to ordering people around, a woman used to having her own way, wasn't going to like taking orders. Only, Burr was determined to stay in control of the situation, even if she was the governor's daughter and had the damnedest blue eyes he had ever seen. Not to mention a few other hard-to-ignore assets.

His gaze slid to the opening in his jacket, where her breasts rose as she heaved in a deep breath and let it out in a shuddering sigh. He had an uncontrollable urge—which he carefully controlled—to put his mouth against her flesh to see if it was as delectable as it looked.

He heard her gasp and lifted his gaze to meet hers. Damn, but her eyes were beautiful! They were wide-set and heavily lashed and large enough for a man to get lost in. He could see why they said she had the bluest eyes in Texas. Except, they weren't blue, really. More a sort of lilac color. But definitely unique and absolutely dazzling.

Now he noticed that the rest of her features were rather ordinary. Her nose was small and straight, her mouth wide and full. Her chin jutted slightly, but he figured that was probably because she made a habit of leading with it. She was always going to attract male attention with her lush figure, and her mane of golden hair was indeed a crowning glory.

It was said she used those eyes of hers to put a man on his knees and get her own way. Well, those baby blues weren't going to work on him.

All the same, he felt a jolt of guilty shame when she accused him of wrongdoing with her eyes and followed that with the outraged statement, "You hit me!"

With an effort, he managed a shrug. "It was your own damn fault. I warned you not to scream."

He watched as she pulled the jacket closed. So. She had caught him looking at her. She must be wondering what his intentions were. Hell, he wouldn't mind having her under him in bed. What man wouldn't? But he knew better than to think he could have what he wanted. She was the governor's daughter. He was a man who had grown up on the wrong side of the tracks.

He bent down on one knee beside the open door and realized with an inward sigh that she had brought him to his knees, after all. "Look, Blue Eyes—Miss Major—we have to talk."

She swallowed hard but said nothing.

He was uncomfortable kneeling beside the door, and there was always the chance she would get it into her head to scream again. He stood and closed the car door and started around the front of the Jaguar to the driver's side.

Before he had gotten halfway around the car, she shoved open her door and ran, screaming at the top of her lungs.

Burr caught her before she had gone twenty feet, tackling her like a football player, the two of them rolling over and over until they were stopped by a concrete abutment in a dark corner of the garage. He came to rest lying on top of her, uncomfortably aware of the feminine shape beneath him. His body reacted instantly, instinctively.

Burr was embarrassed and unable to stop the slow flush that climbed his throat. His body had responded like some randy teenager's to the feel of her flesh between his thighs, rather than like the rational, professional, thirty-six-year-old Texas Ranger he was. Hell, he was probably going to have to answer to the captain for that, too.

Lindsey recognized the hardness pressing against her abdomen and felt a renewed terror at her predicament. Worse, Burr's weight kept her from taking a breath, which she desperately needed since the fall had knocked the wind from her.

She knew frustration when she saw it. Her father rarely lost his temper, though he could become dangerously angry. Burr's dark eyes burned now with that same controlled fury.

"Damn you. I ought to..." He didn't finish his threat. His eyes searched the garage, looking for whoever might have heard her scream.

Her mouth worked as she gasped, "Please... Please. I...can't breathe."

He eased his weight onto his arms, but held her captive with his lower body—his aroused lower body. "That was a stupid thing to do, Blue Eyes."

She noticed he had given up the deferential *Miss Major.*

She felt a surge of hope when she saw a couple come out of the elevator and start toward their car.

"Don't make a sound," Burr hissed in her ear.

Lindsey opened her mouth to scream.

And Burr covered it with his.

There was nothing sensuous about his kiss. It was brutal, intended to keep her silent until the couple was gone. She bucked with all her strength at the same time she tried to bite him.

His mouth flattened, but he didn't otherwise respond to the pain she knew she must be causing him with her teeth. His hips pressed her down, so she felt the roughness of the concrete against her legs and back where her gown was rucked up.

She heard a car starting and the squeal of rubber on cement as it drove away. She closed her eyes so Burr wouldn't see the defeat she felt. A moment later he caught both her hands in one of his, while his other hand replaced his mouth to silence her.

"Look at me," he demanded. He used his hold on her to force her face toward him when she didn't respond and repeated, "Look at me!"

Lindsey opened her eyes and looked at him defiantly.

"In a moment I'm going to let you go. If you scream, I will knock you out—all the way out. Blink those pretty blue eyes of yours if you understand."

She blinked her eyes once, slowly.

He removed his hand, then stared at her, daring her to scream.

Burr watched in consternation as tears welled in the bluest eyes in Texas. They made her eyes luminescent and, he decided, even more attractive. He was aroused again—or still. And she was obviously terrified of him because of it. He quickly levered himself off of her and reached down to help her up. She refused his hand, stumbling to her feet.

Burr was just about to start explaining things when she ran again. He quickly caught her, shoving her up against the concrete wall. He stapled her hands flat on either side of her head against the rough surface and snapped, "Damn it, I'm a Texas Ranger! I've been working undercover. You're safe. Do you hear me? You're safe!"

"A Texas Ranger?"

Burr nodded curtly.

He felt her whole body relax against him. Then the tears came in earnest. It was obvious she was fighting them, and he debated whether he ought to try to comfort her. But that sort of thing could be easily misconstrued, and he already had enough to answer to the captain for.

The heartrending sound of a broken sob moved him to put his arms around her and, once he had done that, it seemed the most natural thing in the world to pull her into his embrace and murmur calming words in her ear. His body once again reacted in a totally male way to her femaleness.

Burr had never had much use for prima donnas, and Lindsey Major certainly qualified as one. Unfortunately his body didn't know a thing about her personality; it was reacting strictly to the primeval need of male for female. He tightened his hold, feeling the swell of her breasts against his muscular chest.

Lindsey had thrown her arms around the Texas Ranger in relief, and they caught in the ponytail at his nape, which was surprisingly silky. She trembled at the feel of Burr's lips, soft and soothing against her forehead as he crooned words of comfort. And she was aware, again, of the fact that he was attracted to her in a way that was totally inappropriate to the situation.

Now that she was no longer in terror for her life, however, she realized with no little distress that his arousal had sparked an answering response from her. It was easiest to attribute her reaction to the Ranger as simple relief that he wasn't one of the bad guys. It couldn't possibly be more than that. She didn't know this man and, judging from the looks of him, he wasn't someone she would ever want to know. It would be best to defuse the situation as quickly as possible.

"You can let me go now," she said.

"What?" Burr had been so caught up in the pleasure of what he was doing that he was slow to notice the governor's daughter withdrawing from his embrace.

He met her gaze and saw the tears were gone, replaced by an icy look of disdain. The governor's daughter—a woman the newspapers had recently labeled an elusive ice princess because she was never seen twice with the same male escort—was back.

Burr stepped away, grabbed Lindsey's arm and, without looking back, dragged her toward his car.

Naturally she resisted. "Where are you taking me?"

Burr raised a brow at her commanding tone of voice. "Somewhere you'll be safe."

"I demand that you take me home."

"I'm afraid that isn't possible right now."

She dug in her heels, and he was forced to stop or hurt her. He didn't want to be accused of using unnecessary force.

"I insist you let me call my father right now and tell him I'm all right."

"Not here." Anticipating her argument, he explained, "There's still a chance one of Hector's goons may show up."

She hesitated, evaluating what he had said. "All right, I'll go with you. But we stop as soon as it's safe, and I call my father. Agreed?"

"Agreed." Of course, her idea of when it might be safe to stop and his probably differed. But Burr didn't think this was the time to bring that up.

The Jaguar was the kind of car Lindsey expected a man like Burr to own. Racy. Fast. Dark. Dangerous. She wondered if he had been given the car as part of his cover and realized she was having trouble making the leap from "bad guy" to "good guy" where he was concerned. Burr simply didn't look the part of guardian angel.

Burr opened the passenger door, shoved Lindsey in less carefully this time, and slammed it behind her. He slid over the hood and got in on the other side. The engine started with a roar that became a purr as he pulled out of the garage. He slipped from the city street onto I-35 and accelerated.

Lindsey blinked her eyes against the bright sunlight. The instant she realized Burr had gotten onto the interstate, her alarm returned. "Where are you going?"

"I told you, somewhere Hector can't find you."

Her eyes widened. "You never intended to let me make a phone call, did you?" She reached for the door handle.

"Don't even think about jumping out," he said. "You'd end up seriously injured or dead. Trust me."

"*Trust* you? First you hit me, then you fall on me like a beast in rut and manhandle me like I was some criminal, and now you're driving me God knows where and threatening me with dire consequences if I try to leave your august presence! Give me one good reason why I should trust you."

"I saved your life."

There was a moment of silence. "Well, there is that," she conceded ruefully.

"Look, I can't take you anywhere near the governor's mansion until I talk to my captain. Hector may have someone watching the place. I don't want to be seen returning you home. In fact, I've got to find someplace to hide us both."

"Why do you have to hide?" Her eyes went wide with a sudden horrible thought. "You weren't lying about being a Ranger, were you?"

His lips curled in a bitter smile. "No, I'm a Ranger, all right. But there's a slight problem nobody counted on."

"What's that?"

"Hector is liable to be a bit perturbed when he finds out I killed his brother."

"His brother?"

"Epifanio."

"Oh, no!"

Lindsey bit her lip worriedly as Burr exited west onto U.S. 290 heading toward Fredericksburg and the hill country. A long, poignant silence developed as she watched the miles fly by. Her glance slid to the man driving the Jaguar. Maybe she simply hadn't given him the right incentive to take her home.

"I'm sure my father would reward you generously—with a great deal of money—if you would just take me home."

"Do you think you're worth it?"

She arched an aristocratic brow. "What do you mean?"

"I know for a fact you were warned not to go out last night. Why did you?"

"That's none of your business."

"You made it my business when you got yourself kidnapped."

"I had promised to attend the ball. I had to go."

"So you were just doing what spoiled little rich girls do, is that it?"

"Spoiled—" Lindsey bit back her retort. She wasn't going to argue with a man wearing a ponytail and a diamond earring. "You know nothing about me."

"I know what I read in the papers."

Lindsey laughed. "I suspected you were a fool. Now I've got proof."

He glanced sharply at her.

"Anyone who believes what he reads in the papers—"

"Is a fool?" he interrupted. "But then, I've had a chance to judge you for myself now. At least one thing they said is true. You've got the bluest eyes I've ever seen. And from the looks of you, I'm inclined to believe there's some truth in the rest of what I've read."

"You mean, that I'm spoiled rotten, the 'very much indulged' daughter of a very powerful man?" Lindsey said, her voice rife with indignation as she quoted a recent society news article.

"If the panty hose fit..."

He took his eyes off the road long enough to give her a thorough perusal with eyes that held their share of disapproval and disdain.

Lindsey gave him a withering look of scorn. "Appearances can be deceiving."

He snorted. "You can say that again."

She noticed with some alarm that he had turned off the highway onto a winding dirt road that was shaded by live oaks. "Where are we going?"

"Someplace private where I can use the phone."

"Remember, I want to talk to my father."

He brought the Jaguar to a stop in front of a small wooden cabin with a roofed porch and a stone chimney. The cabin was unpainted, and the split wood had been aged by wind and weather. There was a picture window in front, with a door to one side of it.

"Get inside," he said.

Lindsey sat where she was.

"Go on," he said. "There's no one here but us."

Lindsey stayed where she was. "What is this place?"

Burr exited the car, slid over the hood and opened her door. "Are you coming out of there on your own, or am I going to have to drag you out?"

Lindsey dipped a bare foot out of the car. She winced when she encountered the small, sharp stones on the drive. Before she had taken two painful steps,

Burr swept her up into his arms. She instinctively grabbed his shoulders. The muscles beneath the T-shirt were rock hard. Her eyes met his, questioning.

"You don't weigh as much as I thought you would."

She flushed at the insult buried in the compliment. She was five-ten in her stocking feet, and nobody had ever accused her of being skinny. Fortunately, he was easily six inches taller. He carried her up to the porch and set her down.

She didn't thank him. After all, it wasn't her fault she didn't have any shoes.

Burr opened the door and gave her a nudge inside.

Lindsey lifted her chin and, once she regained her balance, walked past him as regally as a queen. She thought she heard him grunt in disgust, but refused to give him the satisfaction of a response.

She looked around the cabin, which was sparingly furnished. There was an old leather couch and a rawhide-covered chair in front of the stone fireplace. The hardwood floor was polished to a high sheen, but there were no rugs of any kind on it. Nor were there curtains on any of the windows.

She could see the kitchen from the living room. It contained a small wooden table and two ladderback chairs. She suspected the other doorway led to the bedroom and bath. There wasn't room for much else.

She turned to face Burr with her hands folded in front of her. "Now what?"

"Now I have to make some calls."

Lindsey looked around for a phone, but didn't see one.

"Not here," he said. "I have to go into town."

"What am I supposed to do while you're gone?"

"Wait here for me."

Lindsey swallowed her outrage and managed to say in a reasonable voice, "Why can't I go with you?"

"I can't take the chance you'll draw attention with those blue eyes of yours. You'll be safer here."

"I can always wear sunglasses," she snapped.

"I don't have a pair handy. Do you?"

Obviously she didn't.

"You'll be safer here," he said.

"Safer?" she asked in a sharp voice. "What if one of Hector's men finds me here? I'm totally defenseless!"

Burr snorted. "I wouldn't say that. You didn't do so badly at the hotel."

"You know what I mean," she said with asperity. "I know what Hector had planned for me. I heard you talking through the door." She paused and admitted, "I'm scared."

Burr's eyes narrowed. He seemed to debate a moment before he spoke. "You've got nothing to fear if you stay here."

Lindsey looked at him, really looked at him. At the long hair. The earring. The twice-broken nose. The snake tattoo. "I repeat, I don't see anything that leads me to believe I can trust you to have my best interests at heart."

"As someone recently told me, appearances can be deceiving."

"I won't stay here alone," she said. "The moment you're gone, I'll walk back to the road."

"I'm sorry to hear that."

He moved amazingly fast, catching her arms and dragging them behind her. He found rope in the kitchen and tied her hands. He wasn't precisely rough, but he yanked the clothesline cord tight around her wrists. He pushed her toward the open doorway that led to what turned out to be, as she had suspected, the bedroom.

He picked her up and dumped her on the bed before tying her ankles together. "You should do all right here until I come back."

"How long is that going to be?" She felt humiliated and indignant, and both of those emotions were apparent in her voice.

"Not long enough for you to work yourself free of those ropes," he said, as though reading her mind. "Just lie still and be good. I'll bring you back something to eat."

Lindsey suddenly realized she was famished. It had been almost twenty-four hours since her last meal. But she refused to be mollified by the bone he had thrown her. "My father will have your badge when he hears about how you've treated me. You'll be writing parking tickets for the rest of your life!"

"I'm sorry to have to do this," he said as he tied a pillowcase around her mouth. "I don't think there's anybody around to hear you if you scream, but I can't take the chance."

Then he was gone. She heard stones scattering as he left the driveway. She immediately tested her bonds, but they didn't give. She began looking around the room to see what she might use to cut herself free. Then it dawned on her that he hadn't tied her to the bed. There was nothing to keep her from just getting up and hopping away.

Burr was worried. He wondered whether it might not have been smarter to take the governor's daughter home, after all. But he knew that wouldn't have solved anything. Hector would just make some attempt on some other member of the family. No, this had to be solved while Hector still thought someone on his side had the woman.

Burr was also angry with himself for not finding some other way to rescue "the bluest eyes in Texas" without having to kill Hector's brother. But he hadn't been given a choice. At least he had the girl—the woman, he corrected himself—to bargain with. And what a woman!

Lindsey Major was the kind of woman he had always dreamed about, whenever he let himself dream. She was tall, with lush curves and soft skin. He knew about the soft skin because he'd had to touch her to tie her up. And he knew about the curves because he had picked her up and held her in his arms.

Burr felt his body respond to the memory of how she had felt with her warm breasts nestled against his chest. He cursed under his breath. He might as well desire some image on a movie screen. He had about the same chance of intimacy with the governor's blue-eyed daughter.

He found a phone booth in the small town closest to the cabin. The town consisted of a gas station and a general store, which also contained a post office. People stopped here for gas or to get a soda on their way to hunt in the hill country, or on their way to go floating down the many streams in the area on an inflated inner tube. He hadn't come here once in the eighteen months he had worked for Hector, and he was pretty sure there was no way Hector could trace him here.

He called the governor's mansion, knowing that was where the captain would be. It took a while for someone to acknowledge who he was and to get the captain on the phone.

"I've been compromised," Burr said.

"Damn!" A pause and then, "Is she safe?"

"I've got her."

"Where?"

"At my cabin in the hill country."

"What happened?"

"I had to kill Hector's brother."

"Come on in, Burr. The game's up."

Burr shook his head, then realized Captain Rogers couldn't see him. "No, Captain. I haven't spent the past eighteen months undercover with these bastards to have it all go down the drain now. I think I can still get Hector. But I need to do something with the governor's daughter. Is there someplace I can drop her off?"

There was a long pause, and Burr heard Captain Rogers discussing the situation with those around him.

"You there, Burr?"

"Yes, sir."

"I want you to call Hector and tell him you're willing to deal for the governor's daughter." Frank continued speaking, telling Burr the details of the plan he had worked out with the other law enforcement officials who had responded to the governor's call for assistance.

When Frank had finished, Burr said, "I don't like it. I could manage better without the woman."

"She's safe with you. We'll take care of Hector."

"Hector's not going to deal unless he sees me in person," Burr said.

"You call him. Offer him the deal. Then sit tight with Miss Major."

"I think Miss Major would be happier if she went home."

"That's not an option, Burr."

"But, sir—"

"Don't waste your breath arguing. The decision has been made. Miss Major stays with you."

Burr heard someone ask for the phone.

"This is Governor Major. Who am I speaking to?"

"This is Ranger Lieutenant Covington," Burr replied.

"How is my daughter?" the governor asked. "Is she all right?"

Burr heard the emotion in the governor's voice. *He's going to have my head, all right. Just like she said.* "She's fine, Governor."

"She's not hurt?"

"No, sir. She's just as beautiful as the newspapers say. And just as contrary." Burr swore under his breath. *Why did I say that? I'm going to get my tail kicked all the way back to Austin for insubordination.*

He heard the governor chuckle. "That's my girl, all right." He gave a patent sigh of relief. "Thank you, Lieutenant Covington. Take care of her for me."

"Yes, sir. I will, sir."

"You heard the governor, Burr," the captain said. "I'll get back to you when we've taken care of Hector. Until then, you take care of Miss Major."

"Yes, sir." Burr waited for a click, then slammed the phone onto the hook. A moment later he picked it up again and began to dial.

When Hector came on the line, Burr pricked him by asking, "Did you lose something?"

"Where is she?" Hector demanded.

"I've got her."

"What happened?"

Burr said nothing.

"I asked you what happened."

"They gave me no choice."

"The girl belongs to me. I want her."

"I want to make a deal, Hector."

"You bring her to me now, and I might let you live," Hector said. "Otherwise, I'll hunt you down. And kill you and the girl both."

Burr quickly gave Hector the terms Captain Rogers had outlined. When Hector arrived at the rendezvous site, there would be law enforcement officials of all kinds waiting to apprehend him.

"I'll keep the girl as insurance," Burr said. "You'll get her when you show up with the money."

"You're a dead man, Burr," Hector said.

"If you don't get the girl back, you can't negotiate with the governor for the Turk's life," Burr reminded him.

Burr hung up the phone on Hector's threat to kill him slowly when he caught up to him. After a stop to buy supplies, he was careful not to be seen leaving town and watched to make sure he wasn't being followed when he turned onto the dirt road that led to the cabin.

It was time he had a talk with the governor's daughter. He went directly to the bedroom where he had left her.

She was gone.

Chapter Three

If she had possessed a decent pair of shoes, Lindsey thought, she could have made it to the main road. But the men's cowboy boots she had found in the closet of the cabin weren't doing the job, even with two extra pairs of socks.

She hid behind a tree when she saw the Jaguar returning along the dusty road. Burr would know in a moment or two that she was gone, and he would come looking for her. There was no sense running. Not in these damned boots. But she wasn't sure she wanted to give up, either. Being in Burr's custody hadn't exactly been a picnic so far.

She rubbed her shoulder where she had bruised herself falling out of the high, four-poster bed, and ran a gentle finger over the cuts at her wrists where she had used a knife from the kitchen to free herself. It had been stupid to try to escape. In all probability, her father had demanded her return, and Burr had come back to set her free.

She hadn't decided yet whether she was going to complain about what Burr had done to her. He was responsible for more than a few of the bruises she now bore. She moved her jaw cautiously. It was swollen and sore, but she was pretty sure he hadn't hit her as hard as he could have.

"Have a nice walk?"

Lindsey stiffened at the sarcasm in Burr's voice. She turned slowly to face him, gritting her teeth when she saw the amusement in his eyes at the outfit she was wearing.

"You look like a little girl dressed up in her father's clothes."

Lindsey looked down at the oversize orange University of Texas sweatshirt, men's jeans, and boots she was wearing. The jeans were held up with some of the rope that had been used to tie her hands. "This was all I could find."

"If you'd just been a little patient, I would have solved the problem for you. I bought some things for you in town."

"I won't need them, because you're going to be taking me home," Lindsey said in a firm voice.

He shook his head. "I'm afraid not."

"My father—"

"I spoke to the governor personally. He agreed you'd be safer with me until Hector's been picked up."

Lindsey felt her chin begin to tremble. "How long is that going to take?"

"Until tomorrow, if we're lucky."

"And if we're not?"

"We'll worry about that when the time comes." Burr reached out a hand and traced the bruise on her jaw. "I'm sorry about that."

Lindsey jerked her head away. "You've got a lot more than that to be sorry for!"

His eyes grew cold. "I was doing my job the best way I knew how. If you had paid attention to the warnings you were given—"

"I had no warning about anything like this!"

"You were told Hector was making plans."

Lindsey bit her lip. "I didn't think—"

"Your kind never does," Burr interrupted.

Lindsey's face flamed with anger "This isn't my fault!"

"It sure as hell isn't mine!" Burr retorted. "I spent eighteen long, lousy months undercover with the Texas Mafia, trying to get enough information to prove Hector Martinez ordered the death of a friend of mine. Thanks to you, prosecuting Hector for that crime isn't going to happen now."

There was a pause while Lindsey absorbed what he had said. "I'm sorry."

"Yeah, well, sorry doesn't cut it, Blue Eyes."

"Don't call me that!"

"I have it on good authority—the news media—that you're the lady with the bluest eyes in Texas."

"My eyes have nothing whatsoever to do with who I am."

"What you are is arrogant and uncooperative."

"How dare you—"

"You ready to walk back now?"

Lindsey stuck her chin in the air and began walking back toward the cabin. Her stride was hampered by a broken blister on her left heel.

"Something wrong with your leg?"

Lindsey heard the concern in Burr's voice, but answered haughtily, "Nothing that concerns you."

She continued her determined limp toward the cabin.

Lindsey gave a cry of surprise as Burr swung her up into his arms, shifting her until he was holding her close, with her breasts crushed against his chest. Her arms involuntarily circled his neck. She sought out his face and was surprised to find his eyes hooded, his nostrils flared. She was unnerved by the male energy vibrating from the man whose arms had closed securely around her shoulders and under her knees. Her eyes came to rest on his mouth, which was partly open, the lips full, the mouth wide.

"What do you think..." Her voice was raspy, so she cleared her throat and tried again. "What do you think you're doing, Mr. —? What *is* your last name, anyway?''

''Covington,'' Burr replied. ''I thought I'd give you a lift back to the cabin.'' He had already started walking, in fact. He kept his eyes focused straight ahead.

''Did it ever occur to you that I would rather walk than be put in the position of accepting your help?''

''There are a lot of things that occur to me when I think about you.'' *Like how good you feel in my arms. Like how those blue eyes of yours would look if I was inside you making sweet, sweet love to you.*

Lindsey didn't bother asking Burr to explain himself. She didn't want to exacerbate the situation. She held on to his neck because that eased the weight he had to carry in his arms, not because the silky hair at his nape felt good. She snuggled closer so he wouldn't drop her, not because she liked the feel of hard muscle pressing against her breasts. And she laid her face against his throat so she wouldn't have to look at him, not because she wanted to smell the essence of him on his skin and clothes.

When they arrived at the cabin, Burr set her down on the porch and offered her an olive branch. ''Look, if we're going to be stuck together for the next twenty-four hours, we may as well call a truce.''

''I wasn't aware there was a war going on.''

Burr snickered. "Fine, Blue Eyes. I don't mind the sniping if you don't."

"Wait!" Lindsey laid a hand on Burr's arm. She recoiled when she realized she had touched the snake tattoo.

His lips curled in a cynical smile. "Not the kind of thing you're used to, is it?"

Lindsey's eyes narrowed. "I don't understand why you're so determined to insult me. And I should mention, it isn't doing your career any good."

"Is that a threat, *Blue Eyes?*" Burr said in a low voice.

"That would be rather foolish under the circumstances," Lindsey conceded. "I am, after all, at your mercy for the next twenty-four hours. It would seem discretion is the better part of valor. Truce?" She held out her hand for Burr to shake.

Burr's hand enveloped hers, and she realized for the first time how big he was, and how strong, and that his palm and fingertips were callused as though he worked with his hands. Perhaps he did in his spare time. She knew little or nothing about him.

"You can change in the bedroom while I cook us something to eat."

Lindsey disappeared into the bedroom and shut the door behind her. She was surprised at how well the jeans fit, not to mention the tennis shoes. However, she decided she would rather walk barefoot until she could find a Band-Aid for the blister on her heel. She pulled on a T-shirt that pictured a dead armadillo on the front with the words Road Kill blazoned across it and headed back to the kitchen.

Burr was dismayed at how the jeans fit her. They outlined her legs and fanny too well. And the T-shirt was downright dangerous. She had obviously abandoned the merry widow, and he could see the soft curve of her breasts beneath the cotton. He frowned when he realized she was barefoot. The sight of her toes curling on the hardwood floor made her look as vulnerable as a child. Only she was a full-grown, red-blooded woman. And his body responded to her like a full-grown, red-blooded man.

"The shoes didn't fit?" He was amazed at how rough his voice sounded. He turned back to the stove to hide the bulge that was making his jeans uncomfortably snug.

"I was wondering if you have a Band-Aid."

At his look of confusion, she set her bare foot up on the counter beside him and showed him the blister on her heel.

"See?"

Whoever would have thought an ankle could be such a source of erotic stimulation? Burr stared at her foot until his eyes glazed, then forced his attention back to the potatoes he was frying on the stove. "Don't have a Band-Aid. I'll get one tomorrow when I go into town."

"Guess I'll have to go barefoot until then." She put her foot back on the floor and wiggled her toes. "It feels kind of nice," she admitted. "I can't remember the last time I walked around barefoot. Oh, yes, I do," she said.

To Burr's relief, she wandered to the kitchen table and sat down. He bent over and checked the steaks in the oven broiler to hide his state of arousal.

"I was six, and my mother and father took me to Padre Island, to the beach. My mother was pregnant with Carl—he's my younger brother—and I got to race up and down the beach barefoot. I loved it."

"That was a long time ago," Burr said.

"Yes, it was. Those were some of the last carefree days my family had. Father entered politics that year. I didn't see as much of him after that. He was always on the road campaigning, first for state representative, then for congressman, and finally for governor."

Talk about Lindsey's father reminded Burr of who she was, and why he'd had to keep his distance. If he was lucky, he would get out of this situation with no more than a reprimand. If he let his libido get out of hand, there was no telling what the consequences would be. Only, it was damned hard to remember who she was when she was slouched back comfortably in the kitchen chair with her fingers meshed behind her head, raising the tips of her breasts against the T-shirt. Her right ankle was crossed over the opposite knee, in a naturally sexy pose.

He checked the steaks again. "These are about ready. How do you like yours?"

"Pink."

The word brought to mind all kinds of things Lieutenant Burr Covington would rather not think about. Lips. Blushing cheeks. Nipples. *Damn it, Covington, get your mind off the woman! She's out of bounds. Got it?*

"Do you have any wine?" she asked.

Burr stared at her in confusion.

"To go with the steak," she explained. "I love a dry red wine with steak."

Burr snorted. "I've got some beer."

"Lite?"

He snorted again, only this time it turned into a rumbly sort of laugh. "Hell, Blue Eyes, how about a diet cola?"

Her eyes reflected her disappointment, but she said, "I'll take it." And then, to explain herself, added, "I never learned to like beer, but the lite beers don't seem to taste as bad."

"You wouldn't have lasted long in my neighborhood," Burr muttered.

"What neighborhood is that?" Lindsey inquired.

"The wrong side of the tracks in Houston."

"Is that where you got the tattoo?"

Burr held his arm up and looked at it as though the tattoo had suddenly appeared there. "Yeah."

"May I look at it?"

He held his arm toward her. To his chagrin, she got up from the table and came over to him. He held his breath as she traced the shape of the coiled, hooded cobra with her fingertips.

Then she looked up at him, catching him like a deer in a set of headlights with those blue eyes of hers. "Does the snake mean something special?"

"It was an initiation rite of the gang I was in as a kid." He rubbed his skin, which was suddenly covered with goose bumps, brushing her hand away in the process.

"You were in a street gang in Houston?" Her eyes went wide with astonishment.

"Yeah."

"What? I mean . . . how . . ."

"The steaks are done," Burr said. "Sit down and I'll serve up supper."

Burr knew she was curious about his past, but she could just stay that way. He had decided talking to her wasn't such a good idea after all. He managed to think of grisly things all through supper, which kept his mind off the woman across the table from him. Or mostly kept his mind off her. She ate like she was starving, not at all like a dainty debutante. She cleaned her plate with a gusto that made him wonder if she did everything—and his mind was picturing all sorts of indiscrete activities—with that sort of relish.

"That was delicious," Lindsey said when she finished.

She made no offer to wash the dishes, not that Burr had thought she would. He didn't suppose a governor's daughter got KP duty too often. He thought about just taking care of them himself, but damn it, he was tired. And he had done the cooking.

"You'll find the dish soap under the sink."

Lindsey stared at him blankly for a moment, until she realized what he was implying. "Oh."

In case she wasn't perfectly clear on what he meant, Burr said, "I cooked, you clean."

"I suppose that's fair." She rose and began clearing the table.

Burr was impressed by her willingness to do her share. Unfortunately, he was unable to sit and be waited on. His mother hadn't allowed it when he was growing up, and he couldn't make himself do it now just to spite a woman who couldn't help the fact she had been raised with a silver spoon in her mouth.

"I'll scrape the dishes," he said. "You wash and I'll dry."

"All right."

She was so careful with the dishes, he knew the job wasn't one she was familiar with. "I don't expect you have to wash dishes in the mansion too often."

"No," she said with a quick grin. "I hadn't realized how much fun it is."

"Fun?" He felt his body draw up tight as he watched the way she caressed a plate with a cloth hidden by a mound of white soapy bubbles. Then she rubbed the cloth around and around inside a coffee cup. Burr felt his cheeks heat. He had never realized washing dishes could be such a sensuous experience. He threw his towel on the counter and headed for the living room. "We can let the rest dry in the drainer. I'll light a fire. It's getting cool outside."

He knelt down in front of the stone fireplace and dropped his forehead to his knee. In twenty hours he would be free of her. He just had to hold on until then. He busied himself building a fire and soon had it crackling. When he turned around, he found Lindsey sitting cross-legged on the couch behind him.

"This is nice," she said.

Too nice, Burr thought. The fire lit up her eyes and made her skin glow with warmth. He had liked it better when she was fighting him. At least then he was being constantly reminded why getting personally involved with the governor's daughter—an ice princess and a spoiled brat, not to mention the girl with "the bluest eyes in Texas"—was a bad idea.

He sat down where he was and crossed his legs, keeping the distance of the room between them. It wasn't enough, of course. But it would have to do.

"What's it like to live in the spotlight?" he asked.

"You wouldn't like it," she replied.

He raised a brow. "Why not?"

"People who don't know a thing about you are always making judgments about you."

"No, I wouldn't like that. I suppose you believe you've been judged unfairly."

"I'm not what the newspapers say I am," she said.

"And what is that?"

"I'm not arrogant, for one thing. Or cold-hearted."

Burr cocked a disbelieving brow but didn't say anything.

"It's just that I don't suffer fools gladly."

"I see."

"I don't think you do," she said in a voice that dripped ice. "There is another side of me, a private side, that no one ever sees."

His lips curled in a mocking smile, which suggested that if she believed what she was saying—about not being arrogant or coldhearted—she didn't see herself very clearly. "I guess I haven't met that other woman yet."

"Nor will you," she said in her haughtiest voice. She rose imperiously. "I'm tired. I think I'll go to bed now." Then she turned her back on him and stalked to the bedroom, her fanny gloriously displayed in the skintight jeans.

Burr gritted his teeth. Eighteen hours. She would be gone then, and he would never have to lay eyes on her again. He stayed where he was until he was sure she had the bedroom door closed. Then he rose and settled himself on the couch, using a pillow and the afghan to make himself a bed. He lay staring at the fire for a long time before he finally fell asleep.

Meanwhile, Lindsey was finding it impossible to relax. She didn't want to turn off the lamp, but it had a high-wattage bulb that flooded the room with light. When she tried the dark, it was too frightening. Memories of her kidnapping returned, of waking up in the hotel room, and the deaths of the two villains

Burr had been forced to kill. She wanted to go home, to return to the somewhat normal life she had led before all this had happened.

She kept remembering Burr's accusations about her character. If she had been disdainful of the men she met, it was because they treated her like some stone goddess, not a flesh-and-blood woman. Or they were so puffed up with their own consequence they expected her to fall gratefully at their feet. Or they were more interested in her father's political power than in her.

Burr fit none of those neat categories. He wasn't intimidated by her position, and in his arms she was anything but a woman of stone. Her father's power had failed to influence him. She found it amazing and utterly frustrating that a man she found so intriguing seemed to be doing his level best to ignore her!

Her attraction to Burr surprised her more than a little. After all, he was a gang member from Houston who had somehow become a Texas Ranger. And he certainly looked the part.

Appearances.

Lindsey, who had spent her life being judged by her looks, was appalled to realize she had been equally judgmental of Burr's outward trappings. There must be more to him than what showed on the surface. Otherwise, why had she been so drawn to him?

Maybe she found Burr so fascinating because he was different, because he came from the wrong side of the tracks, because he was dangerous. Burr possessed a different kind of power than her father wielded, but there was no doubt Burr Covington was a powerful man. And one who was far more likely to get himself shot than any politician or businessman or financier she could have chosen to fall in love with. And yet, she had been willing to give in to the powerful attraction she felt toward him.

He had made it clear he wasn't interested.

That was another totally new experience for Lindsey Major, debutante and governor's daughter. Normally, men fawned on her and begged for her favor. She refused them; they didn't refuse her. She felt humbled, humiliated, and hurt by the Ranger's rejection of her.

Those feelings lasted about as long as it took Lindsey to acknowledge them. They were replaced almost instantaneously by annoyance and determination. She had spent a lifetime using her famous eyes to cajole, entreat and demand what she wanted and rarely failed to get her own way. She didn't want Burr Covington, but she did want a little revenge to assuage her ego. It would be a simple matter to get him to admit he wanted her and then refuse his advances.

Lindsey figured she had about seventeen hours to bring Burr Covington to his knees.

Chapter Four

Lindsey woke to a steady thudding sound, which she finally recognized as an ax striking wood. She got out of bed, crossed to the curtainless window and looked out onto the backyard of the cabin.

Burr was dressed in nothing but a pair of worn jeans, and goose bumps rose on her arms at the sight of him. He had shaved, and she was surprised to see that he looked almost handsome. The broken nose gave his face character, she decided. His hair, free of the ponytail, was plastered to his forehead by sweat and hung in damp curls on his bare shoulders.

He had been working hard enough splitting logs that his muscular torso glistened. Her gaze was drawn to a crystal drop of liquid as it rolled downward across a washboard belly toward his navel. She noticed the scabbed-over cut near his ribs where Epifanio had slashed him with his knife. It wasn't the only mark on his body. There was also a scar near his collarbone that looked suspiciously like a healed bullet wound. She wondered whether he had gotten it as a kid in a Houston gang, or during his duties as a Texas Ranger.

As she watched, he paused and wiped his forehead with a bandanna he pulled from a rear pocket of his jeans.

And noticed her staring at him from the window.

She leapt back out of sight, then realized that was foolish, since he had already seen her. She took a deep breath, shoved the window open and leaned out, unaware that the V-necked T-shirt she was wearing gave Burr a revealing glimpse of female pulchritude. "Good morning," she called.

"There's coffee and cereal in the kitchen," Burr replied curtly. He began swinging the ax again.

She had been dismissed.

Whatever second thoughts Lindsey might have harbored about her plan to bring Burr Covington to his knees flew out the window along with a fly that had been buzzing by her ear. So he thought he could ignore her, did he?

You're being childish about this, Lindsey.

Am I?

The man is only trying to do his job.

That Ranger has insulted me for the last time.

He doesn't strike me as the kind of man who'd ever kowtow to a woman.

Just wait. I haven't been labeled the girl with the bluest eyes in Texas for the past seven years without learning a few things about how to manipulate the male of the species.

Lindsey stripped off the overlarge T-shirt she had slept in and took a quick shower. Then she put on the T-shirt, jeans and tennis shoes Burr had bought for her in town, using some tissues to cushion the blister on her heel.

She didn't normally have more than toast and coffee for breakfast, but the colorful box of sugar-coated kids' cereal on the table looked tempting. She poured herself a bowl, doused it with milk, then surprised herself by eating ravenously. Maybe being kidnapped had given her an appetite. As she munched the last few bites of cereal, Lindsey pondered how she could best seduce the Ranger.

Now you're going to seduce *him?*

How else am I going to lay him low?

How about an intellectual argument?

Somehow that wouldn't be the same.

It sure sounds safer than bearding the lion in his den.

He may look like a lion, but by the time I'm through with him, he'll be following me around like Mary's little lamb.

It dawned on Lindsey that while she had gathered a large male following over the years, she had done nothing purposely to garner their attention, other than having blue eyes, of course. Unfortunately, Burr hadn't fallen under her spell. For the first time, she was going to have to do something other than flutter her eyelashes to attract a man. Since everything else about her was rather ordinary, she wasn't sure exactly what she was going to use for bait. Maybe having an intellectual discussion with Burr wasn't such a bad idea after all.

Burr was immediately aware of Lindsey when she headed out the back door toward him. She had a graceful walk without the limp. Her hair was tied up in a ponytail that made her look a lot younger and more approachable. She wasn't wearing any makeup, either. She looked about twenty and as innocent as a lamb. However, he knew that wasn't possible. A woman like Lindsey Major was sure to have put a few notches in her bedpost. Not that it was any of his business. Besides, having been around more than a little himself, he was in no position to be throwing stones at glass houses.

"Is there anything I can do to help?" Lindsey asked when she reached Burr's side.

"I need to haul some of this wood inside, but otherwise, I'm done here."

"I'd be glad to help with that, but do you suppose we could go for a walk first?"

Burr's gaze shot to her feet. "Are you going to be all right in those shoes?"

"If not, I'll just take them off and go barefoot."

Burr noticed Lindsey was looking everywhere but at him. He set down the ax and mopped his chest and back and under his arms with the T-shirt he had taken off when he had started working.

An enchanting flush rose on Lindsey's face.

Surely this isn't the first time she's seen a man working without a shirt! Burr thought. But she was clearly affected by the sight of him, so he stuck his arms in the plaid Western shirt with folded-up sleeves that had come off at the same time as the T-shirt and buttoned a couple of the buttons.

"I'm ready when you are," he said.

She gave him a gamine smile and headed off toward a cluster of pecan trees in the distance that surrounded a pond deep enough to swim in. He followed after her, wondering why she was being so friendly all of a sudden. He didn't think she had changed her opinion of him overnight, so he was naturally suspicious of her intentions.

He kept his eyes on her, which was easy, considering how her fanny moved in the tight-fitting jeans. There was a sexy little sway to her walk that was as enticing as any perfume he had ever smelled. He realized that if she had walked off a cliff, he probably would have followed her over the edge. The sunshine did something magical to her hair, revealing a dozen different shades from red-gold to golden chestnut. He saw the pleasure on her face as she closed her eyes and tilted her head back, basking in the sunlight.

Burr felt his body responding to the woman in front of him. More disturbing, however, was the way his mind recorded all the sensual data about her. As a Ranger, he was used to making snap judgments about people based on their actions. The way she walked told him she liked being a woman, and that she had a great deal of self-confidence. The sun-streaked hair told him she spent a lot of time outdoors, and that she probably had an expensive hairdresser. And the way she turned her face up to the sun told him she was a sensual person, ready to greet with open arms whatever life had to offer.

He tried to make that evaluation of Lindsey Major mesh with what he had read about her and what he had experienced so far in her company. The pictures didn't match.

"Penny for your thoughts?"

Burr hadn't even realized Lindsey had stopped. She was facing him with her hands on her hips. He took one look at the beautiful woman in front of him and said, "Why aren't you married?"

"I don't think that's any of your business."

"I suppose not. I just wondered why a beautiful woman like you hasn't found herself a husband and settled down to raise a family."

"I've already got a family."

Burr frowned. "I don't understand."

Lindsey turned and started walking toward the trees again, and Burr fell into stride beside her.

"Since the Turk killed my mother five years ago, I've been responsible for raising my younger brother, Carl, and my sister, Stella."

"Seems to me your father ought to be doing that."

She turned and gave him a bittersweet smile. "He doesn't have the time. He's a public servant who takes his duties seriously. I also act as my father's hostess at dinners. You can see why I don't have time to go hunting for a husband."

"I wouldn't think you'd have to go hunting," Burr said frankly.

Lindsey glanced sideways at Burr, and his heart jumped. Her eyes seemed to invite all kinds of things he knew she couldn't possibly intend. Her next words suggested she meant everything her sultry gaze had conveyed.

"I haven't met anyone I was interested in getting to know." She paused. "Until you."

Burr stopped in his tracks. He was used to keeping his feelings to himself, but it took a great deal of effort to keep the astonishment—not to mention the suspicion—off his face. "I find that a little hard to believe."

"You're . . . different."

Burr smirked. "I see. Is it the broken nose or the tattoo you find so fascinating?"

"That's not fair!" Lindsey retorted.

The heat in her face told him he had hit the nail on the head.

"I'm sure there's more to you than your appearance suggests," she said, compounding her error.

Burr laughed out loud.

"I was trying to *compliment* you!"

"I don't think I've ever been damned so well by such faint praise."

"What I meant is that I don't think I've seen the real Burr Covington yet, and I'm curious what's behind the 'bad boy' facade."

"What you see is what you get."

She shook her head, sending her ponytail swinging in the breeze. "I'm convinced there's more to you than meets the eye, and I'm determined to get to know the real Burr Covington before the day ends."

"What's the sense of that?" Burr asked. "After I return you to your father this afternoon, we'll never see each other again."

"It doesn't have to be that way," Lindsey said in a quiet voice.

Burr's lips curled in a cynical smile. "What kind of rig are you running, Blue Eyes? What is it you want from me?"

She looked at him with those stunning eyes, and he felt his heart skip a beat. He hadn't expected to be as vulnerable as the rest of the pack that worshipped the bluest eyes in Texas. But he found himself wondering what it would be like to wake up to those eyes every morning for the rest of his life. He shook his head to break free of her spell.

"Well?" he demanded. "What is it you want?"

"I'm attracted to you," she blurted. "I thought—"

"Oh, no, you don't. I am not, I repeat, *not* getting involved with the governor's daughter. I'm supposed to be guarding you, for Christ's sake!"

He didn't know quite how it happened, but she took the few steps to reach him and laid her hands on his chest and looked up at him, her lips parted.

"I want you to kiss me," she said in a husky voice.

Burr's hands clamped down on Lindsey's arms so hard they were liable to be bruised when he let go. But, hell, better that than the other alternative, which was to kiss the woman—which he had to admit had crossed his mind as a potentially pleasant experience—and damn the consequences.

"We are *not* going to do this."

"Why not?"

"Because you are who you are, and I am who I am."

"That's not a very good reason to deny ourselves."

"Then I'll give you a few more. I grew up in a gang in Houston—you grew up as Texas royalty. I live life in the trenches—you amble along up top. And this situation is only temporary. You wouldn't look twice at me if we weren't stuck here together."

Her eyes flashed, and she stabbed a forefinger against his chest. "Hogwash. The only thing that matters is whether or not you're as attracted to me as I am to you. Are you?"

He let her go and forked a hand through his hair in agitation. "All right, I'm attracted to you! Is that what you wanted to hear?"

She grinned from ear to ear. "It's a start."

"Just remember you asked for this."

Burr captured her in his arms and lowered his mouth to hers. He felt her catch fire when he put his tongue in her mouth to taste her, but he didn't stop there. He had wanted to hold her breasts since he had first caught sight of them. He shoved his hand up under her T-shirt and palmed her flesh. She made a sound of protest before arching into his hand. He used his other hand to hold her close while he rubbed himself against her with a body that was stone hard. When he let her go at last, there was a stunned look on her face.

He took a step back and let out a shuddering breath. "Is that what you were after, Blue Eyes? Be sure it's what you want before you start playing games with me again." He didn't recognize his voice. It was harsh and grated like a rusty gate.

"I wasn't...I didn't mean..." Her denials fell flat because she had goaded him, and she had meant to provoke exactly the response she had gotten. Only the encounter had been far more devastating for her than she had imagined. She felt shattered. Overwhelmed. Aroused. And afraid to act on what she was feeling for fear of the consequences.

"Now you know the real difference between the two of us. I'm not into playing games, Blue Eyes."

"And you think I am?"

"Aren't you?"

"I wasn't thinking about the differences between us when you were kissing me."

"That's good, because when I look at you I see a woman I want to get so deep inside I can't see daylight, a woman I want underneath me panting and scratching and as eager for me as I am for her. How about it, Blue Eyes? You ready for that?''

Burr watched Lindsey's jaw drop. Then she whirled and fled back to the cabin as fast as her legs could carry her.

You're a damn fool, Covington. She was asking for it. You should have given it to her. Why did you scare her off?

She doesn't know what she's getting into. I would be taking advantage of her at a vulnerable time.

She came on to you.

She's a woman who doesn't know what the hell she wants.

You had your chance to make love to her and you blew it.

Yeah. Sometimes those are the breaks.

Acknowledging his folly didn't make Burr feel any better. He headed toward the pond situated among the pecan trees. He needed a dip to cool off. He couldn't remember a time when he had been so turned on by a woman. Why the hell did it have to be her? They had nothing in common. There was absolutely no future for the two of them. He simply wasn't the kind of man who chased after windmills.

Lindsey had been shocked and not a little shaken by Burr's prompt and devastating response to her sexual invitation. She was used to a more civilized male creature, one who would ask permission and accept limits. Burr had given her fair warning and then taken what he wanted from her.

Not that she had protested much...or at all. In fact, she had quickly found herself a willing participant in anything and everything he'd had in mind to offer her. And she had to admit there was every bit as much give as there was take in what he had done.

So why did you run, Lindsey?

The answer to that was simple. She had been frightened by the powerful feelings Burr incited. She had no explanation for her attraction to the Ranger. She only knew she wanted to feel his arms around her, wanted to put her arms around him and hold him close. She was as appalled as she was astounded that she could be so attracted to a man like him. He didn't mince words; he didn't play games. He had a tattoo, for heaven's sake! But his need for her, his intense desire, was a strong aphrodisiac.

She had thought she could tease the lion and escape unharmed. But this beast had sharp teeth and dangerous claws that could drag her down and destroy her if she let him.

She remembered the avid look in Burr's eyes as his hand had cupped her breast. It was impossible to forget the taste of him, the rough feel of his tongue as he probed her mouth, the way his teeth caught her lower lip, and how her body had drawn up tight as he sucked on it. Her hips had met his thrusts and sought more of the delicious feelings as he brushed against her through two layers of soft denim.

Lindsey had fooled around in high school, done a little petting, but she had never gone "all the way." Somehow, the things her mother had told her about saving herself for marriage had made sense. Since she had expected to meet her future husband in college, that hadn't seemed like such a long time to wait.

Then her mother had been killed, and her life had been turned upside down. For the past five years she had lived as celibate as a nun. Perhaps it was those years of deprivation that had caused her to respond so wildly to Burr. Or maybe grown-up hormones were more powerful than the teenage ones. All she knew was that what she had felt with Burr far surpassed anything she had ever experienced in the past.

Lindsey felt confused and still half aroused and wasn't sure what her next move ought to be. Maybe the smart move was to make no move at all. She would let Burr set the tone for the rest of the day. Much as it irked her to concede any battle, she knew when she was outgunned. It would be better to retreat while she still could.

She spent the next hour carting firewood into the house and wondering where Burr was. When he returned, she realized he must have gone swimming. His hair was slicked back and his skin was pearled with drops of water. She had a fierce urge to taste his skin, to lick up those crystal drops. She forced herself to stay where she was.

"You took a swim."

"Yeah."

They stared at each other for a moment without speaking. Then Burr said, "It's time for me to call in. If we're lucky, Hector's been picked up, and you can go home."

Lindsey was torn between wanting to go home and wanting more time with Burr. She had been attracted to him because he was so different from the men she usually met. She felt certain that if she didn't discover the man behind the mask before Burr Covington, Texas Ranger, dropped her off in front of the governor's mansion and said goodbye, she never would. Lindsey found that a very painful thought.

"You won't get any crazy ideas while I'm gone, like walking to the road, will you?" Burr said.

"No. I'll wait here."

"I shouldn't be more than an hour. You'll be safe here." He reached out a hand and tucked an errant curl behind her ear. The instant he realized what he had done, Burr withdrew his hand. A moment later he captured her head between his hands and kissed her hard on the mouth. "Be here when I get back."

"I will."

Chapter Five

Lindsey stepped out onto the porch as Burr shut off the Jaguar's engine. "What's the news?"

Burr joined her on the porch, his face solemn. "Hector escaped the trap that was set for him. The captain thinks he may have left the country for South America."

"Now what?"

"The captain says we stay here," Burr said flatly.

"How long?"

"Until the Turk's sentence is carried out."

"That's four days!"

"I know."

Lindsey was amazed that she didn't feel more disappointed. In fact, what she felt was elated. She had four more days to find out everything there was to know about Burr Covington. Four more days to figure out the source of the riotous feelings that had bombarded her when Burr had so solemnly announced they were stuck together for a while longer.

To her consternation, Burr completely avoided her the rest of the day, which wasn't easy, since they both had to eat and sleep in the cabin. Somehow, he arranged it so she ate before he did and retired to bed before he returned from taking a late evening walk.

Lindsey lay in bed chewing on a fingernail. Maybe Burr had the right idea. Maybe it was better if they didn't get to know each other. She tried to imagine introducing Burr to her father as someone she cared about and had a pretty good idea what he would say: she was suffering from some kind of kidnapping syndrome and had fallen for the man who had rescued her from the bad guys.

Lindsey admitted she had something like an adolescent crush on Burr. She refused to dignify her desire to have him kiss her and hold her in his arms with any other label. How could it be more than infatuation? She had only known the man for forty-eight hours. She wasn't even sure she liked him. But there was no doubt she was physically attracted to him.

It occurred to her that perhaps the best way to get over her physical attraction to Burr was to find out what kind of man he really was. Personality flaws were bound to show up that would make him repugnant to her as a lover. Her crush would die a quick death under the weight of his unattractive character traits.

However, her plan required her to spend time in Burr Covington's company, discovering the unattractive man behind the fascinating "bad boy" facade. Which meant she had to find a way to keep Burr from disappearing before she had a chance to ask him a few questions. She decided to rise early the next morning and make a breakfast he wouldn't be able to resist sharing.

The smell of frying bacon woke Burr.

"Breakfast is ready!" Lindsey called from the kitchen. "Come and get it!"

Burr wasn't a morning person. His mind didn't start functioning until he had washed the cobwebs out with a shower, and he needed several cups of coffee before he could face the day. He met the call to come directly to the breakfast table with wariness. He needed his wits about him to deal with Lindsey Major.

He had managed to avoid any contact with the governor's daughter the previous day, but if he was any judge of the situation, he wasn't going to be allowed to repeat his disappearing act. He rubbed a weary hand across his bristly jaw. He hadn't gotten much sleep because he had spent the night dreaming in lurid detail of what it would be like to make love to her.

He struggled upright, shoving the afghan off his bare legs. He pressed his palms against eyelids he would have sworn were endowed with spikes the way they scraped against his eyeballs. Maybe if he got up on the wrong side of the bed—make that couch—and let Miss Major see him at his worst, it would discourage her.

Burr felt a grin struggling to break free. If Miss Major wanted him, she was going to get him. Warts and all.

He pulled on his jeans and zipped them, but didn't bother buttoning them. They caught on his hipbones. He headed for the kitchen barefoot, scratching his naked chest, his hair stuck up every whichaway and a dark stubble on his cheeks and chin.

When he reached the kitchen doorway he grabbed hold of the molding above his head and held on, letting his body sag slightly forward. "Got any coffee?"

Lindsey turned toward him, and he nearly laughed out loud at the look on her face. Her features ran the gamut between disappointment and delight. Clearly she was glad he had joined her for breakfast. Equally clearly, she hadn't seen a man in his condition at the breakfast table.

He let go of the molding and took the three steps necessary to sit at the table, which had been adorned with china and silverware—his mismatched plates, chipped cups and stainless-steel flatware—in a way that would have pleased Miss Manners. He leaned his head on his hand and blatantly stared at Lindsey while she filled his coffee cup. "Thanks."

"How would you like your eggs?" she asked.

"Over easy."

She cracked a couple of eggs into the pan she had used to cook the bacon. He noticed she watched the eggs as though they might run away and ignored his presence in the room.

"This is a nice surprise," he said.

She looked over her shoulder at him somewhat nervously. "I thought this might be a way to repay you in some small measure for all you've done for me."

Burr grunted. "You don't owe me anything. I'm just doing my job."

"It may not seem like much to you, but I can't help thinking what might have happened to me at the ho-tel if you hadn't been there."

He saw her hands were trembling but resisted the urge to get up and go comfort her. Black knights didn't comfort ladies fair. He watched her visibly calm herself.

"I thought maybe we could walk down to the pond after breakfast," she said.

Burr knew why he wanted to spend time with her. What made no sense was why she apparently wanted to spend time with him. He had already warned her what would happen if she exhibited an interest in his attentions. She was damn well going to get them! Well, she was a big girl, and she knew the consequences of playing with fire. He figured he might as well enjoy her company while he could. It was a choice he might not have made if he hadn't still been fuzzy with sleep.

Almost a full minute after Lindsey had asked him to go walking with her to the pond, he replied, "Yeah, I'll go with you." After all, he was supposed to be keeping an eye on her.

"Do you suppose it would be all right if I went for a swim?"

Burr had just taken a gulp of hot coffee, and he choked and sputtered as a vivid picture rose before him of what Lindsey would look like with water dripping off her naked body. He felt his groin tighten with anticipation. "Sure. Why not?"

Burr was surprised when Lindsey set a plate of eggs, bacon and toast in front of him that were cooked to perfection. He gave her a look of admiration.

"I took some classes in French cooking. We practiced a lot with eggs," she explained as she joined him on the other side of the table with a plate of her own.

They ate in uncomfortable silence, which Lindsey finally broke when she said, "I was wondering how someone who belonged to a street gang ended up as a Texas Ranger.''

Burr hadn't told the story to very many people. Maybe if Lindsey knew the truth about him, she would back off and leave him alone. Maybe a dose of reality would cure what ailed her.

''My father died when I was two,'' he began. ''My mother went to work as a waitress in a truck stop outside Houston. She didn't have any family, so she brought me with her to work and kept me behind the counter. I sort of grew up there.''

''In a truck stop?''

Burr's lips curved at the look of horror and disbelief on Lindsey's face. It was just dawning on her that they came from two different worlds.

''It wasn't such a bad place. The truckers sort of adopted me, but none of them ever stayed around very long, so I never got attached to any of them. The problems started when I turned fifteen. The Cobras—that was the gang I eventually joined—all showed up one day at the truck stop. I was fascinated by them. They talked hip and looked cool. Most of all, they were a family.

''At the time, I needed to belong. So I joined up. I had to do a lot of things, initiation rites, before I could be a part of the gang. It was mostly petty thievery, vandalism, that sort of thing. And they beat you up to see if you could take it."

"That's terrible!"

Burr shrugged. "That part wasn't any fun. But afterward I was one of them, so it seemed worth it. Once I was in, I got the tattoo." He brushed his fingertips absently against the coiled black snake.

"There's no telling what might have happened to me if my mother hadn't married a Houston cop." He smiled in remembrance. "Joe Bertram came into the truck stop to investigate the theft of some video equipment—which I had stolen. The minute he and my mom laid eyes on each other they fell in love. I've never seen anything like it.

"Joe became my stepfather a month later. You could say my life of crime came to a rather abrupt end. He laid down the law and made me toe the line. He forced me to quit the Cobras. When I look back on it now, I can see he was a pretty terrific guy. At the time, I hated his guts.

"The long and the short of it is, the week after I graduated from the University of Texas at Austin with a degree in business, he was killed in the line of duty."

He paused and swallowed hard.

"I didn't even know I loved him till I heard the news." Burr turned away so she wouldn't see the tears that stung his eyes. "I felt cheated that I had lost him just when I was starting to appreciate him. And I felt bad that I hadn't ever thanked him. I figured one way I could repay him for all he'd done for me was to become a cop myself.

"Fortunately, the Rangers provide a natural stomping ground for renegades and loners like me. I put in my time as a cop and applied for the Rangers as soon as I was eligible." He spread his hands wide. "Here I am."

Burr had spent his life trying to make up to his stepfather for the trouble he had given him. In all these years he had never forgiven himself for the hateful things he had said to the man who had given him such tough love, even though his mother had assured him that his stepfather had forgiven him—had known his stepson cared for him—long before his death.

"Where's your mother now?" Lindsey asked.

"She died two years ago."

"So you're all alone?"

"I don't have any family left, if that's what you're asking."

"Why haven't you married?"

"I suppose I never found the right woman."

"What would she be like?"

"I haven't really thought about it. There's no such thing as perfection, so I guess I'd settle for a woman I loved who loved me back."

"Sounds pretty simple."

"Not many women want to be married to a law enforcement officer."

Lindsey nodded. "I suppose they don't want to wind up widows. I can understand that."

"And agree with the sentiment?"

"I lost my mother to violence. I live every day with the fear that an assassin will kill my father. So, no, I don't think I've ever imagined myself marrying a man whose life would constantly be on the line."

Burr rarely pondered his mortality. He couldn't afford to because it might distract him from the job he had to do. But he couldn't deny he was involved in a dangerous profession, and he couldn't blame a woman who considered that risk when choosing a husband. Even if it put him squarely out of the running.

While they were talking, Burr had finished the food in front of him and drunk a second cup of coffee. When Lindsey started clearing the table, he rose and took his plate from her. "You cooked, I clean, remember?"

She gave him a quick look from lowered lashes before saying, "I'll go change into something I can swim in."

Burr wondered what she would find to serve as a swimsuit and was rewarded when she arrived back in the kitchen a few minutes later with a sight that made his whole body go taut.

Her face looked fresh and innocent as she glanced quickly up at him from blue eyes masked by dark, lush lashes. Her mouth was slightly parted, and he could see her breasts rise and fall in a T-shirt that made it plain she wasn't wearing a bra. Her hair was a silky mane of gold that spilled over her shoulders and begged for a man's hands to grasp handfuls of it to pull her close. The T-shirt was tied in a knot above a pair of his cut-off jeans that revealed the length of her tanned, shapely legs.

It was an outfit designed to drive a man's imagination wild. Burr turned toward the sink so she wouldn't see that his body had promptly responded to the sexual invitation she had unconsciously thrown out.

"I'll be finished here in a minute and we can go," Burr said in a voice that was surprisingly husky.

"I'll wait for you on the porch."

Burr was grateful for the respite to get his libido back under control.

Whoa, boy! That sexy little siren is the governor's daughter!

She's also a very desirable woman.

Who's off limits!

Why?

You know damn well why! She wouldn't look at you twice if the circumstances were other than what they are. What kind of future could the two of you have together?

So what's wrong with a little fling?

With the governor's daughter? Get a grip, man. Think of the consequences!

Burr tried to imagine the possible consequences of slaking his lust with Lindsey Major. The mind boggled. Better to grit his teeth and bear the pain of unsatisfied passion. In the long run that was the smart move.

His resolve lasted until Lindsey came up from her first dip in the creek in the wet T-shirt. Her nipples had peaked from the cold, and he was treated to a sight that made idiots of adolescent males at beach parties. Burr told himself he was an intelligent grown man who knew better than to succumb to such riveting sights.

When Lindsey called, "Why don't you join me?" he responded with a muttered oath and stood his ground.

"I promise the water isn't too cold," she teased.

Maybe that was what he needed, Burr thought, a dip in some cold water. He yanked off his black T-shirt and sat down to remove his boots and socks. Then, still wearing his jeans, he strode into the icy water.

He wasn't consciously heading for Lindsey at first. Not until she began to back away from him. She should have known better than to run. A hunter could never resist the chase.

He saw the teasing smile on her face begin to fade as she realized he was coming for her.

"Burr...Burr..."

When she turned and raced for the bank, he ran after her. He caught her in the grassy verge and pulled her down. They rolled several times before he pinned her beneath him.

She didn't fight, but lay panting, her eyes wide, her body pliant. She slicked her tongue over her lips, leaving them wet. Her gaze met his, and he waited for a sign that she wanted to be freed. It didn't come.

He lowered his mouth to hers, tasting the dampness, and heard her moan low in her throat. He pressed his hips down and felt her arch upward to meet him. This time he groaned.

"Lindsey, if you don't want this, say so now."

"I want you, Burr. Please, don't stop."

He had the wet T-shirt and shorts off her moments later and shimmied out of his wet jeans a moment after that. He settled himself between her thighs and then raised himself up on his elbows to look at her.

"You're so beautiful!" He watched the flush steal up her throat to stain her cheeks. Her eyes were closed, the lashes a fan of coal across rose-petal skin. "Look at me, Lindsey."

Lindsey had closed her eyes on purpose, not wanting Burr to focus on them because she had been judged for so long by their uniqueness. She wanted to be appreciated for who she was inside, not because she had the bluest eyes in Texas. She raised her lids slowly, first to a slit, then wider as she saw the admiration and approval in his tender gaze.

He brushed his thumb across her cheek and then slid it across her parted lips. She dipped her tongue out to taste him and heard his hiss of pleasure. His dark eyes seemed to bore into her, seeking the person within. She willed him to see her as she was—innocent, needing him, wanting him, not quite frightened, but anxious about the unknown.

They didn't speak again. At least not with words. He caressed her skin as though it were the most fragile silk, and finally lowered his mouth to suckle her breast as his hands explored her body.

Lindsey bit her lip to keep from crying out, but couldn't suppress the guttural sounds that escaped her throat. She had never imagined it could be like this, never imagined the powerful response her body could have to the touch of a callused male hand. His mouth kept moving over her, up to her throat, then to her ear, inciting pleasure wherever it roamed. She felt a shiver of desire when his teeth nipped her shoulder, and sought out his skin with her mouth to return the pleasure.

"Your skin is so soft," he mused. "And your hair." His hand tightened around a fistful of the silky stuff and pulled her head back to expose her throat for his kisses.

Lindsey was overwhelmed with feelings. She responded with the desperation she felt, tunneling her hands into Burr's hair and grasping hold to keep his mouth where it was as her body arched beneath his. She relished his groan of delight as she brushed against his shaft.

His invasion came swiftly and without warning. She stiffened and cried out.

Burr froze. He didn't pull away, merely lifted himself on his palms to stare into Lindsey's face. He caught the remnants of pain in her eyes. And the growing exhilaration.

"You should have told me," he said in a harsh voice.

"Would you have done this if I had?"

"Hell, no!"

"Then I'm glad I didn't say anything."

Burr let out his breath in a sigh. "I hurt you."

"The pain is gone now." She still felt stretched, and her body ached, but that was bearable. And she knew the worst was over. "Please don't stop."

Burr snorted. "I'm not about—"

She put her fingertips across his mouth to silence him and let her eyes plead for what she wanted. She raised herself enough to replace her fingertips with her mouth. Her tongue traced the crease of his lips and when he parted them, slid inside. She moaned with delight as Burr's tongue forced hers back into her mouth and claimed the honey to be found there.

His hands cupped her shoulders and pressed her back down as his body began to move in tandem with hers. His thrusts were slow and easy at first, but as she began to answer him, his body plunged deeper, seeking pleasure, giving it, until they were slick from sweat, until their bodies begged for air, until each cried out as he spent his seed within her.

Consequences.

It was the first thought that popped into Lindsey's head as she lay atop Burr, still gasping for air, totally enervated. They hadn't used any kind of protection. She knew better, and he must certainly be aware of the dangers of unprotected sex.

"Do you...? Have you...?"

"It's a little late for that, Blue Eyes, don't you think?" Burr said in a quiet voice. "But, no, I don't have anything you can catch. And I don't expect, under the circumstances, that I'm going to catch anything from you. That leaves pregnancy. Is this the right—or wrong—time of the month?"

Lindsey's face was beet red. She kept her eyes lowered. "I just got over... It's the wrong time of month for me to get pregnant," she blurted.

He pulled her close to his chest and held her there. "Thank goodness for that, anyway." He was quiet for a long time before he said, "Why me?"

"It's not what you're thinking."

"What am I thinking?"

"That this is just a fling."

"Isn't it?"

Lindsey was silent for a moment. Is that what Burr had thought? That she just wanted to have sex with him for the fun of it? That she didn't care for him as a person? But, honestly, what else could he think? They barely knew each other. They were strangers. The likelihood of them continuing any kind of relationship once she returned to the governor's mansion was small indeed. So why had she allowed—be honest, Lindsey—*encouraged* this to happen?

"I don't know what it is," Lindsey admitted. "I think I wanted to see if I could make you want me. I didn't realize until... until you caught me that I wanted to be caught. And then..." She shrugged. "I'm not sorry it happened, though. I have feelings for you that are..." *Stronger than I'm willing to admit even to myself, let alone to you.* She didn't dare speak of love. It was an absurdity under the circumstances.

"No regrets?"

She shook her head. "It had to happen sometime, and—"

Burr rolled her off of him and was on his feet an instant later. "And I was convenient," he finished in a hard voice. "Don't fool yourself into thinking I'm something I'm not. I'll always be a man more used to walking alleys than streets. There's no getting rid of my past, like there's no getting rid of the tattoo on my arm. And if it's all the same to you, Blue Eyes, I've had enough of being a convenience."

Burr was aware of a tightness in his chest. It had dawned on him that he would give anything to have a woman like Lindsey for his own, to hold and to love. He couldn't stand the thought of another man touching her, loving her. Only, he had no right to those feelings. Their situation wasn't real; it was contrived. How could he even think about proposing to the governor's daughter?

His hurt turned to anger when he realized the situation Lindsey had put him in. He was furious she hadn't told him that he would be the first man to make love to her. He sure as hell hadn't been thinking in terms of forever, as any woman who had saved her virginity as long as Lindsey had must have been. He knew, even if she didn't, that the governor's daughter wasn't going to marry a former Houston gang member, a man with a snake tattoo on his arm and an earring in his ear, even if he was a Texas Ranger.

"You should have waited for the right man to come along, Blue Eyes, instead of wasting your innocence on me."

She had hurt him, Lindsey realized, and he had snapped back with something equally hurtful. She sought some way to make amends. "I didn't mean—"

"I know what I am, Miss Major, and what I'm not. The question is, do you?"

"Now wait just a minute, Burr Covington," Lindsey said. "You can't use that snake tattoo or your broken nose to scare me off! You aren't so tough."

"Oh, yeah?"

"Yeah!" She poked him in the chest with her forefinger. "There's a fellow inside there somewhere who makes my heart beat fast, a guy who leaves me breathless. So there!"

Burr was tempted by her speech to take her back in his arms. But he already had his wet jeans on, which helped immensely to dampen his ardor and keep him from doing something that foolish. "Get dressed."

"I won't let you ignore me." Lindsey reached out and stopped him from buttoning his jeans. "I wanted *you* to make love to me, Burr. You."

Burr grabbed her wrists to keep her from touching him. His body was on fire, and he knew if he let her arguments sway him, he would be the one who got burned. If he let himself believe her, he would start thinking about a future together, and he knew better than that. "Get dressed," he repeated. "I can't leave you out here alone."

He glared at her while she tugged on her cut-offs and pulled her soggy T-shirt over her head. The flimsy cotton did nothing to hide her lush body, and he felt his loins tighten at the sight of her nipples through the thin cloth. The minute she was dressed, he grabbed her wrist. "Let's go."

"How can I make you believe that I mean what I'm saying?" Lindsey said as he dragged her along beside him.

"I should have known better than to let myself lose control like that," he muttered.

"I do care about you. I—"

He jerked her to a stop. "Don't you dare use words like that when you don't mean them! You have no idea what it means to care about anyone but yourself. You're exactly what the papers call you—a pretty pair of blue eyes without any substance behind them!"

"How do you know what I feel?" she cried. "Why are you acting like an insensitive, uncaring brute?"

"So now I'm a brute? You're the one who came after me, so what does that make you, lady? You asked for it, and I gave it to you!"

"Oh, you...you..." Lindsey was so furious and hurt, nearly blinded by the tears she was furiously blinking back, that she couldn't find an epithet bad enough to use on him.

"Who are you to be judging me," Burr demanded with a sneer, "when you don't have a life of your own? You're a substitute wife for your father, a substitute mother for your siblings. You wouldn't know how to be yourself, because there's nothing more to Lindsey Major than a pair of pretty blue eyes."

Lindsey was appalled at how close Burr had come to describing her life and enraged that he had rejected her because of it. "And you'll never outgrow your roots," she taunted back. "You'll always be a street hood at heart."

They stood glaring at each other. Each wanting desperately to be the kind of person the other wanted and sure they fell far short of the other's expectations.

Burr wondered what would have happened if they had met under different circumstances, when labels could have been dispensed with, when they could just have been a man and a woman meeting for the first time without the concealing masks they had both worn for so many years.

"Hey, you two, what's the problem?"

Lindsey and Burr turned to stare openmouthed at the man dressed in a ranger uniform who stood on the porch of the cabin.

Burr cleared his throat. "Captain Rogers? What are you doing here?"

"Hector fooled us. He didn't get on that plane to South America, after all. One of our informants saw him and tipped us off. We picked him up a couple of hours ago. You can go home now, Miss Major."

Lindsey turned stricken eyes toward Burr. "I can go home."

"Yes, ma'am," the captain continued, oblivious to the powerful undercurrents between Burr and Lindsey. "Your father's waiting for you at the mansion. I'll give you a lift there."

"I'll give her a ride," Burr said. Unspoken was the knowledge that they would finish their conversation on the way. Only, what was there left to say?

Lindsey shoved a fist against her mouth to keep a sob from escaping and raced into the cabin.

"What the hell did you do to that woman?" Captain Rogers asked.

Loved her. Burr thought. *I just loved her.*

Chapter Six

In the face of the accusations each had made against the other, both Lindsey and Burr remained silent during the first part of the drive back to Austin.

It's over too soon, Lindsey thought.

I never had an even chance with her, Burr thought.

I'm not what he thinks I am.

There's more to me than she knows.

Maybe I need to look more closely at who I am, Lindsey thought.

Maybe I ought to look at myself and see what's really there, Burr thought.

"I never realized before how thoroughly I took my mother's place after she died," Lindsey murmured, her voice barely audible. "At first, after my mother's death, my father was so desolate he couldn't function. I saw a void, and I filled it. I suppose I should have stepped back sooner, but the role was comfortable for me. I felt needed. I *was* needed. Now...I don't know. Carl and Stella are old enough to resent it when I try to parent them. And my father...I think he wouldn't have the heart to tell me he didn't need my help anymore."

"But you think he could survive now without you?"

Lindsey made a face. "He hired a new secretary last year. She's quite good at what she does."

"I see."

Lindsey was afraid Burr saw too much. "At least I'm willing to admit I need to make a change. What about you? How well do your stepfather's shoes fit, Burr?"

Burr kept his eyes on the road, refusing to meet her gaze. "You don't pull any punches, do you, Blue Eyes?" And of course she was right. It was time he figured out whether he was in this line of work for his stepfather's sake . . . or his own.

Burr had spent so many years giving mental lip service to the idea he was a cop to repay his stepfather, that he hadn't thought about how much he enjoyed his work. He liked being a Texas Ranger; he was good at it. And it was a satisfying job, giving him the independence his soul craved along with the opportunity to serve a noble purpose.

But was the role of Texas Ranger sufficient for the husband of a woman like Lindsey Major? He would never be rich, and his first devotion was to duty. Although he would cherish Lindsey if she were his, there would necessarily be times when his job would take him away from her. It might even kill him. He didn't want to think about how she would feel if that happened.

Lindsey snuck a peek at Burr and wondered what traits he wanted in a wife. She was beautiful, but what else did she have to offer a husband? She had a great deal of experience as an organizer and a hostess, but somehow she didn't think the wife of a Texas Ranger needed those skills. She was frightened of the danger he lived with day in and day out. Her heart caught in her throat when she admitted the perilous danger of his chosen profession.

Life with a man like Burr would never be easy. But she understood now why her mother had endured the trials and tribulations of life as a politician's wife. Loving, caring, left no choices.

Lindsey stared straight ahead as the interstate flew by, unwilling to speak again because she was afraid all the things she was feeling would pour out of her mouth. Her relationship—if you could call it that— with Burr was over before it had started. She was going back to her world. He was going back to his. Their paths wouldn't cross again, not without some effort on one or both of their parts. She was leaving it up to him to make the first move. That might be old-fashioned, but she wasn't willing to lay her heart on the line without some indication from him that he was willing to do the same.

The governor's mansion was in sight before she finally asked the question that was foremost in her mind. "Will I ever see you again?"

"What would be the point?"

Lindsey looked down at her hands, which were knotted in her lap. "I thought we started something by the river."

"If there are consequences, by all means call me."

Lindsey shot an angry look at Burr. "You know that wasn't what I meant. And I wouldn't call you now even if I were expecting triplets!"

"It wouldn't work," Burr said in a quiet voice. He glanced at her for an instant, then focused on the road in front of him. "You and me, I mean. I think in our case appearances aren't at all deceiving. You're a princess living in an ivory tower, and I'm—"

"Prince Charming. Or you could be."

Burr shook his head and laughed. "Whoever heard of Prince Charming with a snake tattooed on his arm? Can you imagine what your father would say if he saw the two of us together?"

"He wouldn't care."

Burr raised a skeptical brow, and Lindsey conceded, "At least, not after he got to know you."

"Both of us know appearances count, Blue Eyes. Think of the heyday the press would have if the two of us showed up in public together."

"What's printed in newspapers doesn't have to affect us."

"What about your friends? What will they say?"

"If they can't—or won't—accept you as you are, they won't be my friends for long."

Burr sighed. "It won't work, Blue Eyes. We're too different."

"We both want the same thing," Lindsey argued. "Someone to love…someone who'll love us back. We could have that together, Burr. Nothing else matters."

"Now I know you've been living in an ivory tower. We wouldn't have a snowball's chance in hell of surviving the rebuke that would be leveled against us from all directions. Me for stepping out of my place, and you for stooping down from yours. Think of the headlines—Bluest Eyes In Texas To Wed Former Gang Thug, or Texas Ranger Nabs Bluest Eyes In Texas."

"If you don't want me, just say so."

"Wanting you has nothing to do with it! I want you like hell. I'm just trying to be realistic about the situation."

"If your mind's made up, I don't suppose I can change it," Lindsey said. "But I'm stating here and now for the record that I think you're wrong. If you decide you want me bad enough to fight for me, you know where to find me."

She was out of the car and running inside the mansion before he had a chance to stop her. Not that he would have known what to say to her if he had. She was wrong. There was no way they could have a life together. He wasn't Prince Charming. He was an ordinary man with a slightly crooked nose and a snake tattoo and a few scars he had earned along the way. When the governor's blue-eyed daughter had recovered from the trauma of being kidnapped, of being held captive by a Ranger against her will, of being made love to for the first time, she would be glad he had bowed gracefully out of her life.

Lindsey threw herself into her father's embrace and sobbed with relief as his arms tightened securely around her.

"Are you all right, Lindsey?" he asked. "Are you hurt?"

"I'm fine, Dad," she managed between gulps as she fought back her tears. "It's just...it was *awful!* There was so much blood and those two men dead, and Burr... Oh, Dad!"

"I know sweetheart. I know. You'll be fine now. Nothing bad is ever going to happen to you again. I'll see to that."

Lindsey heard the remorse in her father's voice that she had been forced to suffer through the kidnapping and his determination to protect her from harm in the future. She could feel the walls closing in on her. It was a gilded cage her father wanted her to inhabit, but it was still a cage. If the governor got his way, she would never see Burr again, that was for sure. A brilliant idea popped into Lindsey's head, and she acted on it.

"If it hadn't been for Lieutenant Covington, I would have been brutalized and blinded before I was murdered. He saved me, Dad. Isn't there something we can do for him? Some way to thank him?"

"I don't know. I'll have to think about it."

"Could we have some sort of ceremony and give him a medal? We could invite him to dinner, too, couldn't we?"

The speculative look her father gave her brought a telltale blush to Lindsey's cheeks.

"You seem to have gotten along pretty well with this Covington fellow."

"He saved my life," Lindsey repeated.

"Hmm."

Lindsey held her breath.

"All right. I'll talk to Captain Rogers and see if a commendation of some sort is appropriate."

"And we'll invite him to dinner?"

"Sure. Why not?"

Burr slipped a finger into the collar of his tuxedo shirt and tried to loosen it. He felt like a mustang running with a herd of high-priced Thoroughbreds. He was wearing black cordovan dress shoes instead of boots, and his hair had been trimmed so much it curled at his nape. There was no earring in his ear and the snake tattoo was far out of sight. Except for his broken nose, he looked like most of the other men in tuxedos who had been invited to the governor's mansion for dinner.

Only, he was a fraud. They looked comfortable in the clothes they wore. They smiled and nodded and chatted with ease. He knew the moment he opened his mouth the wrong thing was going to come out. This wasn't his milieu. He would always be more comfortable in alleys than on streets.

He had learned from the captain that this reception in his honor was all Lindsey's idea, supposedly a way to repay him for what he had done.

"I was only doing my job," Burr had protested.

The captain hadn't been willing to take no for an answer. "You're going to dine as the governor's guest, and I don't want to hear any more argument!"

So here he was, all dressed up and fighting the bit to be somewhere else.

"Hello, stranger."

Burr turned and his breath caught in his throat. He had forgotten how beautiful she was. She was wearing a dress similar in style to the one she had been kidnapped in, only this one was black. He wondered fleetingly if she was wearing a black merry widow beneath it.

She smiled at him as though divining the direction his thoughts had taken. The look in her eyes made him want to haul her off somewhere and kiss her silly. He settled for taking the hand she extended and holding it in his own.

His thumb caressed her wrist, and he felt her pulse leap beneath his fingertips. "It's been a while," he managed to force past his constricted throat.

"Three weeks and two days."

"You've been counting?"

"Haven't you?"

He grinned. "Three weeks, two days, and eight hours."

"I've missed you." Lindsey couldn't take her eyes off Burr. The crisp white shirt contrasted against his tanned skin, and the black tux jacket emphasized his broad shoulders. He looked distinguished, but no less dangerous. For the first time in her very social life, Lindsey was incredibly nervous. She didn't know how to act and took her cues from Burr.

Burr ignored her invitation to admit to feelings that were only trouble. The orchestra at the far end of the ballroom had just begun a waltz, so he asked, "Would you like to dance?"

"I'd love to dance."

He led her into the waltz, a dance he knew because it was popular in country bars. But the count was the same, and she was as light on her feet as he was, so they moved easily around the dance floor.

"I didn't know you could dance so well," she said.

"There are lots of things you don't know about me."

"I'd like to learn."

Burr took a deep breath and let it out. "There's no time like the present, is there? Let me introduce myself. My name is Burr Covington. I'm a Texas Ranger. I grew up in Houston, but I've been assigned to the office in Austin for the past two years."

"It's nice to meet you, Mr. Covington," Lindsey said with a shy smile.

"Please call me Burr."

"I'd be pleased to...Burr. My name is Lindsey Major. People claim I have the bluest eyes in Texas, but they're greatly mistaken. They aren't blue at all. They're—''

"Lavender," Burr finished for her. "And what have you been doing to keep yourself busy these past few weeks, Miss Major?"

"Oh, please, call me . . . Blue Eyes."

"Well, Blue Eyes?" Burr said, a tender smile teasing his lips.

"I've been talking to my father about going back to college. I never finished my degree in journalism, you know. I've decided to return to Baylor in the fall."

"Then you can be the one to do the writing, instead of being written about."

"That thought has crossed my mind," she said with a mischievous smile.

"I just might be transferring to that area of Texas," Burr said.

"As a Texas Ranger?"

"Yeah. One of my rewards for saving the governor's daughter was my choice of assignments. And I got a raise. So I was thinking about settling down and finding me a wife."

"Oh?"

"Would you by any chance be interested in the job?"

"Why, I think I might be willing to consider such a position. So long as you don't mind getting up every morning to the bluest eyes in Texas."

"No," Burr said as he pulled her close and lowered his mouth to hers. "I don't think I'll mind that at all."

* * * * *

Dear Reader,

I don't believe most seductions are planned. A look. A kiss. A touch. Then nature takes over. The need to mate—the sexual instinct—is powerful, because in order for the species to survive, males and females must couple. Happily, nature has given women the means for attracting men—

Scent. Perfumes to pheromones, they're potent aphrodisiacs.

Sound. There's nothing like a whisper of suggestion—in words or song—to put your lover in the mood.

Sight. Beauty is in the eye of the beholder. If you feel beautiful, you are, and some man will find you so.

Taste. Sharing an orange together can be a sensual experience. Tasting each other can be even more fun.

Touch. A man's callused hands on a woman's skin; fingers tunneling through silky hair; the press of lips to lips, tongues to tongues; the ultimate joining of a man and a woman.

Ah, seduction... Ain't it grand?

Happy (seductive) trails,

Joan Johnston

THE BOUNTY
Rebecca Brandewyne

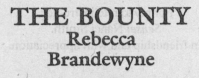

Come to me in the silence of the night;
Come in the speaking silence of a dream;
Come, honky-tonk woman, with eyes as bright
As sunlight on a stream;
Hold back the fears,
The memories; there's hope in your tears.

O dream how sweet, so sweet, so bitter sweet;
I have wakened in the arms of Paradise,
Where souls brimfull of love abide and meet;
Where a ramblin' man's eyes
Watched a wild door
Open, let me in, but out no more.

We became as one in dreams, that we might find
Our very lives again, once cold with death:
Became as one in dreams,
the chase that would bind
Pulse for pulse, breath for breath:
Speak low, lean low,
The bounty's here, my love, how well I know!

—adapted from *Echo*, by Christina Rossetti

For my karate instructor,
Sensei Nanci Smith.
In friendship and with appreciation.

Chapter One

The Watering Hole
Wyoming

Twenty-five thousand dollars. That's what Dolan Pike represented to Hayley Harper. Money in the bank, money she desperately needed and could make last a year, if she were careful. So, no matter what it took, she wasn't about to let it—or Pike—get away. Thus resolved, she deliberately leaned forward to provide him a better look at the swell of her full, generous breasts displayed by her liberally unbuttoned, red-bandanna blouse as, after collecting the empties, she plunked another ice-dripping, long-necked bottle of beer down on the cork coaster lying on the chipped, wood-grained Formica table before him. The wide, inviting smile she flashed him had in the past beguiled criminals even more hardened and cunning than he, and like that of Pavlov's dog, Pike's tongue was already hanging out in response.

"Will there be anything else, lover boy?" Hayley drawled, just softly enough that he had to bend near to hear her above the blaring jukebox and the raucous talk and laughter of the Saturday-night crowd gathered at the Watering Hole, the local favorite—possibly because it was just about the only—honky-tonk for miles around. Despite that outside the spring night air was cool, the barroom itself was hot. Perspiration glistened on Hayley's upper lip and trickled down her exposed cleavage, mingling sensually with the potent, musky fragrance of her perfume. Pike's nostrils twitched as he inhaled the scent of her. "I like to keep my customers happy... if you know what I mean?" Her heavily green-shadowed, kohl-rimmed eyes spoke volumes as her tongue darted forth to suggestively moisten her mouth, bright red with lipstick.

The man would have had to be a complete fool to misunderstand her—and Pike hadn't managed to commit more than a dozen armed robberies, to jump bail after his last arrest, and subsequently to evade recapture for the last two and a half years, by being a fool. He might be a high school dropout, but what he lacked in education and intelligence, he compen-

sated for with a dangerous, animal cunning and a vicious dearth of morals. Inside his skull lurked a brain
as sly as that of a weasel stealing eggs from a hen
house before bolting back to its hidey-hole. He'd got
away clean from all but the last of his several bank
jobs by being clever enough not to step foot inside any
bank itself. Instead, his MO—as in modus oper-
andi—had consisted of his pulling his pickup up to
one of a branch bank's drive-up windows and loading into the receptacle not a withdrawal slip, but a
bomb triggered by a remote-control detonator, whose
explosive device he'd then sent through the tube to the
teller, along with a note threatening to blow up the
bank if the teller didn't empty the contents of all the
cash drawers into money pouches, which were then to
be hand delivered to him outside. With a pair of high-
powered binoculars, Pike, his face concealed by a
black ski mask, had watched from his truck through
the bank's windows to be certain his instructions were
carried out to the letter. With everybody in the bank
terrified at the thought of his depressing the red button on the bomb's detonator should he hear the
sound of sirens wailing or see patrol cars approach-
ing, no employee had ever proved brave enough to set
off the bank's alarm system. Still, like most criminals, Pike fancied himself smarter than he really was,
smarter than the law, unlikely to be caught—despite

his rap sheet of previous arrests, all but the last for more minor offenses—and, if ever once more apprehended, able to make good his escape a second time.

Now, a knowing, anticipatory grin split his thin lips, revealing crooked, tobacco-stained teeth as he leered up at Hayley smugly, drunkenly. The beer she'd just brought him was his sixth; she'd kept track, just as she'd kept the black plastic bowl of salty pretzels on his table filled to brimming all night to ensure his thirst. Drink befuddled a man, slowed his wits and reflexes, gave her an advantage that, being a woman, she sometimes needed to hook him.

"Jest lookin' at you's enough to make a man think he'd died and gone to heaven, angel." Pike's beady, bleary eyes roamed over her cascade of gleaming, honey blond hair, her svelte, curvaceous figure licentiously as he lounged in his chair, hips thrust forward to emphasize the obvious bulge in his ragged jeans. Ostentatiously unfolding a wad of bills he took from the pocket of his T-shirt, he peeled off enough to pay for the beer and a generous tip, besides, making sure Hayley noticed the amount of the extra cash he laid on her metal, cork-lined serving tray. Then he slowly slid his hand up her left leg to cup her buttocks, enticingly encased in a pair of very short, very tight denim cutoffs. "How 'bout it, angel? You wanna spread your pretty wings for me, so's I can teach you how to really fly... higher 'n you've ever been before?''

Imperceptibly, Hayley's cat green eyes hardened and her cherry red mouth tightened at his crude, boastful question, and at the unwelcome, offensive feel of his hand upon her backside. Pike was scum, everything she heartily despised in a man: an ignorant, racist redneck; a conceited, sexist pig; a felonious lawbreaker. She wouldn't be at all surprised if, in addition to robbing banks, he belonged to one of the White Supremacist groups scattered throughout the Northwest. No doubt, it was from them that he'd learned how to build the bombs he'd used during his bank jobs, having favored a sawed-off shotgun at convenience- and liquor-store holdups in the past, graduating to the big time only after a stint in prison. It was all Hayley could do to keep from snatching up his beer bottle and bashing him over the head with it, knocking him senseless right then and there. But she'd learned the hard way not to let her temper get the best of her on a job. So, instead, swallowing her revulsion, she forced herself to pick up Pike's money and to make an entertaining show of slowly tucking it down inside her lace, demi-cup bra, so the bills nestled temptingly in the valley between her breasts. All the while she thought with grim satisfaction how she was really, if he gave her any trouble whatsoever later, going to enjoy giving him the business end of her stout *kapo* before handcuffing him, throwing him into her small recreational vehicle and then hauling him off to the nearest sheriff's office, in order to collect the $25,000 bounty on his head.

"You keep those tips coming like that, lover boy, and after my shift ends, we'll be soaring all night." Hayley's voice was low, smoky, sexy, like molasses heating over a fire.

The idea of actually going to bed with Pike gagged her. And not for the first time, she pitied the other barmaids, who, unlike her, were the genuine article and, provided a man had been forthcoming with his tips—and sometimes even if he hadn't—were seldom averse to going home with a customer after closing time. Hayley couldn't have lived like that. She didn't understand how other women did, despite knowing that unfortunate circumstances often drove them to it. Sometimes it was the only way they could make ends meet, especially if they had small children to support—the result, in far too many cases, of their having got mixed up with the wrong man: a worthless bum, an alcoholic, a doper, an abusive brute, or a hard-core criminal like Pike.

Every time Hayley dragged a bail jumper back to face justice, she felt she was striking a blow not only for law and order, but also for every poor woman who had ever suffered at a man's callus hands. Sometimes she even fancied herself on a crusade with her one-woman bounty-hunting agency, cleaning up filth so the streets would be safe for women and children alike—after which women everywhere could direct their attention to educating otherwise basically decent men, who just hadn't seen the light yet when it came to equality of the sexes. During her investigation of Pike's case history, background, acquaintances and habits, she'd discovered that his ex-wife and three little kids were living in a shack, subsisting on welfare and food stamps, struggling just to keep their heads above water. Given his disadvantaged upbringing, typical of so many law offenders, Hayley would have had more sympathy for Pike if he'd resorted to armed robbery for his family's benefit. But it appeared that he'd selfishly blown his loot on himself instead. The purchase of a shiny new "Dually" pickup, complete with a well-stocked toolbox bolted across the bed, and endless bouts of carousing had punctuated his last-known crime spree.

A sucker for beer and beauty both, Pike had clearly taken the bait Hayley had dangled before him; now, all she had to do was reel him in. Surreptitiously she glanced at the round, luminous-dial-faced clock that hung above the mirrors behind the brass-railed bar that ran the length of the barroom's east wall. Another thirty minutes, and it would be "last call." She'd waited two and a half years to nab Pike; if she had to, she could endure another thirty minutes of his crass leering and grabbing, managing to fob him off until closing time, when she'd give him something— although not at all what he was expecting—to remember her by outside in the Watering Hole's gravel parking lot. With feigned reluctance, Hayley turned from her prey, intending to sashay away with a toss of her head that would set her dangling hoop earrings to dancing provocatively, and with a sway of her hips that would keep Pike firmly hooked until the vigorous ringing of the cow bell suspended over the bar, which sounded "last call." But Pike had other ideas. Before she could make good her escape, he grabbed her wrist and, in a slobbering caress, pressed his lips to her upturned palm, his tongue snaking out to lick off the last traces of the melted ice from the beer bottle.

"What's your hurry, angel?" he asked, practically drooling.

Hayley's hand clenched convulsively on her serving tray. Thoughts of whacking Pike in his weaselly face with it, bloodying and breaking his sharp, pointed nose, crossed her mind. But again, with difficulty, she tamped down her temper—although she was unable to repress a shudder that, fortunately, Pike mistook for being sexual in nature.

Just grin and bear it, Hayley, honey, she told herself sternly. *Pike might not be prime stock, but he's still cash on the hoof. And having to put up with a few uncouth passes is a small price to pay for the chance to keep the agency going a little while longer.*

"Oooh, you *are* a lover boy, aren't you? I can hardly wait till closing. But right now, I've got to get back to work. Buckshot gets awful mad if the barmaids slack off on hustling drinks." Hayley nodded toward the big, beefy proprietor of the Watering Hole. He was perched on a high stool behind the old-fashioned cash register that sat at one end of the bar, the buckshot-loaded shotgun that had earned him his sobriquet propped up close at hand as a deterrent against brawls. He was glaring at her censuringly for wasting so much time with Pike when the barroom was packed full with free-spending, beer-swilling customers. "You don't want me to lose my job now, do you?"

Pike snorted at the prospect. "Buckshot'd be a fool to fire a woman like you. Bet you sell more beer 'n a brewery!"

"Miss. Hey, miss! *Miss!* Yeah, you, blondie!" The man hollering at Hayley from the nearby pool table gazed at her coolly as, finally realizing he was addressing her and not one of the other barmaids above the cacophony of music and babble, she glanced over in his direction. As he leaned against the pool table, casually chalking the tip of his cue, his eyes flicked from her to Pike and then back to her again. Then one brow lifted demonically and his lips twisted sardonically, making his disgust for her—and her apparent taste in men—plain. Mortified, Hayley blushed with shame and embarrassment before she reminded herself that she was *not,* in reality, a cheap barroom tramp on the make, for which the pool shooter had obviously and, given the circumstances, understandably taken her. "You think you could pay a little less attention to your boyfriend there and a little more to your customers? I've been waiting so long to be served that my tongue's swollen from thirst. Can I get a beer over here or what?"

Hayley had noticed the man earlier but hadn't paid him much attention. Now, from long habit—her sixth sense beginning to prickle, warning her that he might be trouble—she mentally sized him up.

Perhaps spruced up and dressed in an Armani suit instead of the old, short-sleeved blue chambray work shirt and faded jeans that he was currently wearing he might have been not just handsome, but actually drop-dead gorgeous. Even as it was, there was something curiously, compellingly, attractive about his rough, unkempt appearance. The mane of dark, woodsy-brown hair that brushed his broad shoulders and the small, thin gold hoop in his left earlobe both marked him as a rebel by nature. The stubble of beard that shadowed his lean, hard visage revealed a careless attitude toward what he deemed unimportant. The casually open collar of his shirt, which partially exposed the fine mat of hair on his chest, hinted at sensuality. The copper-tinged skin indicated a strain, somewhere in his genes, of American Indian blood, a heritage not particularly uncommon in the Northwest, but seldom resulting in facial bones so strongly but finely sculpted, the product of noble ancestry and in sharp contrast to those of most of the Watering Hole's patrons. The pool shooter had got the best of both worlds—and his arrogant stance, one thumb now hooked in the leather belt slung low on his narrow, provocatively-thrust-forward hips, said he knew it, too. King only of the barroom beasts, he might be, but he was a king all the same—a lion among jackals, prowling and dangerous.

Framed by thick, unruly brows and spiked with thick black lashes that appeared as though they often concealed long, brooding thoughts, his dark, deep-set hazel eyes held a predatory glitter in the dim, smoky light of the barroom as they raked her. The nostrils of his chiseled nose flared as though he'd caught her musky scent; his carnal mouth curved, baring even, white teeth in a wicked smile that mesmerized and beguiled, as a carnivore might hypnotize its prey in that heartbeat just before fatally striking. His hard, determined jaw, which bespoke a man accustomed to getting what he wanted, was softened only by the cleft in his chin, alone of which suggested that his savage temperament could be gentled, if not tamed, by those who knew the way. He was tall, a couple of inches over six feet, Hayley's expert eye judged, and would weigh more than he looked, because his sleek, rangy body was corded with the kind of muscles that came only from manual labor or regular workouts—probably the former, she speculated, taking in the unusual tattoo on his bare right forearm.

From past experience, she knew that tattoos usually indicated a military, blue-collar, or criminal background. But if this last were the case, she didn't recall the pool shooter's face staring back at her from any of the more recent Wanted posters she'd carefully examined, before stashing them in a drawer in her RV. Regardless, she would have remembered the tattoo—an ''identifying mark''—had she seen mention of it on the sheets. Still, that didn't mean he wasn't bad news. Instinctively she knew he was a man who wouldn't back down from a fight, and beside her, Pike was already bristling like an eager, untried timber wolf about to defend his territory.

"'Last call' isn't for another thirty minutes. So just keep your shirt on, mister. I'll be right with you," Hayley called to the pool shooter, relieved that he'd at least given her a good excuse for pulling away from Pike.

Unfortunately, as she'd feared, Pike didn't see it that way at all.

"Why don't you git somebody else to wait on you—or else git lost, man!" he snarled, slurring his words and glowering threateningly at the pool shooter. "Angel here's taken, ain'tcha, angel?"

Without ruining all her deceitful, demeaning but necessary efforts to gain Pike's interest, Hayley could hardly disagree. Inwardly she sighed, now certain there was indeed going to be trouble. Unwillingly she forced a smile to her lips and nodded her head, silently reminding herself of the role she'd so carefully established and played over the past few weeks, once she had cajoled Buckshot into hiring her. Her success had been based on a not-quite-so-false hard-luck story, a stream of crocodile tears born of an onion in her handbag, and a low-cut, pullover knit shirt coupled with the clinging denim cutoffs she was currently wearing.

"That's right . . . I'm taken," she agreed, disliking the hard glint that had come into the pool shooter's narrowed eyes at Pike's insulting words and knowing how a verbal barroom confrontation more often than not rapidly escalated to a physical one—which, in this case, might wind up totally destroying not only her well-laid plan for tonight, but two-weeks' worth of hard work that she could ill afford to lose. "But I'm sure Jolene there wouldn't mind taking your order," she added hastily, indicating one of the other barmaids, in the hope of staving off an altercation.

"Well, I don't want Jolene. I want *you* . . . angel," the pool shooter insisted perversely, his voice low, insolent. His eyes smoldered like twin embers as they deliberately ravished her, lingering covetously, unmistakably, on her breasts and the juncture of her inner thighs, igniting within her a sudden, jolting heat that coursed through her entire body, as though an electric shock had leapt from him to her. Confused and unnerved, Hayley shivered; she could have sworn that just moments ago, there had been nothing in his glance but contempt for her. Now it was as though he desired her and intentionally aimed to rile Pike by taking her from him, notions the pool shooter's next words appeared to confirm. "So, why don't you go fetch me a beer and tell old ferret-face there to take a hike—preferably a long one."

"Hey, I don't like the way you're talkin', man—and I like even less the way you're lookin' at my woman!" Savagely scraping his chair back from the table, Pike leapt to his feet, enraged. He had a volatile temper, Hayley knew, its fuse frequently shortened, as now, by liquor. As a child, he'd often been beaten by his loutish, backwoods father, besides. As was the result in so many battered children, instead of turning him against violence, his father's brutality had left Pike equally as quick to resort to his fists. "You shut your friggin' mouth, and leave her alone, you bastard—or I'll kick your sorry half-breed Injun ass!"

At Pike's threat, a tight, mocking grin that did not quite reach his flinty eyes curved the pool shooter's lips.

"Well, come on!" he taunted. "If you think you're big enough!"

Even Hayley, her every sense alert, was taken by surprise at the speed with which events progressed. Pike charged forward, fists swinging, connecting, to his astonishment, with nothing but air as the pool shooter stepped lightly, agilely, aside, using his cue like a *bo,* a Japanese long staff that was Hayley's own specialty when it came to martial arts weapons. Turning swiftly to land—legs spread, knees bent—in the traditional horse stance, the pool shooter jammed the butt end of the cue into Pike's stomach, doubling him over. Then, deftly pivoting into a right front stance while bringing the cue level and around, the pool shooter slammed the length of its tip end into Pike's jaw, sending him reeling. After that, flinging the cue onto the pool table, the pool shooter grabbed Pike by both the scruff of the neck and the left arm, the latter of which he twisted up behind Pike's back as—apparently wise to Buckshot's means of settling barroom disputes—he roughly, rapidly, half marched, half shoved Pike through the crowded barroom and out through the Watering Hole's front door. It all happened so fast that Hayley could see from the corners of her eyes that even the sharp-eyed, avaricious Buckshot remained unaware of the brief commotion. He had not budged from his perch to reach for the shotgun with which—as the pitted plasterboard ceiling and walls testified—he maintained what passed for acceptable behavior in his establishment, thereby keeping the cost of glass and furniture breakage to a minimum.

Fury and anxiety roiling inside her at the pool shooter's unwitting interference with her scheme to capture Pike, Hayley tossed her serving tray onto the nearest table and raced after the two men, slapping away grabbing hands and, with fists and elbows, proficiently driving aside the cowboys, lumberjacks,

wildcatters and bikers who formed the bulk of the
Watering Hole's clientele. She pushed past one of the
two burly bouncers to rip open the front door; the
cool, fresh, spring night air and the quiet hit her in a
welcome blast after the heat, smoke and clamor of the
barroom.

For a moment she just stood there on the flat concrete pad of the shake-shingled vestibule, catching her
breath while her eyes and ears adjusted to the rela-
tive darkness and hush beyond. The string of out-
door floodlights that lined the top of the Watering
Hole's painted signboard mounted on top of the
roof—Buckshot was too cheap to spring for neon—
did double duty by illuminating not only it, but also
a portion of the gravel parking lot beyond the vestibule. Still, half the bulbs had been shot out by rowdy
drunks or had burned out on their own. The night
seeped like a black, amorphous stain around the
edges of the light, and the tall trees of the fecund
woods, which threatened to engulf the patch of open
ground upon which the Watering Hole sat, cast long
shadows in the silvery shower of moonbeams that
dripped through the soughing branches. In the parking lot itself, cars, pickups, motorcycles, four-wheel-
drive and off-road vehicles all beaded with droplets
from the sweet, clean-smelling rain that had drizzled
earlier, were parked helter-skelter around the crater-

size potholes that now had become muddy puddles. The vehicles glowed dimly in the diffuse light, like the irradiated refuse of some post-apocalyptic world.

Damn Pike!—and damn that interfering pool shooter! The minute Hayley had taken his measure, she'd known he was going to prove a pain in the butt. Where in the hell were they? Stepping from the vestibule, she spied the two men at last. Pike had somehow managed to wrest free of the pool shooter's tight grip; now, they were engaged in combat beneath the feathery boughs of a towering pine rising up at the dark border of the parking lot. Pike was getting by far the worst of the fray. The pool shooter, it would appear, was indeed—as his stances and the way he'd used the cue earlier had seemed to indicate—a martial-arts expert, a black belt in karate, if Hayley were any judge of competency and style. Despite her own matching rank in that art, she wasn't sure she wanted to take him on. Watching him, she knew he was good. And while she'd found that a man's height often worked against him when battling her, a smaller opponent, the fact that the pool shooter outweighed her by at least seventy-five pounds was *not* to her advantage—his weight alone would take her down if he jumped on her.

On the other hand, the local sheriff might not be too happy if she dragged in Pike, with him having

been beaten to a pulp. Just as they did private inves-
tigators, law-enforcement officers sometimes had a
tendency to treat bounty hunters like second-class
citizens. She was trained in Ryu Kyu Kempo, an Oki-
nawan form of karate similar to the Shotokan style
popularized on film by Jean-Claude Van Damme.
And with her *kapo,* she *had* planned to clobber Pike
over the head if he'd proved recalcitrant—not that the
sheriff would know that, of course. Still, unless Pike
spoke up in her defense, which seemed unlikely if she
turned him in to the law, *she* might be suspected of
having done the number on him. Hayley had enough
problems as it was, keeping her small agency afloat;
she didn't need any additional hassles, especially one
that could conceivably lead to the suspension or even
the revocation of her bounty-hunting license.

Digging her key ring from the pocket of her cutoffs, she ran to her RV parked to one side of the Watering Hole, unlocked the back door and climbed
inside to grab her *kapo* and handcuffs off the counter
within, where she'd laid them earlier next to her
handbag with its gun inside, in preparation for Pike.
The cuffs she shoved down inside her back pocket,
but the *kapo* she kept in her hands. The solid, bur-
nished ebony wood of the Japanese nightstick shone
lethally in the moonlight as, after slamming the RV's

door shut behind her, she started determinedly toward the two men, a martial glint in her eye.

By this time Pike was down on his hands and knees on the ground, scrambling to escape from the well-placed jump kick that caught him in the ribs before he could elude it, tumbling him over onto his back and knocking the wind from him. Groaning, gasping for breath, he curled into a tight ball, rocking to one side, arms clutching his ribs, knees drawn up to protect himself from further blows. Intent on their conflict, neither man noticed Hayley sneak near, flitting stealthily through the shadows, using the trunks of the trees along the boundary of the parking lot for cover, her feet making no sound on the moss, wild grass and weeds that carpeted the earthen floor of the woods.

"Had enough, dirt bag?" the pool shooter demanded harshly, scornfully, his whipcord body bent forward, hands on knees as, breathing labored, he scowled down at Pike.

"Go to hell . . . Injun trash!" Pike ground out between rasps for air. Blood dripping from his nose, he lay there sickly, looking as though he might puke at any moment.

Gingerly, with the back of his hand, the pool shooter wiped away a trickle of blood at the corner of his own lips, then he spat in the gravel to rid his mouth of the bad taste.

"Come on! Get up! You ain't hurt that bad! A broken nose and a couple of busted ribs, maybe, is all. You're lucky it ain't worse. I don't take kindly to insults from pond scum like you. Now, get up, you redneck!"

Still, Pike made no effort to move. At that, with a snarl of anger and disgust, the pool shooter hunkered down, powerful hands grabbing hold of Pike's faded old Jerry Jeff Walker concert T-shirt—which had prompted the last gibe—to haul him roughly to his feet.

She would get no better opportunity, Hayley knew. Stepping up behind the pool shooter, she swung her arm back, raising the *kapo,* then, with an expert flick of her wrist, she brought it down hard. But some sixth sense equal to her own evidently warning him, the pool shooter glanced up over his shoulder at the last minute, snapping his left arm up and over in an upward block, just in time to deflect the intended strike. He grunted with pain as the nightstick buffeted his inner forearm, knocking him off balance so he stumbled over Pike and nearly fell. Quickly, before the pool shooter could regain his footing, Hayley lunged forward to attack again, this time delivering a crack upside his skull, which drove him like a poleaxed steer to his knees. A practiced roundhouse kick to the opposite side of his head finished him off. He stared at her dazedly, disbelievingly, for a moment, before his eyes slowly fluttered closed and he slumped into a crumpled heap upon the ground.

Lord, what if she'd accidentally killed him? Hayley wondered uneasily as she warily crept forward to take a closer look at his fallen figure. That second clout she'd dealt him with her *kapo had* been pretty hard; she'd been so worried about not doing him in with the first, about his getting the jump on her as a result, pinning her with his muscle and weight. As she stared down at him, an image of the pool shooter's hard, corded thighs straddling her, imprisoning her, pressing her down, came unbidden into her mind. She remembered how his eyes had strayed so hotly, so desirously, over her body, the answering heat that had surged inside her; and she shivered—although not entirely with apprehension.

It had been years since her divorce, months since she'd slept with a man. She was a strong, intelligent, independent woman who hunted hardened criminals for a living. Most men couldn't handle that, backing off, like her ex-husband, once they discovered that beneath her beautiful exterior lay not the joke-provoking dumbness of the stereotypical blond bimbo, but a smart mind and a steely will that demanded respect and equal status. Hayley wished that just once in her life she could meet a man unafraid of that challenge, a man willing to face it head-on, to meet it halfway. But, then, even if she did, her gypsy life-style of living in an RV, wandering from place to place, with only a post office box to call home, would in the end no doubt make the relationship unworkable. No matter how he'd looked at her or how she'd responded, the pool shooter was no different from all the rest of the men she had ever known. Only her father, "Gentleman Jim" Harper—so called for his pugilistic abilities, which had been in keeping with those of the famous Gentleman Jim Belcher and which had in his younger days won him a Golden Gloves boxing championship—had valued her strength, her intellect and her abilities, teaching her to value them, too. After all this time since his death, she still missed him.

Kneeling beside the pool shooter's sprawled form and cautiously laying two fingers at the side of his neck, Hayley sighed with relief as she felt his pulse beating steadily. Thank God, he was still alive. Still, his being out like the proverbial light didn't mean he wouldn't come around soon. When that happened, she wanted Pike handcuffed, stashed in her RV and both of them well away from the Watering Hole, in case the pool shooter proved stubborn enough to attempt to finish what he'd started. Rising, stuffing her *kapo* through a belt loop on her cutoffs and jerking her cuffs from her back pocket, she turned to the spot where Pike had been lying, doubled up, a few feet away.

Damn! He was gone!

He must somehow have managed to get to his feet and to stagger off while her attention had been focused on her examination of the pool shooter's unconscious body. Her face tightening with vexation and despair, Hayley glanced about feverishly. She just couldn't lose Pike! She just couldn't! It would mean the waste not only of the months she had spent tracking him, but also of the past two-weeks' worth of hard work, of standing on her feet all night, slinging beers and humiliating herself by dressing up and acting like a cheap tramp, letting Pike paw her—for nothing! Not to mention the loss of the $25,000 bounty she so desperately needed.

The sudden, deep-throated growl of a monstrous 460-HP engine springing to life, the piercing of the darkness by a pair of brilliant headlights, followed by the loud crunching of gravel, alerted Hayley to Pike's whereabouts. He was in his Dually— getting away! Crying out in protest, she bolted toward the black pickup now bumping and fishtailing along a crooked path through the parking lot toward the narrow backwoods road beyond. Each pair of dual rear wheels, which had given the truck its nickname, were spinning, and in their wake both gravel and water came flying out of the puddled potholes.

"Wait! Wait!" Hayley shouted, running toward the Dually, waving her arms wildly in a futile attempt to flag down Pike. He did stop—but only just long enough to plaster a feeble grin on his swelling lips and to yell out the open, driver's-side window, "Some other time, angel." He gunned the pickup's engine deafeningly before he lurched onto the blacktop, tires screeching and burning rubber as he sped west down the road into the darkness.

He was gone. And in the RV she would never catch him—at least, not tonight. She'd lost him. Hot tears of bitter frustration stung Hayley's eyes at the realization. Angrily, ashamed at her unaccustomed display of weakness, she dashed them away with the back of her hand. Then she slowly tucked her cuffs into her back pocket. By God, it was all that damned pool shooter's fault! she fumed. If not for *him,* she'd be on her way to the nearest sheriff's office by now, with Pike securely cuffed and stuffed in the RV. Pike had got away...but maybe all was not yet lost; maybe that pool shooter *was* wanted, she thought suddenly, her eyes narrowing speculatively at the idea. Maybe he was worth something, after all, and she just didn't know it. She'd find out who he was, Hayley decided resolutely, as she strode toward the place where she'd left him. Then, with the internal modem of her laptop computer, which was inside the RV, she would run a make on him.

Good thing for the pool shooter that he was still lying passed out on the ground, because she was so mad right now that if he hadn't been, she'd have knocked him witless again. Her mouth set in a grim, determined line, Hayley bent and, having taken the precaution of cuffing his hands behind his back first, began methodically to rifle the pockets of his jeans. Locating his leather wallet, she slipped it out and flipped it open.

"You've caused me a whole lot of trouble, Pool Shooter. So, now, we'll just see who you are. If there's a warrant out for you for so much as a lousy parking ticket, you're going to be sorry!" she declared aloud, glaring down at his unresponsive figure. Then, manipulating his driver's license so she could get a better look at it in the faint light, she inhaled sharply as she read his name: *Rafer Starr.* "Damn, Hayley!" she whispered to herself, stricken. "You've really done it this time—dumped the fat out of the frying pan and right into the fire! And not a fire extinguisher in sight! Great…that's just great. Way to go, Hayley." A man like him, with a name like his . . . she couldn't possibly be mistaken. It had to be *him!*

Her hands trembling, she hastily unlocked her cuffs about his wrists, then crammed his wallet back into his jeans, her heart pounding as he began to moan and to stir. She had to get away! She had to get away before he came to, otherwise, there was no telling what he might to do her! Leaving him where he lay, she raced to the RV, yanked open the door on the driver's side and clambered into the cab, punching the key into the ignition.

"Come on, come on," she muttered to the engine as it balked and sputtered lamely, *rrr rrr rrr,* refusing to start. Bad battery, bad alternator, bad starter? No, not now, not now! The engine was just a little cold, that was all; please, let that be all. Nerves strung as taut as thong, she pumped the accelerator a couple of times, then turned the ignition again. This time, to her vast relief, the engine roared to life. "Go, Hayley, go!" she urged herself frantically, wondering dimly in some far corner of her mind if, living and working alone for so long, she weren't growing prematurely senile, talking to herself all the time. Maybe she should get a dog or a cat.

Or a man, she could almost hear her father prod . . . and then chuckle at her indignation.

Grimacing wryly at the image, she expertly whipped the RV around, tires slinging gravel as she barreled through the parking lot toward the road, hitting a pothole that jolted her head into the ceiling, causing her to wince and to swear. That was another thing for which she owed Rafer Starr! On the radio, Waylon Jennings was belting out "Ladies Love Outlaws."

"Like hell, they do, Waylon," she muttered with annoyance, abruptly twisting the knob to the Off position.

Rafer Starr was an outlaw—of a sort.

Hayley tried hard not to dwell on that disturbing thought as she swung onto the blacktop and, following Pike's trail, headed west into the night.

Chapter Two

On the Road
Wyoming—1994

She shouldn't have panicked. There had been absolutely no reason for her to panic. In her line of work it was not only unprofessional behavior but also dangerous, as her father had taught her. Panicked people didn't think straight—and she hadn't. Still, as she plowed along the narrow, wending, backwoods road, pushing the small RV faster than she ought, Hayley's hands gripped the steering wheel so tightly that her knuckles shone white in the spray of moonlight through the windshield. And she could not seem to prevent herself from checking the rearview mirror every few minutes, searching for a pair of headlights coming up hard and fast behind her.

Rafer Starr. That name was legendary among bounty hunters. He was the best in the business, maybe the best there ever had been or ever would be. Even her father, Gentleman Jim Harper—himself a bounty hunter extraordinaire—had spoken well of Starr, had respected and regarded him highly.

"The man's something else, Hayley," her father had said once, shaking his head and smiling wryly, although not without admiration, even so. "Before he resigned his commission, he was a captain in the Marines—Special Forces. Even then, as now, he was a law unto himself, they claim, notorious for disregarding orders, daring—downright reckless, some would tell you, especially after that wild stunt he was reported to have pulled down in South America. Plus, it was rumored that he beat the tar out of a fellow officer afterward, calling him a fool who'd jeopardized men's lives on a mission. Still, the fact that, despite his antics and insubordination, Starr was never dishonorably discharged speaks for his abilities. It's said that his men would have followed him to the gates of hell—they had that much faith in him. This I do know, however—whatever else Starr might be, he's one hell of a man—strong, smart and capable, a professional...the kind of man *you* need, Hayley, instead of another namby-pamby like Logan. Money wasn't all *he* reeked of! Why, every time

I think about the night that knife-wielding mugger attacked you, and how Logan went running back inside the restaurant—''

"He went to get help, Dad,'' Hayley had interjected, but her voice had lacked conviction, for she'd felt, as her father had, that instead of fleeing the scene, her ex-husband, Logan Anthony Deverell III, should have come to her aid. As they had so often during their marriage, they'd quarreled that evening; it had long been a bone of contention between them that after their wedding, she'd continued to work for her father. Angry as a result, Logan had been several steps behind Hayley when the mugger had leapt out from between two cars in the shadowy parking lot to grab her around the neck, pressing a bowie knife to her throat and demanding her purse and jewelry. Instead of trying to defend her, Logan—fearing for his own safety, and assuming that, being a bounty hunter, she could take care of herself—had raced back inside the restaurant where they'd just finished eating a late supper, leaving her to deal with the threatening mugger on her own. Shattered by Logan's lack of caring, his callous desertion of her in the face of her endangered life, Hayley had divorced him a month later. "And at least he did call the police."

"Mighty damned generous of him!" Her father had snorted with disgust. "Man was a coward! Always had things too soft, too easy, stepping right into his daddy's shoes, taking over the family's oil business instead of having to work his way up in the world! If he'd have had to get a little bit of that oil, a little bit of that grease and dirt from his daddy's oil fields on his hands, it might have made a man of him instead of his turning out to be such a wimp! But Rafer Starr, now . . . there's a man! *He* wouldn't have cut and run, abandoned you to the mercy of a mugger's knife! No, ma'am! Too bad he's such a loner; we could use him in the agency now that my old ticker's not what it used to be and you've still got some learning to do, puddin'.''

"Don't you worry about me, Dad. I'll be fine," Hayley had insisted, distressed at the idea of her father's bringing an outsider into their small agency. She knew she would do everything in her power to look after Harper & Daughter and her father both, just as he'd always taken care of her since she was a child and her mother had died in a car accident. Further, although Jim Harper had never liked or approved of her ex-husband, he'd loathed even more the thought of her being left all alone someday, he being her only family. To Hayley's dismay, after his heart attack, her father had taken up matchmaking on her behalf. She hadn't liked the notion he'd had about Rafer Starr's being the man for her. Logan had taught her that no man, no matter his profession, wanted a "macho-woman" bounty hunter, as her ex-husband had called her, for a wife, and she wasn't about to make another mistake when it came to men. "And besides, the doctor says you'll be back up to speed in no time, Dad."

But much to Hayley's deep shock and grief, instead of regaining his former good health, Jim Harper had unexpectedly suffered a second—and fatal—heart attack. It had taken Hayley a long time to recover from his death. Holidays, especially, had been hard, with her having no other family to turn to. On top of her sorrow, she'd soon discovered how difficult it was going to be for her to keep the agency solvent without her father—how few people, despite all her training and credentials, took her, a woman, seriously as a bounty hunter. Still, determined not to fail her father, to keep the agency that was his legacy alive, she'd thrown herself into her work, managing somehow to survive. It had been three years now since Jim Harper's death, three years since she'd thought of their conversation—and of Rafer Starr.

"What's Starr think he's doing...poking his nose into my business, anyhow?" Hayley asked herself crossly as she glanced nervously at the rearview mirror again. "Dolan Pike is *my* bounty, damn it!—not his."

Still, deep down inside, she had a sinking feeling that not only was Starr *not* going to see it that way, but also that he was going to see *her* just as she'd seen him: as an unwelcome interference, one to be got rid of as quickly as possible. That's why she'd panicked. His reputation was such that she wouldn't have put it past him not just to have subdued her physically, but actually to have gagged and handcuffed her and left her locked in the toilet stall of her RV or something. He was wild, brazen, unpredictable and ruthless—an "outlaw" in the country-western vernacular—not known for being a particularly nice guy if he felt that someone was poaching on his preserve. Without exception he always worked alone, never in tandem with another bounty hunter. His one-man agency— Shooting Starr, Incorporated—was one of the most successful in the business, renowned for bringing down the big game. Pike's $25,000 bounty was hardly even worth Starr's time—and it meant everything in the world to her!

Now, some of her anxiety fading at the lack of headlights behind her, and her anger rising at the thought of Starr snatching her hard-earned bounty right out from under her nose, Hayley wished perversely that she'd hit him even harder, had taken a chapter from his own book and had cuffed him and stuffed him into the Watering Hole's Dumpster out in back of the rundown building, where he might have been stuck for at least a day or two before being discovered, giving her a jump on him. He'd treated rivals similarly in the past, she'd heard through the grapevine, so it would have served him right to have been given a dose of his own medicine. Now, not only did she have to worry about catching up to Pike, but she'd have to be constantly looking over her shoulder, too, for Starr. He'd seen her face when she'd whacked him and he would remember it. If he ever saw her again, he'd probably leap at the chance to even the score between them, especially if he learned that she was after Pike, also.

Hayley was so tired and upset that she drove off onto the sandy verge when a deer suddenly crashed from the woods to bound across the road in front of her. When the glare of her headlights illuminated it, she had just time enough to slam on her brakes and to swerve to avoid hitting the startled animal. It came within inches of being clipped by her front bumper but, to her relief, somehow managed to escape. Still, since she was an animal lover, the incident rattled her so badly that after she'd recovered her composure and spent several minutes searching for a turn-off, she found a place to park the RV in the woods on the side of the road for the night.

After making sure all the doors were locked and the blinds drawn, she stripped to her French-cut lace panties and pulled on her favorite old nightshirt, which had the words *Hard-hearted Woman* emblazoned across the front. She'd bought it after her divorce, to remind herself never to be a fool in love again. At the sink she gratefully scrubbed off all the makeup that, in keeping with her barmaid role, she'd applied with an atypical heavy hand to her face; then she brushed her teeth. After that she retrieved her automatic pistol from her purse and climbed into the wide bunk over the cab. Making sure the gun had a round in the chamber, she tucked it securely into one of the berth's cubbyholes in which she kept it at night, within easy reach. It was a Glock 19, given to her by her father. The polymer used in the construction of the compact pistol made it lighter and so gave it less of a recoil than most nine-millimeters, so it was easier for a woman to handle. In addition, it fired fifteen rounds and had a trigger safety, meaning it was always ready when she needed it. Hayley had been compelled to use it only a few times in her career, but she was always prepared to do so. A woman in her line of work couldn't be too careful.

Flipping the light switch, so only the RV's nightlights glowed, she flopped over onto her stomach, pulling the blankets up about her and her down pillow sideways under her head, so she could wrap her arms around it—not so comforting as the presence of another human being or even a teddy bear, perhaps, but it was all she had. Somewhere in the night, a solitary animal cried, echoing the loneliness she resolutely kept at bay, locked away in her heart.

To her perturbation, when she slept, her dreams were of Rafer Starr.

With her laptop computer's internal modem, knowing there was no time to go through proper channels, and reminding herself that she was leaving the files exactly as she'd found them, Hayley spent the better part of the morning guiltily hacking into various credit card data bases to see if Dolan Pike had used any major credit card late last night or early this morning—to pay for a motel room or breakfast—so she could pick up his trail. But much to her frustration, her investigation proved fruitless; she turned up nothing under his real name or any of his known aliases. He could be anywhere by now. That being the case, she saw no choice but to keep traveling west until she reached the next town. It wouldn't be much of a town, Wyoming having the smallest number of residents in the nation. Even its largest city, Casper, had a population of only 51,000 people. But at least she could purchase some groceries at the local market, ask around, find out if anybody had seen Pike or the

Dually. Her biggest fear was that Pike would head deep into the wooded mountains, where she'd lose him for sure, because to track him there, she'd have to possess special knowledge and training—like Rafer Starr—which she lacked.

Finding nothing worth listening to on the radio to entertain her while she drove, Hayley popped Styx's *Paradise Theater* CD into the compact disc player, programming the song sequence so only her favorite tune by the '70s rock band would play, over and over—a habit that had driven her ex-husband up the wall. He'd never understood how certain music put her in certain moods, how she wanted to listen to a song until she couldn't stand to hear it again for a while. Right now, she wanted the sounds of what she'd always thought of as hard-driving, bluesy rock wailing in her ears. Generation X didn't know what it was missing, she thought as the opening strains of "Snowblind" filled the RV; today's music was synthesized and digitized to the point that in exchange for clarity of sound, it had lost much of the rough-and-tumble heart and soul that had characterized the music of the sixties and seventies belonging to the Baby Boomers.

Nowadays, musicians didn't have to be able to play their instruments, only to produce a few chords; singers didn't have to be able to sing, only to "rap."

There were no Lennons and McCartneys, no Hendrixes and Claptons, no Joplins and Arethas anymore. At the thought, Hayley reflected wryly that she was getting old; in a few more years, forty would be just down the road for her, through the woods and over the mountain—or over the hill, as the case might be, although not if she had anything to say about it. Still, her "biological clock" was ticking. Although she didn't regret divorcing her ex-husband, she did wish that they'd had children, that something to be treasured and celebrated had come of their marriage. She would have liked to have had a family. But Logan hadn't wanted any kids—something else, like assuming she'd give up being a bounty hunter, he'd neglected to tell her until after their wedding.

As she listened intently to the lead guitar's intricate, soaring, sliding notes, emphasized by the Marshall's preamp being kicked on overdrive; to James Young's and Tommy Shaw's powerful, emotion-filled vocals; to the dark, soul-stirring lyrics about emptiness and being "snowblind" with a desperate, aching hunger and need, which emotions were adroitly only implied by and so must be derived from the words, Hayley unwittingly recalled the way Rafer Starr's eyes had appraised her in the Watering Hole, making his desire for her plain; and again, that strange, thrilling heat shot through her. Unlike Logan, she couldn't imagine that Rafer Starr would have any inhibitions about stating flat-out what *he* wanted and expected from a woman. Somehow she knew instinctively that he would mate like an animal, would be blind with passion, savage in his hunger and need for a woman he wanted above all others. Her heart pounded peculiarly at the notion. For the umpteenth time since hitting the road after lunch, she glanced in her rearview mirror but spied no one behind her. Starr must have passed her by in the night or else had taken a turnoff somewhere between the Watering Hole and town. Either way, she'd succeeded in eluding him, Hayley thought, confused and disconcerted to find that she felt not elation, but a curious pang at the realization.

The men once under his command would have recognized that not only was Rafer Starr's present mood an ill one, but also that while it was upon him, he should be avoided at all costs. He was not, under the best of circumstances, a man to cross; when in the grip of one of his infamous black rages, he was lethal. Last night, Dolan Pike had escaped from him, and even now, his head still ached and bore a lump on it the size of a goose egg where he'd been struck by Pike's beer-slinging, *kapo*-wielding girlfriend—a real knockout in more ways than one. Damn her! Rafer still couldn't believe how she'd managed somehow to sneak up behind him and to cosh him, conking him out cold. It had been a long time since a man—much less a mere woman—had got the best of him like that! She'd made him feel like a complete fool, a raw greenhorn in the bounty-hunting business. Because she was a woman, a cheap barroom tramp, Rafer had broken the number one rule of survival: know your enemy. He'd not only underestimated, but wholly discounted Pike's girlfriend as a player in the events that had unfolded at the Watering Hole. He would *not,* however, make that mistake again, Rafer assured himself grimly as he stared at her through the leafy branches of the bushes behind which he was currently crouched for cover.

His off-road Jeep could go where her RV couldn't and was a hell of a lot faster, besides. Last night, having lost Pike, he'd decided that the woman represented his best chance of sniffing out his quarry's trail, that sooner or later she'd lead him to her ferret-faced boyfriend. In fact, given how she and Pike had hung all over each other in the Watering Hole, Rafer had thought that it was a pretty good bet that Pike was living with her in the RV, which doubtless, like the Dually, was an ill-gotten gain bought with the loot from the bank jobs. Thus reasoning, Rafer had turned off the two-lane blacktop onto an unpaved road that, while a good deal rougher, was a shorter route to the nearest town west, and that had put him there ahead of Pike's girlfriend.

At first, when she hadn't shown by lunch, Rafer had been afraid that his hunch had been misplaced, that instead of heading toward town, she'd turned off somewhere along the way and that he'd lost her and Pike both. But just when he'd been fixing to start up the Jeep to backtrack toward the Watering Hole, Rafer had spied the woman finally rolling into town. She'd stopped at the local market on the corner, buying a bag of groceries, chatting at some length with the clerk at the checkout counter while she'd paid for them. Then she'd stepped outside to survey her surroundings carefully, either looking for Pike or making certain she hadn't been followed, Rafer had surmised as he'd watched her covertly from his Jeep.

When she'd finally driven out of town, he'd fallen in behind her, taking care to hang well back so she wouldn't spot him, since, obviously, she'd suspected she might be tailed. No doubt Pike had warned her not to lead anyone to him. At sundown she'd pulled off the road into a little clearing in the woods, placed a call on her cellular telephone—presumably to Pike—then pitched camp, building a fire over which she was currently cooking a pot of chili and a pan of spoon bread. Rafer's mouth watered at the savory aromas. For lunch he'd wolfed down a couple of packaged ham-and-cheese sandwiches he'd bought at a convenience store. But they hadn't done much to sustain him, and now he was hungry again. Still, that the woman's supper was nearly done indicated that her boyfriend, Pike, ought to be showing up anytime at their rendezvous. Had she been his woman, Rafer knew that he himself would already have been here, eating his fill of her food and drinking in his fill of her beauty.

Her silky, honey blond hair, parted on the side in the style immortalized on film by Veronica Lake decades ago, cascaded down past her shoulders, a luxurious mass that framed a pale, oval face with high cheekbones skillfully emphasized by a light dusting of dusky rose blush. Beneath gracefully arched brows, her cat green eyes were wide and luminous, lined with a heavy fringe of sooty lashes that, in the firelight, cast crescent smudges upon her cheeks. Her classic nose was set above a mouth that was as lush as a full-blown rose and a gamine chin with a decidedly stubborn tilt. Ripe, round breasts strained against her short-sleeved, oversize, pullover burgundy shirt. Its wide neckline bared her swanlike throat, delicate collarbones and one white shoulder, and, despite its bagginess, did little to conceal her slender, hourglass figure. Her long, shapely legs were accentuated by clinging burgundy stirrup pants and a pair of high black boots.

There was something different from last night about her now, Rafer mused as he studied her. In the subdued light cast by the snapping and sparking flames of the campfire, she looked softer somehow, fragile, vulnerable and pensive—traits he would not previously have associated with her. Maybe she was not so hard as he had at first supposed; maybe she'd just had the bad luck to get mixed up with the wrong man—although why she'd picked a weasel like Pike to begin with, Rafer couldn't fathom. With that face and body she could have had any man.

Get a grip, Rafe, he told himself sternly as he abruptly realized the unwise direction of his thoughts. *Don't be a fool again. Behind that angel face lurks a devil of a woman. She damned near killed you, for God's sake!*

This stringent reminder was reinforced by the fact that the woman had a Winchester 1300, the Defender model, propped up against a rock beside her. The 12-gauge, pistol-grip shotgun had an eighteen-inch barrel and fired eight rounds, and there was not a doubt in Rafer's mind that, like the *kapo,* she would use it, if need be. That was why he intended to secure her before Pike arrived. There was no reason to have the odds stacked two against one unless necessary.

Checking the wind, then moving low and sound-lessly through the brush, Rafer began to circle around behind her, an expression of grim determination upon his hard visage.

Hunkered over the campfire, a potholder in each hand, Hayley carefully lifted the ceramic lid on the big, white-speckled, blue stockpot perched on the open grill and, with the ladle resting inside, stirred the homemade chili, sniffing its steaming aroma appreciatively. It was hot, ready to eat, and she was hungry. She replaced the lid. Then, so the chili would stay warm but not burn, she slid the pot off the grill, setting it alongside the pan of spoon bread on one of the rocks that ringed the campfire. Her plate, bowl and utensils sat nearby, waiting, along with a large, gay, red-checkered cloth napkin. Just because she was eating alone didn't mean she shouldn't pamper herself with a few niceties, she'd always thought, having resolved after her divorce not to fall into a miserable rut. Now, was there anything she'd forgotten? she asked herself. Oh, yes. The butter for the spoon bread was still in the small refrigerator in the RV.

Under normal circumstances, the snapping of a twig would have warned Hayley that she was no longer alone. But as she stood, turning to fetch the butter from the RV, she mistook the sound for the crackling of the cheerily blazing campfire and so let out a startled scream when she spied Rafer standing less than six feet away, looking like some wild animal looming out of the surrounding woods' long shadows, which had come with nightfall—a dangerous predator stalking his prey. She hadn't heard him. He moved like a panther, she thought, and resembled one, too, half crouched, fixing to pounce—on her! There was not a doubt in her mind that he'd crept up on her, seeking revenge. As it had last night, unaccustomed panic rose within her. Resolutely, Hayley fought it down.

"*You!* What are you doing here? What do you want?" she asked, annoyed by the nervous note in her voice, which she knew he must have heard.

"A bowl of that chili and a slice of that spoon bread would do me for a start," Rafer rejoined lightly, slowly straightening up but not making any other move, sudden or otherwise, hoping to allay her apparent fear and suspicion, thereby still to take her off guard. "It smells real good, and I'm famished. Look, you don't have to be afraid. I'm not going to hurt you. I just want to talk, okay?"

"Yeah, right. My dinner guests always show up looking like they're on the warpath or a covert military operation!" Hayley's voice dripped with scorn as her eyes took in his appearance: the two eagle feathers braided with a narrow, beaded rawhide thong into his otherwise loose mane of hair; the wide black band, its long ends trailing, tied around his forehead; his handsome face daubed with camouflage grease, and his soldier-of-fortune attire—a pair of black combat boots, jungle fatigues and a black T-shirt that, across the front, boasted a wickedly grinning white skull wearing a Special Forces beret. Framing the skull was the wry catch phrase *Mercenaries never die. They just go to hell to regroup.* Being something of a mercenary herself, Hayley didn't need to ask the obvious question, why the word *old,* which customarily prefaced the majority of all such similar slogans, was absent. There were no old mercenaries—and no old bounty hunters, either. Neither was the automatic pistol in the shoulder holster he wore nor the knife in the leather sheath at his belted waist apropos merely for a meal and a friendly chat. "Where are your tomahawk and Uzi, Rambo?" she prodded sarcastically, wishing that her heart were not drumming so hard, so crazily, at his proximity. What was the matter with her that she continually lost her professional cool in this man's presence?

"I must have forgotten and left 'em at home. And it's Rafer, not Rambo."

"Gee, you could have fooled me!"

"Consider yourself fooled then. Now, how about that chili?"

"The only 'chili' you're going to get is a chilly goodbye, Rambo. Now, get lost—before I lose my temper and do something you'll regret even more than that crack I gave you upside the head," Hayley threatened with false bravado.

"You're making a mistake," Rafer declared, maddeningly unruffled, casually beginning to walk toward her.

"I don't think so!" she shot back defiantly, although she was shaking inside as she warily backed away from his approach.

Given his appearance and knowing his notorious reputation, she didn't trust him an inch. No matter what he'd said earlier to the contrary, he had—garbed like some half-breed Indian commando—sneaked up behind her, hoping to catch her unaware. There was no telling what he intended, only that whatever it was, it wasn't anything good—at least, not for her. Despite her caveat, he hadn't left—and didn't look as though he were planning to, either. In fact, at any moment, he would be close enough to grab her. Her gaze narrowing, Hayley swiftly gauged the distance between her and her shotgun, then her and the RV. The shotgun was closer, loaded and ready for action. Abruptly moving, she dove toward it. But Rafer was a professional, too, and in that fleeting moment in which she'd assessed her situation and selected her best option, he'd read her decision in her eyes. Springing forward at the same time as she did, he seized the wrist of her outstretched hand and began to drag her struggling figure toward him.

"Let go of me—or you'll be sorry, I swear!" Hayley warned through gritted teeth as she settled into a back stance, digging her heels into the ground and exerting a determined pull in opposition to Rafer's own, while trying to wrench her wrist loose.

"You're the one who's going to be sorry," he insisted coolly as, before she realized what he intended, he withdrew his handcuffs from his back pocket and swiftly locked one steel ring into place around the wrist he held imprisoned with a grip like an iron band, deliberately cutting off her circulation. "Woman, this is one battle you can't win, so why don't you just give up now and save us both a lot of grief."

"Like hell I will!"

Unable to haul him off balance, terrified that he would capture her other wrist and finish cuffing her, Hayley took him by surprise with a side kick, slamming her right foot straight into his chest, causing Rafer to grunt with pain and to release his tight hold on her as he stumbled back, sprawling onto the ground. Again, she lunged toward her shotgun. But he came up fast, trying—as he realized he was indeed, as he had previously suspected, dealing with a woman trained in the martial arts—to grab her around the knees so he could yank her legs from beneath her, then flatten her with his greater weight. To counter the offensive move, Hayley delivered a powerful roundhouse kick to the left side of his ribs, pivoting around. But before her spinning hook kick could connect, Rafer grasped her ankle, twisting her leg so she fell, although she did manage to take him down with her by hooking her arm around his elbow.

Grappling for supremacy, they rolled on the earth together, she catching his booted foot behind her knee as they edged perilously near to the campfire. Despite the heat cast by the flames, which she could feel uncomfortably close against her skin, Hayley determinedly maintained her grip on Rafer's arm, finally maneuvering him into a joint lock, so he was forced facedown against the ground. Normally she could have held him immobile while she handcuffed him, but her own cuffs were in the RV, and she was on her knees instead of standing as she ought properly to have been for the hold, besides.

As she reached to pull his automatic from his holster, Rafer, with his strong right leg, captured her ankle again, roughly hauling her sideways, while, simultaneously, his fist shot out. His pistol skidded away as, adroitly, she parried the blow, following through with a back fist to his jaw, which they both knew would leave a bruise in its stunning wake. Blood spurted anew from the split corner of his mouth, wounded last night in the battle with Pike. But tumbling to the side as she was, Hayley was in no position to defend against Rafer's sweep, as she normally would have done by jumping over his foot, which hit hard behind her knees, jerking her legs up and out from under her so she landed, with a cry of pain, flat on her back, the wind knocked from her. Instantly, as she'd feared, Rafer was on top of her before she could recover, mercilessly pinning her down with his heavier weight, his corded legs imprisoning her own, his strong hands snatching her arms up over her head and locking upon her unsecured wrist the open ring on his handcuffs, so both her wrists were now caged and, regardless of how she tussled, he could hold her firm with just his left hand, leaving his right one free for whatever he might choose to use it.

The sudden, explosive battle had lasted less than ten minutes, but both Hayley and Rafer were breathing hard and fast from their exertions, each all too aware of the other—hot, flushed and sweating, adrenaline still pumping, their lithe bodies pressed together intimately, his covering her own as though he were making love to her. Hayley's nerves thrummed at the thought. Her head was spinning; she couldn't seem to catch her breath as Rafer stared down at her, taking in her blond hair tangled about her in sexy dishabille, her eyes that flashed sparks of fury at him, her shirt—torn somehow in their struggle—now half revealing her lace, demi-cup bra and heaving white breasts. As she saw where his gaze strayed, realized how she was exposed to him, she inhaled sharply, shivering with both fear and some other equally strong, wild, primitive emotion she did not want to name. Deeply misliking the rapacious glint in his narrowed eyes, she began anew to struggle fiercely to liberate herself—to no avail.

"Let me go! Let me go, damn you!" she cried.

"Not a chance in hell, baby," Rafer replied grimly, a muscle flexing in the taut jaw he rubbed gingerly with his free hand, wiping away the blood that trickled from the broken corner of his lips. "I've got a knot a broody hen would mistake for an egg on my head, and now, my jaw may never work right again, thanks to you. The FDA ought to require you to come with a label—one that reads Warning: Seriously Hazardous to a Man's Health! Talk about your blond bombshells . . . woman, you are definitely nitro."

Rafer thought he'd never before seen a woman at once so wildly beautiful and so dangerously beguiling, like a tigress—one that badly needed taming.

Undoubtedly ranked a black belt in karate, she was so damned good that if not for his superior strength and weight, she might well have won their confrontation. In a million years he had not thought to find her like—a woman who was his match, his equal, a fit mate for a man who feared no one and nothing but what lay coiled deep within his own dark, brooding, solitary soul, the emptiness, hunger and need that, being such a loner, he had too long suppressed and denied—and that now, as he lay atop her, stirred forcefully within him, no longer willing to be restrained and rejected.

For, as fighting often did a man, their conflict had not only enraged, but also excited Rafer. The soft, sensuous feel of Hayley herself—her half-bare, ripe breasts pressed enticingly, however inadvertently, against his broad, muscled chest, her long legs spread and pinioned by his own—did the rest. As though somewhere inside him a floodgate had burst, arousal abruptly surged through him, swept him up on a strong, overwhelming wave. His breath caught harshly in his throat; his loins tightened sharply. He could tell by the sudden, alarmed widening of her eyes, the flaring of her nostrils, the ragged little gasp that issued from her own throat, that Hayley, too, felt the burgeoning hardness of his heavy, heated sex against her, at the vulnerable, opened juncture of her inner thighs. In that highly charged moment of their mutual awareness of his desire, Rafer had a powerful, unbridled urge simply to rip open his fatigues, to take her then and there on the grassy ground, to fill her until she moaned and writhed beneath him, cried out her surrender, begged him for release—a primal male instinct that she sensed, he knew, and that, even though she obviously feared and would fight it, her eyes said she nevertheless understood. Her lashes sweeping down to conceal her betraying thoughts from him, Hayley turned her head away, swallowing hard as she perceived the depth of her sudden peril. Surely, he would not force himself on her! Her moist, tremulous mouth parted.

"Please," she whispered, her voice at once importuning and husky with the emotions and sensations coursing through her wildly, setting the pulse at the hollow of her throat to jerking visibly. Never had a man made her feel as Rafer did now—like a quintessential female, fragile, vulnerable, opened, waiting to be taken, to be thrust hard and deep inside of, again and again, undeniably claimed, indisputably possessed. Unbidden images of Rafer doing that to her filled her mind, filled her body with an irrepressible, wanton desire that licked like tongues of flame through her, making her go weak and molten at her core. Stricken by the sound of her soft, beseeching voice, fearful of losing control, of being swept up, too, by the hot, dark, dangerous thing that had seized Rafer in its grasp, Hayley bit her lower lip so hard that she drew blood to hold back the further entreaties that rose in her throat and that she thought would prove fruitless. Forcing herself to concentrate on the pain she'd deliberately caused herself with her teeth, she strove to regain mastery of herself and her situation, trying desperately to push him off her.

But her frantic writhing did not win her freedom; indeed, it only enkindled Rafer all the more. For what was happening so unexpectedly between them was as lethal to him as it was to her. It had been a very long time since he'd experienced such strong feelings toward a woman. He'd thought himself dead inside; now, he knew beyond a shadow of a doubt that he was still alive. The fragrance of her perfumed body was like jasmine on the wind—heady, intoxicating—as he breathed it in deeply. Her flushed skin, as luminescent as a flawless pearl, glistening with perspiration born of the closeness of the campfire and of their conflict, was as soft and delicate as a rain-showered rose petal as, with his free hand, he caught Hayley's jaw, deliberately twisting her countenance back up to his. Slowly, sensually, making her shudder, her heart leap, he drew the pad of his thumb across her generous lower lip, tugged at it gently.

"You scrubbed up real fine." Rafer's own voice was as low and smoky as hers as his dark, glittering hazel eyes drank in the beauty of her face no longer overpowered by an excess of cosmetics, but, instead, subtly enhanced by their light, skillful application.

"Too bad I can't say the same for you, Rambo!" Hayley hissed in return, staring up at his camouflage-greased visage, longing fervently to deny how the feel of his warm breath against her skin and the heat of his sex against her own were like a fever in her blood, dizzying her. Inhaling sharply, she caught the woodsy, musky scent that clung to him—vetiver, her favorite. Her heart beat fast with mingled dread and a perverse but undeniable excitement at his nearness, his dominant-male position. For the first time in her life, she'd met a man stronger than she, was at his utter mercy. To Hayley's bewilderment and dismay, despite her fright, she could not seem to suppress the inexplicable thrill that shot through her at that knowledge, exhilarating her, like a harrowing ride on an old wooden roller coaster, in the last car, which always skipped the tracks. She lived on the edge, as did Rafer. Now, they were both there together—and he was as savage as his Indian forebears in war paint; a warrior, a dog soldier, wounded but forever unbowed, unconquered, she thought, although she did not speak the words aloud. "You look like a grease monkey!'' she spat out instead, fighting him, fighting herself and all he had evoked inside her. ''Now, for the last time—turn me loose, you... you... *barbarian!*''

''I don't think so,'' Rafer muttered thickly, an echo of her own words to him earlier. His eyes darkening with passion, he abruptly crushed his mouth down on hers hard, taking her breath and stifling the whimper of protest that rose to her captive lips.

Hayley was shattered, shaken to her very bones by the ruthless kiss that was like none other she had ever before known—practiced, powerful, possessive, coercing her compliance, demanding her response to the mouth that devoured hers hungrily. No! she thought frantically, no! She would *not* let this happen! She would not! Marshaling her wits, she bit down hard on Rafer's lower lip, causing him to snarl with pain and then to swear.

''So, you still want to play rough, do you, tigress?'' he grated softly as he jerked his head back, licking away the blood from the tiny wound she'd inflicted. ''All right, then. We'll do it your way....'' He laid his hand upon her slender throat, deliberately tightening his fingers there ever so slightly, threateningly. ''Kiss me,'' he demanded, his voice low, urgent, raw with desire, his breath sultry against her flesh as his mouth brushed hers electrifyingly. "Kiss me, damn you...."

Before Hayley could speak, his lips claimed hers savagely again, swallowing her breath. Despite how her mind yet rebelled against his onslaught, the pressure of his hand at her throat compelled her mouth to part, to yield pliantly to the inexorable intrusion of his probing tongue. It found her own, touching, twisting, tasting, exploring her moist inner recesses until, at long last, with a low moan, she ceased to struggle against him, melted beneath him, began to kiss him back with a fervor to match his own, unable to continue the futile attempt to deny the feelings he was inciting inside her. At that, Rafer's hand slid from her throat, stroking her bare shoulder before seeking and cupping her naked breast beneath the lacy material of her bra. A powerful eruption of excitement and desire radiated through her at the bold caress; her nipple puckered and hardened beneath the slow, sensuous circling of his palm, the taunting motions of his thumb and fingers. His hips thrust provocatively against hers, rubbing his hard sex between her spread legs. Unconsciously Hayley strained against him, instinctively positioning herself so the pressure kneaded her soft mound, where a desperate, burning ache was building inside her. It had been so long since she'd had a man—and never one who'd made her feel like this. Certainly, Logan had never made her feel like this. Despite herself, she wanted Rafer inside her, deep inside. . . .

Oh, God, what was she thinking? What was she doing? Hayley asked herself abruptly, mortified as she strove dazedly once more to recapture her senses. She didn't even know Rafer; and here she was letting him kiss her, fondle her, stroke himself against her. In moments he would be ripping off her clothes and his own, pushing himself inside her. She'd been under such a strain lately that she must have lost her mind, must have gone absolutely mad! What must Rafer think of her? That she was a cheap barroom tramp? But, of course, that was exactly what he thought, Hayley realized, sick inside as she understood then what had prompted him to fall like some ravaging animal upon her. With difficulty she tore her mouth free from his, thrashing her head from side to side as he sought ardently to reclaim her lips and, when he couldn't, pressing searing kisses on her temples, throat and breasts instead.

"Wait . . . please!" Hayley gasped out, afraid she wouldn't be able to contain what she'd inadvertently unleashed inside him. "Listen to me! Please! You— you don't understand. I'm—I'm not what you think—"

"What I think is that you're too damned good for a loser like Pike," Rafer growled. But then the thought of his quarry brought him abruptly to his senses, and he swore softly. "Damn!"

He must be completely out of his mind—letting his lust rule his brain! Pike would be here at any moment, and he, Rafer, would be caught with his pants down—literally! He was a bounty hunter, a professional; he knew better than that, a good deal better! What was it about this woman that had inflamed him to the point where he'd permitted his desire for her to override his every ounce of common sense, his every instinct for survival? She was nothing but a cheap barroom tramp, Pike's girlfriend, and probably his accomplice, as well. No doubt, with her seductive feminine wiles, she'd hoped to keep him, Rafer, occupied until Pike arrived, and things had just progressed too fast for her to handle. Naturally she wouldn't want Pike to show up and to find her actually getting it on with another man. His eyes narrowing, his mouth tightening with anger and disgust at himself, Rafer drew back from her a little so he could see her face, although he didn't release her, even so.

His gaze took in her long blond hair, tumbled in wild dishevelment about her; her thick-lashed green eyes dark not only with apprehension, but also with the passion he'd aroused in her; her upper lip beaded with perspiration; her tempting, tremulous mouth, bruised and swollen from his hard, savage kisses; the tiny pulse beating erratically at the hollow of her pale, slender throat; the quick, shallow rise and fall of her breasts, their generous swell above her lacy bra, the trickle of sweat that moistened the valley between them.

At the sight of her, it was all Rafer could do not to finish what he'd started. But instead, his voice low and taunting, he asked, "What's the matter, baby? Did you suddenly remember your boyfriend Pike's jealous temper, grow afraid he might beat you if he should come upon us in flagrante delicto? Or did you just get more than you bargained for, taking me on?"

"Oh, God, I never dreamed that you thought Pike was...that I'd actually let him...when even just the *thought* of that weasel touching me makes me ill! But no wonder you believed that you could...that I would—" Stricken, Hayley broke off abruptly, biting her lower lip. Then, seeing Rafer's slow, puzzled frown, that he had got hold of himself, however difficultly he'd restrained his turbulent emotions, that he could at least be reasoned with now, she continued. "Look, if you'll just listen to me a minute, I can explain everything. I—I know how things must have appeared to you last night, but you've simply got to believe me. Pike is *not* my boyfriend. I don't even have one at the moment, and even if I did, it sure as hell wouldn't be *him!* And I don't sling beer in a bar for a living, either—"

"Yeah?" Rafer quirked one eyebrow devilishly, his skepticism plain, his tone sarcastic as he went on. "Well, you sure fooled me."

"I understand that, and I don't blame you for thinking what you did. But you were wrong—although, to be honest, I don't think you're going to like the truth much better—"

"Oh? And just why might that be, I wonder?"

"Because I'm a—I'm a bounty hunter, just like you." At his startled, darkening glance, Hayley rushed on, not giving him a chance to interrupt again. "I was working undercover at the Watering Hole, so I could get to Pike. I'd learned through my investigation, just as you must have, that he dropped in there on occasion. My—my name's Hayley Harper. And even if that doesn't mean anything to you, the fact that my father was Gentleman Jim Harper should. We used to be Harper & Daughter, but since his death, it's just been the Harper Agency, and I've been running it alone. I...ah...rifled your pockets last night, after I knocked you out. When I found out who you were—are...Rafer Starr, I'm afraid I just kind of...ah...panicked. You've got quite a—a notorious reputation in the business, you know, especially for dealing with rivals. So rather than stick around and try to sort things out with you when you came to, I just drove off. Frankly, I thought I could get the jump on you and locate Pike before you did.''

''Pike now knows I'm a bounty hunter. He would surely have told you that—and for all I know, you might have concocted this story specifically for the purpose of deceiving me in the event that I ever got my hands on you—no pun intended,'' Rafer added mockingly, causing her to blush furiously as his gleaming eyes roved over her again lewdly. ''So why should I believe you?'' he queried dryly, although his gut instinct told him that Hayley was, in fact, telling him the truth. He *was* familiar with Jim Harper's name and work, had heard through the grapevine about Harper's death and now vaguely recalled some tale about the daughter's having taken over the agency—and having a hard time making a go of it, too.

''My ID and license are in my handbag, in the RV. If you'll let me up, I'll get them.''

''Pardon me if I insist that we get them together. But I'm sure you'll understand that regardless of what you've just told me, after your whacking me with your *kapo* and back fisting me in the jaw, quite frankly, I don't trust you, woman.'' Rolling off her at last, Rafer stood and, reaching down, hauled her to her feet. But he didn't unlock the handcuffs about her wrists; and although after retrieving his automatic and Hayley's shotgun, he returned the pistol to his holster, he checked the shotgun to be certain it was loaded and that the safety was on, and then he trained the barrel on Hayley. "Just in case you have any bright ideas about pulling another fast one," he explained at her inquiring glance, then motioned with the shotgun toward the RV. "Now, lead the way... nice and slow."

Once inside the RV, Rafer instructed Hayley to sit down on the bench to one side. Then, carefully placing the shotgun on the counter so it was within his easy reach, he took stock of his surroundings, his gaze lighting on her nearby *bo* and *kapo*. Eyeing her askance, he removed both from her proximity and put them next to the shotgun. Then he picked up her black leather purse she pointed out to him, which was cleverly constructed to appear as though it were all one piece but that, in reality, was like a pair of saddlebags stitched almost completely together along the edges. The concealed opening on one side between the two pouches gave way to a holster inside, in which she kept her Glock 19 during the day, so she didn't even need to unzip the handbag in order to get at the gun. Plus, in the event that the purse were ever forcibly taken from her, it could be opened up and its contents checked without the automatic's presence being discovered, so the handbag—and the hidden pistol—would more than likely be returned to her. But Rafer was wise to the tricks of the trade, and the first thing he did as he examined her purse was to slip his hand between the two pouches and to withdraw her gun.

"My, my. You're just chock-full of nasty little surprises, aren't you?" With one corner of his wryly twisted mouth, he *tsk-tsked* with feigned dismay as, slowly shaking his head, he slid out the magazine and emptied the chamber before laying the automatic alongside her shotgun. Then, saying, "Turnabout's fair play, don't you agree? I mean, after all, you *did* go through my pockets and wallet," he unzipped her handbag and began to rummage through it. "What've you got inside here? A pair of brass knuckles? No, don't tell me…a stun gun. Of course. What else?" Experimentally he depressed the button on the weapon, causing a loud crackle of electricity to erupt between the two small poles. "Bring down a lot of big game with that, do you?" He tossed the stun gun onto the growing arsenal on the counter.

"It's come in handy a time or two," Hayley said tersely, because even though she knew that the charge from the stun gun wouldn't consistently drop an assailant, particularly a heavy one or one high on drugs or alcohol or both, she believed in always carrying a couple of back-up weapons, just in case; and for that purpose, the stun gun worked well enough.

"Uh-huh. I'll bet," Rafer grunted. "If Dolan Pike only knew what a narrow escape he'd had from your clutches, he'd thank his lucky stars that I was at the Watering Hole last night. No wonder you don't have a boyfriend; most men wouldn't dare to risk closing their eyes around you, woman. You know, it belatedly occurs to me that perhaps I ought to have...ah...frisked you more thoroughly. You've probably got a knife stuck in your boot, too."

"Frisking? Is *that* what they're calling it these days?" she drawled derisively, her lashes hooding her eyes to cloak her thoughts. But she could do nothing to hide the betraying stain of color that crept upon her cheeks. And the next thing she knew, Rafer was slipping from her right boot the black-handled switchblade she'd purchased at a gun show a few years back.

"I prefer a butterfly knife myself." Grimly he pushed the catch that released the blade, testing its spring before he snapped the blade closed and tossed it onto the heap of her weapons he'd already confiscated. "You wouldn't by any chance happen to be a Boy Scout, would you?" he asked acidly as he impatiently resumed his rifling of her purse, even opening and digging through her cosmetics bag before finally withdrawing her French-style leather billfold and unsnapping it to reveal her driver's license, bounty-hunting license, gun permits and a couple of major credit cards. "Or do you just share the same motto?"

"Be prepared? Listen, Starr, I shouldn't have to tell you—of all people—what it's like out there on the job these days!—especially for a woman!"

"Well, well. We're making progress. I've been elevated from Rambo to Starr—and you are, indeed, Hayley Harper, would-be Honey West." He flashed her a tight, mocking smile as, at last satisfied as to her identity, he returned her billfold to her handbag and threw the purse aside. Then, folding his muscular arms over his broad chest, he lounged against the counter, gazing at her speculatively, thoughtfully. "Bet she was your idol when you were just a kid in pigtails. You even resemble Anne Francis a little— got that same blond hair and that beauty mark at the corner of your mouth."

"I had a ponytail. And Honey West was a private detective, not a bounty hunter, and, yeah, so what if I used to watch the show every week on TV? Anne Francis broke new ground for women everywhere with that part. She played a woman who did what was considered a man's job and who managed to retain her femininity while doing it, just as Angie Dickinson's Sgt. Pepper Anderson did in later years. What's wrong with that?"

"Not a damned thing from where I'm standing." Once more, Rafer's eyes appraised her, lingering on the swell of her breasts revealed by the tear in her shirt. "Except that I've got the strangest feeling that, also like them, you intend to get the job done— whether I like it or not."

"That's right. Pike's federal—you know that. He robbed banks and crossed state lines on his little spree. He's fair game for anybody. So, how about these?" Hayley hastily held up her cuffed hands, afraid that, knowing she wouldn't back off, Rafer might be getting any number of unpleasant ideas where she was concerned, a suspicion his next words appeared to confirm.

"What're you going to give me in exchange for the key?"

"What—what do you want?"

"You? Is that what you thought—hoped—I was going to say?" he asked, with a wide, sardonic grin as he spied the look in her expressive eyes. "Sorry to disappoint you, Ms. West, but right now, my hunger is leaning more toward a bowl of that chili and a slice of that spoon bread that I can still smell warm on the fire outside."

"Don't flatter yourself, Rambo!" Hayley rejoined, incensed and humiliated that he should so correctly guess her equally apprehensive and anticipatory thoughts about his finishing what he'd started earlier. "The only way you could disappoint me is by sticking around. So if feeding you is the only way to get you to slink back to whatever zoo you escaped from, I'll be more than happy to oblige, believe me."

"Didn't your daddy ever teach you that it's dangerous to provoke an animal?" Rafer inquired softly, intently. Deliberately he let the sudden silence stretch significantly between them, unnerving her, before, to her relief, he finally dug the key to the handcuffs from a pocket of his fatigues and tossed it to her. "Now, be a good girl and get cleaned up for supper. It is, in fact, a jungle out there, but I don't think you'll be needing any camouflage grease tonight."

Once Hayley had freed herself, a glance in her mirror confirmed that her face was indeed, as Rafer had intimated, smeared with camouflage grease from his kisses ... kisses she tried hard not to think about as, together, she and he washed up at the sink. She didn't want to dwell on what had flared so unexpectedly and explosively between them. But when she forced her thoughts into other channels, Hayley unwittingly recalled her father's words about how it might have made a man out of her ex-husband, Lo-

gan, if he'd ever got a little grease and dirt on him.
And then she thought that, with one of her wash-
cloths, Rafer Starr had just scrubbed off more than
his fair share of both. Why was it that the most attractive, exciting men were always such no-good
rogues? she wondered a trifle bitterly. Why were they
always men who didn't know what it meant to love
and to cherish a woman, to be honest with and faithful to her? Logan had often lied to her and, Hayley
suspected, in her absence while away on business for
the bounty-hunting agency, had cheated on her more
than once during their marriage. Doubtless, Rafer
Starr was an accomplished prevaricator and had had
his share of women, too. That the RV should seem so
inordinately small and cramped because he was in it,
that his maleness and nearness should prove so un-
settling to her was foolish. The sooner she was rid of
him, the better! Unless it were the kind she was dragging back to face justice, she didn't want or need another scoundrel in her life. Logan's rejection had
stung more than she cared to admit. That she was, in
some respects, still punishing him—and even her father, too, for dying and leaving her alone—and, by
extension, all men, by living as she did, tracking down
bail-jumping criminals who'd hurt others whose
loved ones were then left behind to grieve, was a
thought Hayley determinedly shoved from her mind.

She didn't want or need to be psychoanalyzed, either.

In the privacy of the toilet stall, she changed her damaged shirt for a whole one. Then, he adamantly refusing to leave her alone with her cache of weapons, she and Rafer went outside, carefully extinguishing the fire and carrying the chili and spoon bread back into the RV to eat at the foldaway table, since the wind had freshened and the spring night air had grown chilly.

"By the way, just out of curiosity, if it wasn't Pike, who *did* you call earlier on your cellular telephone?" Rafer inquired casually as he ladled the still-steaming chili into bowls, while Hayley sliced the warm spoon bread and spread it with butter from the refrigerator.

"My answering service, to see if I had any messages—not that it's any of your business."

"You're on my turf, Hayley." The statement was blunt. "I'm making it my business."

"You been hired by the bondsman for Pike?"

"No," he conceded reluctantly as they sat down at the table.

"Then I'm not on your turf, am I?"

"Look, Pike's personal, all right?" Rafer's shuttered expression said he didn't want to discuss the matter further, but Hayley didn't intend to be put off.

"In what way?" she probed before spooning chili into her mouth and then breaking off a piece of the spoon bread on her plate, swallowing it down with a sip of bottled dark beer.

For a long time she thought he wasn't going to reply. But then, at last, he spoke.

"Pike's ex-wife . . . Wenona . . . she's the kid sister of one of the men who was in my unit when I was in the service. He was killed on a mission down in South America, and before he died, he told me about Pike and asked me if I'd look out for Wenona. Seems Pike periodically gets his kicks by driving out to her place and slapping her around before raping her. She doesn't have a whole lot of money or education, and she's too afraid to call the sheriff, for fear that the state will step in and she'll wind up losing her three kids."

"I suspected something like that," Hayley admitted. "She wouldn't even let me inside when I stopped by to ask her about Pike, much less talk to me. Look, Rafer, I'm real sorry for Wenona's troubles, but what difference does it make if it's you or me who puts Pike back behind bars, where he belongs?"

"The difference is that I'm going to give Wenona the bounty. I don't need it, and she does. She's attending a vocational school at night, when she can get one of her sisters to watch her kids, and twenty-five thousand dollars will go a long way toward helping her get off welfare and food stamps, and on her feet. You, on the other hand, plan on keeping the bounty for yourself.''

"The truth is...I—I need it. Otherwise, I'm going to be forced to dissolve the Harper Agency, and I just can't let that happen! It was Dad's whole life, his legacy to me!'' Even as she unwillingly confessed her financial problems, Hayley felt miserably selfish in light of Rafer's entirely unexpected generosity toward Wenona Pike. But, then, he could afford to be charitable, she thought bitterly. As the gun in his shoulder holster—a Walther P-88, $1,200 minimum, retail—attested, he didn't have any monetary worries. Neither had she—once. But despite the advice of both her father and her lawyer, she'd stubbornly refused to take so much as a dime from Logan, even though he'd been loaded. She hadn't wanted anything from him; she could make her own way in life, she'd told herself proudly at the time, and it was too late now for regrets. "Maybe we could work together, split the bounty,'' she suggested. "That's fair.''

"I work alone, and I never split bounties.'' Rafer's tone was cool, imperious. "So back off.. walk away from this one, Hayley.''

"And if I don't?''

"You said yourself that you weren't unaware of my...notorious reputation. Wasn't that how you phrased it? It's true. I don't lightly tolerate rivals—not even ones who look like you." His eyes glittered with heat and appreciation, making her shiver as he gazed at her. Then, finishing the last of his beer, chili and spoon bread, he rose, carrying the dirty dishes to the sink and beginning the task of washing up.

"You don't have to do that. In fact, I—I think that it would be best if you left now," Hayley insisted a trifle nervously, as she put the remainder of the food into airtight plastic containers and away in the refrigerator.

The glance Rafer shot her from beneath his lashes was sharp.

"Man eats a woman's cooking, the least he can do is clean up the dishes afterward—and unlike a lot of men, I ain't too proud and arrogant to do my share of household chores." There was silence for a moment as Hayley digested this remark, while he, having completed the scrubbing and rinsing, directed his attention to drying the dinnerware and utensils, neatly stacking them on the counter afterward. Then, slinging the damp towel over his shoulder, Rafer turned back to her, continuing. "Besides, it's late, and I'm tired. And, so, quite frankly, I don't relish the idea of having to sleep with one eye open and one ear cocked all night, in case you get some wild notion about sneaking up on me, bashing me over the head again or jerking the plugs out of my Jeep's distributor cap, stranding me so you can get the jump on me and catch up to Pike before I do.''

''What—what do you mean?'' Hayley asked, her heart starting to pound far too hard and fast in her breast at the wicked, determined glint that now suddenly shone in his hazel eyes. ''What—what are you saying?''

Beginning slowly to stalk her, Rafer answered softly, ''What I'm saying, Hayley, is that I intend to spend the night right here, in your bed, with you.''

Chapter Three

"**Y**ou—you can't be serious!" Hayley cried as she stared at Rafer, stunned and aghast, thinking that, surely, he was only teasing her, even though she knew by the expression on his face that he'd meant every single word. "You can't sleep here—and certainly not in my bed, with me!"

"Wanna bet?" Rafer smiled slowly, mockingly, his eyes raking her in a way that sent a shudder of mingled fright and excitement rippling through her. Then, his voice low, arrogant, insolent, he demanded, "Take your clothes off, Hayley."

"I—I won't!" Her turmoil and trepidation were such that she did not dare to add "And you can't make me!'' because even as the thought occurred to her, she realized how childish it would sound, and she knew, besides, that he could—and that he would—compel her to undress for him, given the slightest provocation. He'd already proved that she couldn't beat him when it came to a sparring match between them—a new and not entirely welcome experience, since she was accustomed to besting and thereby getting her man. Still, her karate instructor had always warned her that, all else being equal, a woman would invariably be defeated by a man's superior strength and weight, that surprise and speed were the only elements on her side—and Hayley had now lost both. Since their battle, Rafer was on his guard against her, and his proximity in the small RV prohibited a quick escape. A verbal demand appeared her only realistic option. ''I want you to leave, Starr—now!''

''I told you—I'm not going anywhere. So, we can do this easy, or we can do it rough, whichever you prefer. Just make up your mind, Hayley.''

For a moment she gazed about the RV wildly, seeking a means—any means—of ridding herself of Rafer's presence, while simultaneously calculating her chances of eluding him. But all her weapons were piled on the counter before which he stood, blocking her access to them, and he was between her and the RV's back door, besides. To get away, she would have to crawl through the cab, and he would undoubtedly catch her before she could reach either the driver's or the passenger's door. She was, in effect, helpless against him, another feeling to which Hayley was thoroughly unused. Still, not being one tamely to submit to her fate, she snatched down her nightshirt, which trailed over the edge of her bunk where she'd tossed it that morning. Then, shooting Rafer a defiant glance and relieved when he made no move to halt her, she flounced into the toilet stall to change, firmly locking the door behind her.

Once inside, Hayley leaned against the wall, trembling. This just couldn't be happening to her, she thought, astounded both by her predicament and by the fact that she was only half scared by the notion of Rafer's compelling her to make love with him. She was a smart, competent woman highly trained in the art of self-defense. That she should be at his mercy galled and unnerved her, even while her body tingled with treacherous, tantalizing anticipation as she unwillingly remembered the feel of his mouth upon hers earlier, of his weight pressing her down, of his hand cupping her bare breast. . . .

"Hayley, open up!" Rafer abruptly pounded peremptorily upon the door of the toilet stall, startling her from her reverie. "Hayley, so help me, I promise you that if you don't hurry up and come out of there,

I'll kick this door in—and you know me well enough by now to know that I damned well will, that I don't make idle threats.''

"Yes, I know. Just—just keep your shirt on, will you? Statistics show that it takes a woman longer than a man in here, or don't you know that?'' she called crossly, motivated into hastily stripping to her French-cut lace panties and yanking her nightshirt on over her head. Nervously, afraid the thin door might come flying off its hinges at any moment from a powerful blow delivered by an impatient Rafer, Hayley used the toilet, then flushed it. Then she unlocked the door and opened it, drawing up short at the sight that met her eyes: a broad expanse of naked, heavily muscled chest matted with fine dark hair that trailed entic-ingly down a firm, flat belly to disappear into the waistband, its top button unfastened, of the fatigues slung low on lean, narrow hips.

"As you can see, I don't take orders well," Rafer drawled with a cocky grin as he tossed his T-shirt aside, having previously, while she was changing into her nightshirt, not only unbraided the eagle feathers from his hair, but also taken off the remainder of his apparel, save for his fatigues. "But at least your bathroom door is still in one piece."

"I suppose you think I should be grateful for small favors, huh?'' Hayley gibed caustically, scowling but still unable to prevent her gaze from straying appreciatively over his coppery flesh: his corded arms, the right fore of which sported what she now knew must be a Special Forces tattoo; his broad chest, at its heart a pair of silvery metal dog tags that hung from a chain about his neck.

"*Exceedingly* grateful," Rafer declared softly, intently, his own eyes slowly taking her in: the wide neckline of her nightshirt, which bared her throat and one creamy shoulder; the way in which the thin, pale pink cotton material clung to her full breasts, outlining her nipples taut with fear and excitement; the short hem that revealed her long, graceful legs. "Hard-hearted Woman," he read aloud the nightshirt's caption, emblazoned across a big red heart on the front. "Is that a fact? Well, I'm a man who enjoys a challenge, actually." Then, before Hayley realized what he meant to do, Rafer suddenly reached out and caught her right wrist in a grip of iron, snapping around it one steel ring of his handcuffs, which he had concealed behind his back, then locking the other circle onto his own left wrist. "Even if I don't always play fair," he added coolly, with a cynical smile at her outraged gasp of protest. "So, here's the deal, Hayley—the key to these cuffs is in the right front pocket of my fatigues. You be a good girl and don't give me any trouble, and we'll both get a good night's rest. But if you wake me up—and I warn you that I am a very light sleeper—I will most assuredly forget where I stashed the key and assume that you're fumbling around in my pants for a whole 'nother reason. Do I make myself clear?''

"Crystal. You know, you really are an unconscionable cad...using sex as a weapon!'' Hayley's eyes shot sparks at him, for she'd thought—half hoped—he was attracted to her. And now, she felt a pang of pique and disappointment at the realization that his desire for her had been born only of their heated struggle earlier.

"Well, correct me if I'm mistaken, but somehow I thought that's exactly what you were doing with Dolan Pike at the Watering Hole last night,'' Rafer jeered, his mouth turning down sourly at one corner. "Or are you denying using yourself as sexual bait to lure him outside after closing, where you no doubt planned to cosh instead of to kiss him?''

Hayley had the good grace to flush guiltily.

"It's different for a woman,'' she insisted defensively, although, even to her ears, the excuse sounded lame. "We're not as physically strong as men, we have to rely on our feminine wiles. Besides, any man so arrogant and fool enough to fall for that kind of an act deserves whatever he gets!''

"Uh-huh. Well, arrogant, I may be—but fool, I'm not. You might want to keep that in mind when you bat those cat green eyes of yours at me in the future, tigress. Now, it's been a long day, and I'm for bed—and since we've been united in unholy deadlock, I'm afraid you'll have to join me, whether you like it or not."

Indeed seeing no other choice, Hayley unwillingly climbed into the berth over the cab, Rafer following close behind her, his free hand casually cupping her backside as he boosted her into the bunk. They settled themselves as comfortably as was possible, given that both the handcuffs and the confined quarters forced them to lie closer to each other than either, all too aware of the other, would have liked. Rafer drew the blankets up about them, then flipped the light switch so only the RV's night-lights shone. In the near darkness and the silence broken only by the sounds of night in the woods, Hayley tried to ignore him lying so near beside her. But that was easier said than done, and after endless, restless shiftings of her position—which precluded sleep's coming to either of them—she finally wound up on her back, staring at the ceiling and heaving a deep sigh of annoyance and frustration.

"This is ridiculous! What if I have to go the bathroom in the night?"

"Wake me up, and I'll take you." Without warning, Rafer wrapped his free arm about her willowy waist and pulled her body up next to his own, so she lay on her left side, with him curled protectively around her. "Now, relax and go to sleep. Much as I'd like to, I'm not going to force myself on you, I swear—that is, of course, unless you want me to. Because I understand, you see, that a woman like you needs an even stronger man, that she can't respect anything less. So...would you like me to take you, Hayley, to hold you down and to make love to you? Because that's what it would be, you know...." His voice was smoky, seductive in her ear, only half-teasing; his breath was warm against her skin.

"No, I would not!" she insisted softly—and knew the words for a lie.

His low laugh sent a wild thrill shivering through her in the dimness.

"I could make you want it...want me." His hand slid up to fondle her breast through the thin cotton of her nightshirt. His thumb rotated slowly, sensuously, across her nipple until it grew rigid with excitement, strained against the fabric as waves of pleasure radiated through her. She could feel his sex stir, growing heavy and hard, pressing against her buttocks through his fatigues. "You see?"

"Please stop, Rafer." Her voice was a whisper, an entreaty—because she knew that if he continued his deliberate assault upon her senses and her body, she would relent, would yield to him in the end. Already, her heart was drumming in her breast, her blood was singing in her ears at his provocative caress. "I don't even know you!"

"Don't you? We're alike, baby, you and me—down to the bone—and you know it. We both play to win, and you're just too stubborn to admit that this is one time you lost."

"I haven't lost anything...yet—and I don't intend to! I'm going to get Dolan Pike, come hell or high water. So if you thought you could make me forget about him by seducing me, you were wrong. Now, take your hands off me!"

For a long, tense moment fraught with significance and expectation, Hayley was half afraid Rafer wouldn't do as she'd insisted. But then, at last releasing her, he turned over onto his back, shutting his eyes.

"All right...if that's the way you want it. Just remember this, baby—all's fair in love and war—so don't say I didn't warn you."

"What's that supposed to mean?"

"You'll find out in the morning. Good night, Hayley. Sweet dreams."

"Damn you, Starr!"

At that, he lifted one eyebrow devilishly and raised one eyelid to stare at her censuringly before closing it again, making it plain he wasn't going to respond. Cursing him under her breath, Hayley flopped over onto her stomach, resolutely turning her head so she wouldn't have to look at him anymore. She tried but failed to fall asleep. But after a while she became aware of Rafer's own rhythmic breathing, and moving gingerly so as not to waken him, she turned to study him in the shadowy light. Slumbering, he looked younger and not so hard as life had made him. She could only imagine what his had been like, what it had taken to belong to a Special Forces branch, to take part in the covert military operations in which she knew he must surely have participated over the course of his career in the Marines. No matter what anybody said, Hayley didn't believe that any man could come through combat unscathed, that it inevitably left wounds and scars, if not on the body, then always on the psyche. Obviously the men in his unit had been comrades, or he would not be so driven where Dolan Pike was concerned. But even knowing that Rafer's motives for wanting to capture Pike were altruistic, while her own were more selfish, Hayley still did not intend to back off. She owed her dead father, just as Rafer owed Wenona Pike's dead brother.

That thought uppermost in her mind, Hayley tentatively stretched out her left hand, inhaling sharply as she made contact with Rafer's flesh, his furry chest. He was warm, much warmer than she, his body generating more heat than hers. Briefly, she was tempted to snuggle closer to him; she'd felt curiously safe earlier, when he'd wrapped himself around her. For the first time in a long while, she'd not gone to bed worried that she might have to use her gun in the middle of the night; she'd known that if anyone crept up to break into her RV—as sometimes happened to campers, especially in the woods—Rafer would defend her. Still, if she could obtain the key to the handcuffs, she could regain control of her situation and fate. Rafer didn't stir at her touch, so Hayley began slowly to slide her hand downward, over his belly, gasping, screaming softly when his steely hand suddenly clamped hard around her wrist.

"You know what they say, Hayley," he murmured drowsily, not even bothering to open his eyes. "Don't do the crime if you can't do the time." He turned, rolling her over onto her side, curling himself around her again, his right hand keeping hold of her left, imprisoning her. "Now, for the last time, go to sleep."

"Yes, Rafer," she replied, reluctantly and only momentarily conceding defeat.

"Hmm. I like the sound of that. I could get used to hearing you say it, to holding you in my arms, like this." His voice was low, husky in her ear.

So could she, actually, Hayley realized to her surprise, as, gradually, the heat of him pervaded her bones and, secure in his embrace, she slept.

She awoke in the morning to the smell of eggs and sausage frying on the stove. For a moment, bewildered, she thought that she was a child again, that her father was still alive and cooking breakfast. Then she spied the indentation in the down pillow Rafer had used last night, inhaled the masculine scent of him that clung to the sheets, felt the warmth of the berth, where he had lain beside her and knew that it was he, not her father, at the stove. Rafer was still shirtless, and Hayley could not help but admire his handsomely sculpted body glowing coppery in the soft morning light that streamed through the open blinds. Seeing her gazing down at him drowsily from the bunk, he smiled engagingly, in a way that made her heart turn over.

"Roust it out, Sleeping Beauty," he greeted her as he popped toast up from the toaster and arranged the slices on two plates. "Time's a-wastin'."

"People who rise and shine with the sun—and who are actually cheerful when they do so—deserve to be lined up before a firing squad and shot," Hayley grumbled as she stirred and stretched, wincing at the feel of muscles bruised and sore from her conflict with Rafer the previous evening. "Still, I can forgive a man almost anything if he cooks. Is this a going-away present?" She indicated the breakfast now on the table, at which she joined him, once he had pulled on his T-shirt and sat down.

"Is that a hopeful note I hear in your voice—or a pang of disappointment?" Rafer grinned as he slath-ered red plum jam onto his toast. "Personally, I like my eggs and sausage hot, so why don't we eat first and talk afterward?"

"Fine with me. It takes me a while to wake up, so I prefer quiet during my morning coffee, anyway." Picking up her brimming cup, Hayley sipped the steaming brew gratefully. It was strong and black, just as she liked it. She could fall in love with a man who had hot coffee ready and waiting for her in the morning, she thought idly, then blushed at the un-witting notion. Thank heavens, Rafer wasn't a mind reader!

Hooding her eyes so he wouldn't guess her thoughts, she hastily and hungrily applied herself to breakfast, hoping he hadn't noticed the color that had briefly stained her cheeks, since he was devilish enough to probe, and she would be at a loss for an answer. But to her relief, he was busy devouring his food, using his toast to sop up the soft-fried eggs. The meal was good, just what Hayley preferred in the morning—although, most of the time, being a night person, she rose so late that she didn't eat until noon—and the silence between her and Rafer was strangely companionable. She hadn't expected to find it so; she'd thought there would be awkwardness. They had, after all, shared the same bed last night, even if they hadn't made love in it. But it was instead as though she'd awakened after twenty years to find Rafer waiting for her; and despite herself, honesty forced her to admit that the sight of him had pleased her.

When breakfast was finished, Hayley washed and dried the dishes, observing, as she did so, that all her weapons were missing from the counter. At that realization she felt her first twinge of uneasiness and suspicion that Rafer's amiable demeanor was meant to lull her into a false sense of security. Still, she made no comment as she gathered fresh clothes, then went into the toilet stall to carry out her morning ablutions. He'd said they would talk, and clearly, they must if they were to work out anything at all between them where Dolan Pike was concerned. It was only when she emerged, clean and dressed, to be grabbed by Rafer and to have one ring of his handcuffs snapped back around her wrist that Hayley cursed herself for her stupidity. She should have known not to trust him!

"What do you...think you're...doing, Starr?" she asked between gasps for breath as she struggled furiously—futilely— against his viselike grasp.

"Settling our disagreement over Pike and the bounty," he rejoined coolly as he dragged her into the cab, then shoved her into the passenger's seat, locking the second circle of the cuffs around the shoulder portion of the seat belt and paying no heed to the invectives she hurled at him until he effectively silenced her. Before she realized what he intended, his hand caught her chin, twisting her furious face up to his, and he kissed her hard on her indignant mouth, his tongue shooting deep, taking her breath until she ceased to fight him, clung to him, trembled against him. At that, releasing her, he calmly slid into the driver's seat, opened the door and hopped out onto the ground, his combat boots scraping on rough pebbles. "That ought to keep you busy for a while." He motioned toward the handcuffs.

"Oh, so we're Mad Max instead of Rambo this morning, are we?" Hayley's voice shook with both outrage and passion. It was all she could do to hold back tears of frustration and hurt that she should prove no different to him from any other rival bounty hunter, that she should have dared to hope...what?

That Rafer might actually have begun to care for her a little? How could she have been so foolish, so naive? "Are you planning to leave me a hacksaw—and to stuff a Molotov cocktail up my exhaust pipe before you go?"

"Nothing so dramatic as that." He shook his head, grinning wickedly. "You know, I think you spend too many nights all by your lonesome self here in this RV, watching too many movies, baby. You need some company, to get out more. It's not good to be alone so much."

"Speak for yourself, Max!" she retorted, incensed, embarrassed that he should have guessed so much about her solitary existence.

"Yeah, well, I've been giving my own life as a loner some thought, I'll admit. Now, the way I see your current situation is like this, Hayley. You're a strong woman. Even so, I don't think you'll be able to tear that cuff loose from that seat belt, and even if you somehow *do* manage to, you'll inevitably ruin your seat belt in the process—all for nothing, because I'll be back before you can get free, I promise you. So, it's up to you, whether you think you can make good your escape in less time than it takes me to return."

"Where are you going, Starr? How do I know that you're really planning on coming back, that you're not just going to leave me out here in the boondocks, chained to my RV? How do I know that this isn't just some rotten trick so you can get the jump on me and capture Pike before I do?''

''You don't,'' he said bluntly. ''You'll just have to take my word for it.''

With that, he slammed shut the driver's door and loped into the woods. Biting her lower lip anxiously, Hayley glowered at his disappearing back. His infamous reputation was such that how could she believe him? He was a scoundrel, a rogue—the list of names she could think of to call him was endless. Yet when she recalled the feel of his mouth upon hers, every ounce of common sense she possessed seemed to desert her. She glanced at the seat belt. With both hands, she gave it an exploratory tug. It was fastened tight to its anchor. She sat there warring with herself, debating whether she could even yank the seat belt loose, much less tear the cuff off it, and knowing that Rafer had been right, that even if she somehow *did* manage the feat, the seat belt would be destroyed— and costly to replace. Oh, surely, he had spoken the truth; surely, he planned to return, was not so unconscionable as to leave her stranded in the middle of nowhere, with little hope of escape or discovery.

No sooner had the thought occurred to her than Hayley heard the sound of an engine and, to her relief, spied a Jeep pulling up. The off-road vehicle's top was off, so she could see in the RV's big side mirror that Rafer was at the wheel. What was he doing? she wondered as he killed the ignition and swung from the Jeep, reaching back in its bed to withdraw a heavy chain. Good Lord. He was hooking the vehicle to the RV's trailer hitch! What else could that possibly mean but that he intended to take her with him? Her heart began to hammer in her breast at the realization.

"This is—this is *kidnapping,* Starr!" she sputtered as, finished with his task, he opened the RV's driver's door and climbed into the seat beside her.

"Tell it to the judge, baby," he drawled, unconcerned, flashing her another insolent grin as he fished *her* key ring from his pocket and, after jangling it before her pointedly to let her know that even if she'd somehow managed to get free, she couldn't have driven away, inserted the proper key into the ignition. The engine sprang to life. Putting the automatic gearshift into drive, Rafer carefully maneuvered the RV and Jeep from the clearing and back onto the blacktop road beyond the woods. "You wouldn't listen. You wouldn't agree to lay off Dolan Pike. You're stubborn enough to keep hounding him and me both, and I've got a sneaking suspicion, you see, that Pike'll find your face a lot more attractive than mine, that if you somehow get the jump on me, you'll sucker him into your clutches. So, I'm just going to make sure you don't get in my way."

"By abducting me? I'll have your bounty-hunting license for this, Starr!"

"I don't think so. It'll be your word against mine, Hayley. And even if the law believes you, you'll look real foolish in the business, admitting that another bounty hunter got the best of you. How's that going to help you keep your agency afloat?"

She'd no reply to that, for the simple reason that it was all too true. Of course, Rafer would have thought everything through before taking such a drastic step as this.

"Do you even have the slightest idea where Pike is, or are you just driving aimlessly?" she asked tartly. "If you'd give me the key to these cuffs, I could do some hacking with my computer, find out if he used any major credit card either last night or this morning."

To her surprise Rafer reached into the front pocket of his fatigues, withdrawing the key to the handcuffs and tossing it to her.

"Don't go getting any wild ideas, Hayley. I secured all your weapons in that closet you use as a gun safe. I've got the key to it, and I will, without a doubt, hear you if you attempt to pick the lock. Furthermore, if you attack me while I'm driving, I will most

assuredly run us off the road, wrecking your RV—
which I don't think you want me to do, especially
since you've got money problems. How'd you afford
this thing, anyway?''

''I bought it with the settlement from Dad's life
insurance policy. It—it seemed the best thing to do at
the time. Dad had been ill...his heart. As a result he
left a lot of outstanding medical bills at his death, and
I needed funds to pay for his funeral and to keep the
agency solvent while I settled his affairs, besides. So
I sold our house to cover everything. But that didn't
matter. It was...so empty afterward, so full of
memories.''

''I'm sorry. I didn't mean to hit a nerve, Hayley.''

''It's all right. I've had time to grieve, time to ad-
just—at least, as well as anyone ever does after losing a loved one, I guess. Dad's been gone for three
years now.''

''And you've been alone all that time—no other
family?''

''None other than an ex-husband, an oil man who
didn't find it quite so exciting, after all, being married to a 'macho-woman' bounty hunter, as he often
called me.'' Her soft, resigned tone was tinged with
bitterness at the memory.

Rafer shot her a penetrating glance from beneath
his lashes.

"Man was a fool. There's nothing macho about you, Hayley." His eyes took in her sweep of silky, honey blond hair, her porcelain skin tinted with rose, her delicate bones and her long, slender fingers with their carefully polished nails. "Strong, yes. Macho, no."

"Yeah, well, maybe I'd do better if I actually *looked* like people seem to expect a female bounty hunter to look." She sighed, for the thought had occurred to her before, yet she'd always rebelled against it. Why should she be compelled to sacrifice her femininity in order to accomplish what was traditionally considered a man's job? she'd wondered—and found no good answer. "What about you? Do you have any family?"

"Nope." For a long moment Rafer was silent, and Hayley thought he wasn't going to say any more. But then he continued. "My folks are dead. My older brother stepped on a land mine in 'Nam, and my ex-wife got 'sick and tired'—or so she claimed—of my being away so much during my stint in the service. She ran off with some homebody while I was down in South America."

There was a world of explanation in those few terse sentences, Hayley reflected soberly, understanding now why he was such a loner, among other things.

"I'm sorry." Having unfastened the handcuffs, she laid them and the key aside. "South America. Is that where Wenona Pike's brother was killed? I mean, I don't want to pry, but... I heard some rumors that you'd pulled some wild stunt down there and had beaten up a fellow officer afterward for his having jeopardized men's lives on a mission, so I—I just wondered...."

"Yeah, that's where Wenona's brother bought it. He was cut down by an Uzi—not a particularly pleasant way to die, I assure you. Afterward I... went a little crazy, charged up a hill, guns blazing, inside the compound that was our target. It was a reckless, fool thing to do, actually, and just sheer, dumb luck that I survived. When it was over, I knew for sure that the officer in charge of the operation had withheld certain vital information that would have made a difference to us, saved some men's lives... so, yeah, in a blind fury after the mission, I attacked him, and we fought. I resigned my commission shortly thereafter."

Rafer didn't need to say any more. Hayley could sense, understand and sympathize with his bitterness and disillusionment. It was terrible to lose faith in what you'd believed.

"Well... I'll go see if I can turn up anything on Pike." Rising, she headed back into the body of the

RV, retrieved her laptop computer and sat down at the table, starting up the internal modem. From long practice, her fingers flew deftly over the keys. Eyes glued to the screen, she scanned the information that appeared, working swiftly and competently. "Jackpot!" she exclaimed after a while, elated as she shut down her system and returned to the cab.

"What'd you find out?" Rafer asked.

"Pike used a credit card last night to pay for a long-distance telephone call placed from the Wind River Motel, which is located in a town some miles up the road." She detailed the particulars she'd discovered about Pike's call.

"Then I'm more certain than ever that he's headed for his uncle's cabin," Rafer said when she'd finished. "It's up in the mountains, way off the beaten path—Pike's bolt-hole, where he goes to hide out when things are too hot for him to handle, according to Wenona. But she gave me directions, so I can find it. You got a map of Wyoming, Hayley?"

"Yes." She was already pulling it from the map pocket in the door panel as she spoke, unfolding it, determining their shortest route as Rafer outlined what Wenona had told him.

Presently they were under way. Hayley was filled with exhilaration, despite herself, at the thought that even if Rafer *had* technically kidnapped her, they were, in reality, now more or less working together as a team.

The next few days passed without incident as Hayley and Rafer headed west toward the cabin that belonged to Dolan Pike's uncle. Even towing the Jeep, they made relatively good time in the RV, with Hayley periodically spelling Rafer at the wheel. They talked as they drove, and when there was nothing worth listening to on the radio, Hayley popped CDs into the compact-disc player. Rafer liked music as much as she did and approved of her extensive collection of jazz, blues, and rock and roll. Although she remained, technically, his prisoner, she made no attempt to escape from him, not even when they stopped for gas and groceries at convenience stores, where she might conceivably have got away from him or at least asked for help. She'd never had any real fear that Rafer would truly harm her physically, that her life was in any way threatened by him. And now that she knew he didn't intend by some devious means to rid himself of her, leaving her behind somewhere, she was perfectly content to stay with him.

They had a great deal in common; he was surprisingly good company when he chose to be—besides being a comforting presence both at night and at roadside stops, during the latter of which previously, when alone, Hayley had on numerous occasions been forced to endure not only wolf whistles and sly suggestions from local male yokels, but also actually to defend herself once or twice from jerks who'd proved overly aggressive. Although she still attracted admiring male glances, no one insulted her with Rafer at her side, his arm possessively around her slender waist, his eyes making it clear that he was not the kind of man to back down from a challenge. Still, Hayley was so accustomed to taking care of herself that it was only after incurring Rafer's growl of displeasure that she stopped automatically reaching for doors and her billfold.

"You don't have to prove anything to me, baby," he declared once, frowning. "I know you're perfectly capable of opening your own doors and paying your own way. But equality of the sexes doesn't have to preclude a man's showing a woman a little common courtesy, does it? And it is *your* RV and not my Jeep we're racking up the miles on. And I don't think you'd argue the fact that I'm eating my share of the food, either, would you? So it seems only fair that I should foot the bills for the gas and groceries."

Put that way, Hayley could hardly disagree. In fact, deep down inside, she was forced to admit that having someone look after her for a change—especially when that someone was as handsome and proficient as Rafer—was a heady experience. She didn't need a man. Still, as time passed, she grew increasingly aware that she did *want* one, wanted Rafer. When he kissed her, touched her, as he did now and then, and when he lay wrapped around her at night in the bunk over the RV's cab, she knew that the only reason she'd not yet let him make love to her was because she feared being used, rejected and hurt again. Still, the realization that Rafer was not Logan *did* cross her mind more than once as they drove along, providing food for thought.

By this time they were deep into the wooded mountains. And now the crude blacktop road they'd been following for some time ended without warning, turning into a narrow, rough dirt track, which led to the cabin where they suspected Pike was holed up. Obviously they could go no farther in the RV. After pulling off into a little clearing and switching off the ignition, Rafer just sat there silently for a long moment, drumming his fingers on the steering wheel. Then, at last, he turned to Hayley.

"I don't suppose I could talk you into staying here while I bring Pike down?"

"No—and if you're considering handcuffing me to the seat belt again, forget it! If something should happen to you, I don't want to be stranded here, at Pike's mercy. If his treatment of Wenona is any indication of his attitude toward women, I doubt he'd be above slapping me around and raping me, too, if he got the chance—especially if he learned I'm a bounty hunter after his hide.''

At the thought of Pike's hands on Hayley, something wild and primal tore through Rafer. He clenched the steering wheel so tightly that he was surprised it didn't break off its shaft.

''I'd kill Pike before I'd let that happen. I hope you know that, Hayley.'' His voice was so grim and intent, his face so dark and murderous, that her eyes were wide as she nodded in response. This was a side of him that she'd known he must possess but that was still frightening to see, making her realize just how considerate his treatment of her these past few days had actually been, how he'd restrained himself in the face of her rebellion and obstinacy. This man could have broken her both physically and mentally had he so chosen. The fact that he had not spoke volumes. ''Get changed, and get your gear,'' Rafer said abruptly, tossing Hayley her key ring before opening the door and sliding from his seat. ''We'll take the Jeep from here.''

While Rafer unhitched the Jeep, Hayley quickly changed into a T-shirt, jeans and hiking boots. Then she unlocked the closet she used as a gun safe, slipping on the shoulder holster in which she carried her Glock 19 when she didn't need her handbag. Withdrawing her sturdy backpack, she filled it with essential food, bottled water, clothing and equipment, at the last moment including, despite its weight, her Kevlar vest. It might have been only the dreariness of the day, the sullen grey sky from which spring rain drizzled, but her sixth sense had begun to prickle warningly, and Hayley had learned from experience always to trust her gut instinct. She closed the backpack, setting it and also her sleeping bag to one side, then stood debating whether to take her shotgun or her assault rifle. At last she selected the latter.

"I prefer the AR-15 myself," Rafer said as he rejoined her, his glance swiftly taking in with approval her appearance, her preparations.

"Of course. It shoots straight and fires more rounds per minute. But you know what they say...straight or not, this baby—" she indicated her Kalashnikov AK-47 "—always at least shoots, and unfortunately, the same can't be said of the AR-15."

"Unfortunately," he agreed dryly.

Hayley pulled on her long, drab green rain poncho she'd bought at an Army surplus store, then hoisted her backpack onto her shoulders and picked up her rifle and sleeping bag.

"So...what do you think?" She flashed Rafer a flirtatious smile that made his pulse race as she teasingly strutted like a model before him.

"I think it's too bad the Marines were only looking for a few good men." His eyes roamed over her
slowly, smoldering like twin coals, making her heart
thud wildly in her breast. "Come on. Let's go before
I forget why we're really out here all alone in the
woods."

Together, after locking the RV, they loaded the
Jeep, to which Rafer had thoughtfully fastened the
loose vinyl top—for her sake, Hayley knew, sensing
that he wouldn't have bothered otherwise, despite the
drizzle. He turned on the heater, too. For although
the top kept out the rain, the cool, damp spring wind
slithered through every crevice where the top's flaps
joined the vehicle. Muddy, the narrow, wending track
they followed was such that the going was slow and
rough. Occasionally Hayley was compelled to hold on
to the roll bar above her head to keep from being
jolted too severely. They'd got a late-afternoon start;
twilight fell swiftly in the woods. At dark, Rafer insisted that they stop and camp for the night. There
was no point in plowing on and becoming lost. It was
not likely that Pike, if he were indeed at his uncle's
cabin, would venture from it tonight.

They pitched the small tent Rafer carried in the
Jeep. But such kindling as they might have found
would have been too wet to burn. So, foregoing a
poor, smoky fire, it was by the soft, glowing light of

Rafer's Coleman lantern that they consumed supper straight out of cans—a meal that Hayley somehow still found the most romantic she'd ever eaten. It was peaceful in the woods; the rain that now fell harder beat a soothing tattoo upon the tent in which she and Rafer huddled, one flap open so they could see out into the darkness. The rich, earthy scents of the rain and woods filled the night air; the boughs of evergreens and the greening leaves on the deciduous trees rustled in the soughing wind. It was as though she and Rafer were alone in all the world. Yet, unlike the previous nights they'd spent together, he was strangely silent, brooding. Hayley didn't know what he was thinking, but she was wise enough not to ask. People had a right to their privacy, she'd always believed. If a man chose to share his thoughts, she was glad to listen; if he didn't, she wasn't the kind of woman to press. So she said little, not even bothering to protest when Rafer handcuffed her wrist to his to ensure that she wouldn't sneak off in his Jeep, like a thief in the night, leaving him behind, as, after a while, they zipped their sleeping bags together to share their bodies' warmth and, extinguishing the lantern's flame, crawled inside the makeshift double bed, Hayley instinctively settling into the now familiar curve of Rafer's strong arms.

After a time it came to her gently, sweetly, as she lay there listening to the drumming rain, that somehow, despite everything, she'd fallen in love with this solitary man who held her so close and secure in the darkness.

Chapter Four

The Mountains
Wyoming

It was Rafer's disjointed, muttered ravings, followed by his hoarse cries and violent thrashing that wakened her abruptly. Disoriented in the darkness and her unfamiliar surroundings, Hayley didn't at first know where she was, and erroneously assumed she was in her RV, under assault. It was only when she tried to bring her right fist up to defend herself that, after a moment, she realized she was handcuffed to Rafer and that he was suffering a nightmare undoubtedly born of his time spent in combat. Her father, a veteran of World War II, had continued in his dreams to relive past battles more than forty years after his service to his country had ended, so she was not unfamiliar with such episodes. With the greatest of difficulty, she finally managed with her left hand to light the Coleman lantern so its soft glow dimly illuminated the tent. Then, keeping her voice low, she spoke to Rafer, careful not to touch him, knowing from experience that he might inadvertently mistake her for an enemy and attempt to kill her in his sleep. Once, when, hearing her father's terrible shouts, she'd run urgently into his room to waken him, he had, deep in the throes of one of his own nightmares, tried to throttle her, unutterably stricken when he'd roused to find his hands at her throat. Knowing what war did to people was why Hayley hated it, why any rational person did. Only madmen and fools started wars; only wackos, mercenaries, and young Turks gloried in them—and it was always women who grieved and tried to pick up the pieces afterward.

"Rafer, it's Hayley. Wake up. You're having a nightmare. Rafer, do you hear me?" Like a litany she repeated the words until, at last, her soothing voice pierced the veil of his subconscious and he suddenly sat bolt upright, glancing about the shadowy tent wildly before, with a growl, he grabbed her roughly, flung her down and pinned her to the ground. He was big and strong; his dark visage was hard with murderous intent in the half-light, frightening her. Still, Hayley forced herself to swallow her fear, to remain calm. Gently she laid her hand against his cheek. "Rafer, it's me, Hayley."

After a long, tense moment his eyes filled with recognition and remorse.

"Hayley. Oh, baby, I'm sorry. I didn't hurt you, did I?"

"No. I've been through this before...with Dad. You were having a nightmare—about South America, I think."

"Yeah, these woods...this rain...it was like being down there in the jungle all over again tonight—" He broke off abruptly, his face bleak, his eyes shadowed before he hooded them so she couldn't read his thoughts.

"It's all right. I understand."

Her heart, so full of her newfound love for him, ached unendurably as she realized then why he'd been so brooding and withdrawn earlier. Instinctively she wanted to heal his wounds, to salve his scars, to make the world and his pain go away. He'd been right: they were alike, he and she, Hayley thought in some distant chasm of her mind. And now, they lay together like two chrysalids, cocooned in the woodland tent beneath the still-falling rain, with only each other for strength, for sustenance, each yearning to feed the desperate hunger of the body and soul, to break free of the restraints that bound them, to metamorphose into something finer, to create life—despite how fleeting—in the face of death, which had haunted them both and perhaps waited for them tomorrow.

Perhaps her eyes revealed her thoughts, Hayley reflected, for no man had ever looked at her as Rafer did then, as though he knew that, in moments, he would possess her intimately, utterly, and that afterward, she would belong to him irrevocably for the rest of her days. In that instant her world contracted sharply to the tent's interior, as though some unknown force had indeed magically woven it into a cocoon, hushing the night, the woods, the wind and the rain, although it was only that her senses shut them out. She became so keenly attuned to Rafer that she and he breathed as one. He wanted her; she could see it in his eyes. His nostrils flared as, slowly reaching up, she wrapped her hand in his glossy mane of dark brown hair, faintly surprised by its softness as she drew him down to meet her moist, parted lips. She hadn't expected that, although his mouth was as starving as her own, he would permit himself only a taste of her before he suddenly tore himself away, swearing softly, shaking with the force of his emotions, his arousal, the aftermath of his nightmare.

"I don't want pity, Hayley—especially not from you!" he grated.

"I'm not offering you any... only myself, if you want me... if you'll have me," she said quietly. "I know about pain, Rafer—and that it's easier shared."

"No. I won't be... any good for you like this. You deserve better than to be dragged down into my hell."

Another woman might have misunderstood, but Hayley didn't. She knew Rafer meant that his current mood precluded slowness and tenderness, that he would use her as he willed to assuage the feral feelings, the urgent desire, the driving need his nightmare had unleashed inside him. Still, he was not so hard and brutal as he thought if he feared to hurt her—and she wasn't afraid.

"I don't care!" she whispered fiercely. "I don't care. Take me to where you are...."

There was between them then an interminable moment as highly charged as a night sky alive with heat lightning, the silence broken only by the gentle rhythm of the rain, the faint cadence of the wind, the harsh raggedness of their indrawn breaths. Rafer's glittering eyes evidenced his brief, internal struggle before they darkened with defeat and desire, and with a low groan he fell upon Hayley blindly, his lips swooping to capture hers savagely, a devouring kiss that was hot and hard, purely primal. Intuitively she acquiesced to his wild, possessive onslaught, her mouth yielding softly for the invasion of his demanding tongue that scalded her own, taking her breath, shattering and scattering her senses as surely and strongly as though she'd suddenly been swept up by some unbridled, atavistic storm, whirled away to a dark, mindless place where she was oblivious of all but sensation. In its wake, reason fled, and instinct prevailed. She knew nothing but Rafer, his lips and tongue and hands, rough, restless, ravaging, covetously claiming her, binding her to him as inescapably as his handcuffs that chained the two of them together.

She was only dimly aware of his impatiently tearing away their clothes, of his muttered imprecation when both their T-shirts and her lacy bra caught and tangled on the cuffs, of the knife that gleamed momentarily in his hand before he ruthlessly cut the garments free, then flung them aside, driving the blade into the ground. Slick with sweat, his naked body slid across her own, dark flesh covering pale as he rolled slightly on his side, one corded leg riding between her thighs, opening her. With his impris-

oned hand, he caught her free one, pinioning her
wrists above her head. Then he drew back a little to
look at her, his eyes like twin flames, scorching her
soft, bare skin as his gaze raked her slowly, lingering
on her breasts and the vulnerably exposed juncture of
her inner thighs. Gratification curved his carnal
mouth as, of their own volition, Hayley's rosy nipples grew as hard and taut as tightly furled buds from
the wild thrill of mingled fear and excitement that
shot through her at his appraising glance, at the tantalizing thought that, soon, he would be a part of her.

Watching her all the while, he deliberately cupped
and squeezed her breast, pressing it high. His thumb
rotated around her nipple before he inexorably lowered his head, and his tongue rasped across the peak,
making her gasp from the potent waves of pleasure
that radiated through her. She longed fervently to
touch him, to run her hands over his beautiful, muscular body, the sheeny, coppery skin, the scars from
old wounds that marked it, a mute testament to his
will to survive. But Rafer held her fast, silently making her understand that this was a quintessential male
act of dominance, of conquering, of possession—as
he'd obliquely warned her that it would be, such was
the dark mood that gripped him—and that he rev-
eled in not only her strength, but also, as a perverse

result, her helplessness against his own greater power. His sex, hard and heavy, nudged with heated promise against her belly as his mouth fastened upon her nipple, sucking greedily, his tongue laving and teasing it until Hayley moaned and strained irrepressibly against him, wordlessly begging for more. Feverishly his lips and free hand moved everywhere upon her then. He kissed her wildly, fiercely—her mouth, her temples, her throat, and then her breasts, burying his face between them, licking away the sweat that moistened their valley. His fingers tangled roughly in the strands of her damp, tousled hair before following the trail his searing lips had blazed, then slipping down her belly and the curve of her hip to roam along her inner thighs, compelling them even wider apart.

His hand sought and found her downy softness, cupped her mound, stroked the moist petals that trembled and unfolded of their own needy accord at his bold exploration. His thumb flicked and taunted the key to her delight until Hayley was frantic, whimpering with desire, bucking against him in a silent plea for assuagement of the hollow, burning ache that had seized her, setting her afire with its atavistic flame. With two fingers, Rafer momentarily eased her desperate yearning, probed her slowly, deeply, only to withdraw them, spreading quicksilver heat before sliding them into her again, harder, faster, his mouth claiming hers, his tongue plunging between her lips, mimicking the exquisitely torturous movements of his hand until Hayley gasped for breath, thought she could endure no more, would go mad with wanting.

"Please," she whispered imploringly. "Please, Rafer."

"Tell me that you want me, baby," he demanded huskily against her mouth.

"I want you! I want you, Rafer...."

With a rasp, a groan, a calling of her name, his body urgently covering hers, his hand burrowing beneath her back, lifting her hips to receive him, he drove down into her then, a single, sudden, hard, deep thrust that pierced her to the very core, making her cry out softly, her breath catch raggedly in her throat at the mingled pain and pleasure of his forceful entry.

"God, you're tight," he muttered thickly, his own breath harsh, hot against her flesh. And such was the note of triumph and satisfaction in his low voice that she knew that he recognized that he was the only man she'd had in a long while, and that he was glad of it. "Tight and wet and hot for me, just as I've wanted you. Damn, how I've wanted you! From the moment I first saw you, I've ached to be inside you, like this...." His eyes sought their joining, then riveted on her flushed face again, mesmerizing her. "You're mine, Hayley...mine...."

He kissed her mouth and breasts again as he lay atop her, his weight pressing her down, his sex pulsing within her, filling her to overflowing, molding and stretching her to accommodate him before, slowly, he began to move against her, driving in and out of her in a rhythm as old as time and that grew increasingly stronger and swifter as what little control he'd had deserted him. Hayley's blood roared in her ears as she writhed against him, wrapping her long legs around him and arching her hips to meet each savage thrust. His hand was upon her mound, kneading her as he plunged into her, bringing her rapidly to a gloriously explosive climax. Her head thrashed; she cried out, bucking wildly against him, then straining, tensing as wave after wave of unbearable pleasure erupted inside her, swept through her, blinding her to everything as the world spun away in a burst of dazzling brilliance. Her muscles clenched uncontrollably around Rafer's sex, maddening him, so he knew nothing any longer but the vibrant throbbing of her body around his, spurring his own exigent, primal need for release. His hands grasped and tightened bruisingly around her wrists, holding her down. He buried his head against her shoulder, his breathing labored, his own low cry ringing in her ears as he abruptly shuddered violently against her, long and hard, spilling himself inside her.

When it was over, he eased himself from her slowly, reluctantly, then searched for the key to the handcuffs and impatiently unlocked them and cast them aside before pulling her into his strong arms, kissing her deeply as he cradled her sweating body against his own. Her head rested against his broad, furry chest; she could feel his heart pounding as furiously as hers. His hand stroked her hair gently as they lay still together in the quiet afterglow, each marveling at the chemistry that had ignited so rapidly and explosively between them.

"I'm sorry, Hayley," Rafer murmured after a long while in the silence.

"Don't be. I wanted it as much as you did."

"It was too quick, too rough. I knew that it would be ... I tried to warn you—"

"It doesn't matter. I understood."

"I know that you did. That was the beauty of it. You gave me what I wanted, what I needed, Hayley. Now, let me do the same for you."

Rafer was already aroused, ready for her again; her very nearness intoxicated him so. But this time when he took her, he was so infinitely patient, so incredibly tender that when it was done and he'd extinguished the lantern, Hayley lay with tears on her cheeks in the darkness at the thought that she was nearly forty years old and she had only just learned what it meant to be made love to by a man.

She awoke in the morning to the feel of Rafer's mouth and hands upon her, once more taking her to paradise before he rose, drew on his clothes and went outside to start loading their gear into the Jeep. Mist cloaked the mountains, and it had begun to drizzle again, so the spring air was chilly, and Hayley was grateful she'd thought to bring along a long-sleeved flannel shirt. She shrugged it on over her T-shirt, leaving it unbuttoned, ends trailing. Once she'd finished dressing, she brushed her hair, then double-checked the spare magazines she'd packed for both her pistol and rifle, stuffing the fully loaded clips into the ammo vest she wore. Then, pulling on her poncho, she stepped from the tent to help Rafer dismantle it.

She knew that her eyes shone when they met his, but Hayley couldn't help it. Not even reminding herself that he'd not spoken of loving her, either last night or this morning, dimmed what she felt in her heart for him. He was a man to whom such words would not come easily; she understood that. Still, she thought he must care for her, wouldn't, *couldn't* have made love to her as he had that second time, otherwise. But she was too proud to ask him, too afraid of being rejected and hurt again. She didn't want to know just yet if their relationship didn't mean to him what it did to her. She wanted to hold on to what they shared, for just as long as she could.

That her thoughts were Rafer's own, she was unaware. He'd never before known a woman like her, had never dreamed he'd find her like in all the world. She was everything he'd ever wanted, needed in a woman—a beguiling mixture of femininity, strength, intelligence, wit, sensitivity and vulnerability. He felt that last night her luminous eyes had looked into the harshest, darkest corners of his soul and that, instead of shrinking in fear as other women had, she'd responded with sweetness and light, opening herself to him unequivocally, trusting him not to hurt her any more than he had. She had not made such a commitment lightly, Rafer knew; nor had he taken it so. He would always be moody and brooding—and, where Hayley was concerned, jealously possessive and zealously protective, stronger than she. But all that, too, she would somehow understand, he sensed instinctively. The thought of losing her was more painful than any wound he'd ever suffered in combat. Still, he could not humble her pride, either, to keep her safe and secure.

"I may be *your* baby, Rafer, but I'm not *a* baby," she'd uttered fiercely when, his mind filled with worry for her, for what they might face this morning if they indeed found Dolan Pike at his uncle's isolated cabin, Rafer had again suggested that she stay behind, wait for him to bring down Pike alone.

Now, as they climbed in the Jeep and started down the track, Rafer bit back the anxious words that sprang to his tongue. Hayley had trusted him; now, he must trust her, must have faith that she knew her job as well as he, that she was indeed his equal in all things that mattered, because deep down inside, he knew he wouldn't want her any other way.

They drove through the mist in silence, not even playing the radio; not only because the sound might carry to the cabin, but also because they needed the quiet mentally to psych themselves up for the expected confrontation with Pike. Despite the light rain, they had the top off the Jeep now, so they could without hindrance scan their surroundings. Now and then, Hayley raised to her eyes a pair of high-powered binoculars to look through the trees for the cabin.

Presently she said, "There's the cabin. I see it. Your hunch was right—Pike's Dually is parked out front."

Wordlessly Rafer maneuvered the Jeep so it blocked the track, then switched off the ignition, cutting off Pike's main escape route.

"We'll go the rest of the way on foot. I don't want him to hear the engine. Hayley, you've got to promise me that you'll stick close behind me—and I mean it. Pike's a woodsman. He's probably got all kinds of traps, snares, pits and maybe even *pungee* sticks rigged up out here. I know I sure as hell would." His voice was grim, and she shivered, both at the thought of what Pike might have waiting in store for them and that Rafer knew how to set such devices himself and doubtless had in the past, maybe had even killed people with them.

Wide-eyed, she nodded, hoping she didn't have to worry about snakes, too. Although Rafer hadn't said as much, she knew he was the expert on this terrain, and that was a whole lot different from his just arbitrarily giving her orders. That being the case, as they hiked through the woods, carefully skirting the occasional trap they indeed discovered, she followed hard on his heels until, from where they stood, they could without their field glasses spy the cabin that sat in a little clearing: a crude, ramshackle affair built of logs and having a corrugated tin roof. From the fieldstone chimney, smoke drifted, permeating the air with a scent Hayley had always loved. Since Pike had made no attempt to conceal the black Dually parked out in front of the porch, when a rundown barn was handy, he clearly thought himself safe from pursuit at his uncle's cabin, had no idea that his miserable, terrified ex-wife had finally worked up gumption enough to dare to give away the secret of his hiding place to Rafer.

"I'll take the front." Rafer kept his voice low so the sound wouldn't carry on the wind and alert Pike of their presence. "You go around back."

Nodding again to show she understood, Hayley withdrew her automatic from the shoulder holster beneath her poncho and checked to ensure there was a round in the chamber. Then she turned to go, startled when Rafer suddenly grabbed her, his eyes searching her face intently, as though to memorize its every detail, before he kissed her, hard and deep.

"Hayley, for God's sake, be careful," he muttered urgently as he released her. "It's only a short step from rape and armed robbery to murder—and Pike's poised to take it."

"I know. I will. Rafer, I—" She broke off abruptly, biting her lower lip. *I love you,* she'd wanted to say. "You take care, too."

Then quickly, tears stinging her eyes, Hayley turned and began to make her way furtively through the thin woods at the edge of the clearing to the rear of the cabin, her heart racing, her adrenaline pumping as it inevitably did when she closed in on a bounty. Only a fool was never afraid, her father had always told her, warning her that if she ever lost that edge born of fear and caution, she would most likely lose her life, as well. But it'd been three long years since she'd had to worry about someone else's life, too; that of a man she loved. That thought was uppermost in her mind as she crept near to the cabin, using the trees for cover until she was able to sprint across the weed-grown yard to where a rusted old pickup perched on cinder blocks out back, not far from the cabin. Crouching down low behind the junked vehicle, Hayley flattened herself against its side and started to inch her way along its length toward the mangled front bumper, from where she'd have a clear shot at Pike should he come barreling out the cabin's back door. Finally reaching her vantage point, she hunkered there for what seemed like hours, waiting for Rafer's move, her mouth dry despite the rain that drizzled down her face in the gray morning light.

At last when it felt as though her limbs had petrified from immobility, she heard Rafer kick in the cabin's front door and then shouts, followed by a frightening exchange of shots.

"Rafer!" Hayley cried softly, her heart leaping to her throat. *"Rafer!"* And cursing the slippery wet ground, she began to run.

She expected Pike, if he'd survived, to come out the back door. Instead, just seconds later, he crashed through one of the cabin's rear windows, sending shards of glass and wood splinters from the frame flying in every direction, before, with a thud, he hit the muddy earth, rolling. Skidding to an abrupt halt some yards away, Hayley took up a firing stance and, both hands wrapped around its grip, leveled her pistol.

"Freeze, Pike!" she yelled.

But wild-eyed, appearing suddenly, strangely, to move in slow motion, he sprang to his feet, discharging the gun in his hands even as he rose. The bullet took only seconds to strike her, seconds in which Hayley realized instinctively that she was going to be hit, that her body couldn't respond in time to her brain's frantic signals to her legs. Then, suddenly, the slug exploded against her chest, the violent impact knocking her flat, ripping the air from her lungs and leaving her feeling as though they were on fire as incredible, searing pain erupted inside her.

Desperately, feeling as though she were suffocating, she gasped for breath, some dark, faraway corner of her stunned mind dimly recognizing that Pike, his weaselly face cold, merciless, now towered over her, that he was fixing to shoot her again. It seemed an eternity that she stared in to the long, blued barrel of his .22-caliber Ruger aimed at her head, knowing with certainty that the next bullet had death written on it, that this was what it was to die, and silently cursing fate that it should claim her now, when she was so newly in love, had everything for which to live, everything she'd never thought to find.

"Nooooo!" Rafer's hoarse, stricken cry echoed through the woods as he jerked open the cabin's back door, nearly tearing it from its hinges, and bounded through the doorframe, his shotgun in his hands.

Pike turned to confront this new threat—and Hayley knew nothing then except that he was going to kill Rafer and then her, that Rafer was going to lose his life because of her. At the realization, she somehow miraculously found the strength from someplace deep inside her to raise her automatic, still clutched in her right hand, and to depress the trigger even as Pike pulled his own. Pike was taken off guard when her first slug bored into his leg, staggering him, the wound spurting blood, spraying her all over before her second bullet slammed into his shoulder, sending him sprawling as, at last, her pistol slid weakly from her grasp and she began trying to crawl toward Rafer, knowing only that he'd been hit, that blood dripped down his arm.

"Hayley! Oh, God, Hayley!" His voice seemed to be coming at her from a distance as, running to her side, pausing only just long enough to kick Pike's gun away, Rafer knelt over her, distraught at the sight of the blood, pinkened by the drizzle, that spattered and trickled down her poncho. He laid aside his shotgun, his hands yanking frantically at the long, twisted garment, its hem caught between her legs. She was dully aware that all the while he tore madly at her clothing, he was alternately muttering, shouting, swearing, threatening to murder Pike, who still lay moaning, writhing and bleeding on the ground. "If she dies, I'll kill you, you bastard!"

"V-v-vest," Hayley managed to rasp faintly, her eyes fluttering from the dizziness that assailed her.

"Don't try to talk, sweetheart." Rafer's expression was grim as, having hauled off her poncho, his fingers now fumbled with the lacings of her ammo vest. He was shaking so badly that he couldn't pull the wide strips from their metal loops. Snatching his knife from the leather sheath at his waist, he quickly sliced through the troublesome lacings, staring down at her chest, dumbfounded by the sight of the now misshapen bullet lodged in the Kevlar vest she wore beneath, over her flannel shirt and T-shirt. Understanding dawned; overwhelming relief pervaded his body. The blood was not hers; it was Pike's. Overcome with emotion, Rafer gathered her into his arms, rocking her, stroking her damp hair, kissing her face and mouth feverishly and murmuring, "Oh, Hayley, Hayley, my brave, beautiful, intelligent woman! You wore a vest. Thank God, you wore a vest! I couldn't have borne to lose you! I love you! I love you...."

She'd never before known such joy as she knew in that moment. Her heart soared. It was, she thought dazedly, actually worth being shot to hear him speak those words—although she knew he wouldn't have agreed.

"Love you...too...Rafer," she croaked as her labored breathing finally began to ease, the pain in her chest growing less agonizing.

After a long while, he drew away, brushing the dripping strands of her hair from her face and kissing her brow gently before he rose and went to attend to Pike, tearing away strips of Pike's T-shirt to staunch his bleeding and bandage his wounds until the first aid kit in the Jeep could be accessed. To Hayley's relief, Rafer's own injury was only a flesh wound; Pike's bullet had just nicked Rafer's arm. Hayley's shots had spoiled Pike's aim, had saved Rafer's life, just as he'd saved her own by appearing in the cabin's doorway when he had. When Rafer had finished his makeshift ministering, he handcuffed Pike's wrists behind his back and roughly hauled him to his feet, nudging him forward with the shotgun.

"I heard you always worked alone," Pike grumbled as he glared at Rafer angrily.

"Not anymore. I think you've met my partner, Hayley Harper," Rafer's reply was spoken coolly, casually, as he turned to help her up, his arm around her waist to keep her from falling when her legs trembled weakly beneath her—and not solely from her ordeal, either.

"Yeah, some angel she turned out to be!" Pike sneered.

"Dolan, that's probably the one and only thing you're ever going to get right in your entire life," Rafer observed, his eyes unmistakably alight with love as he gazed tenderly at Hayley by his side before, together, they started down the mountain.

She was now both poorer and richer than she'd ever been in her life, Hayley thought with a sigh as, her eyes closed, she leaned back in the passenger's seat, grateful to be resting, while Rafer wheeled the RV, towing the Jeep behind, down the dirt road that led away from Wenona Pike's shack. For capturing Dolan Pike and turning him into the local sheriff's office, all Hayley had to show was a massive, ugly, black-and-blue bruise tinged with yellow on her chest—and the memory of a tearfully overjoyed Wenona with a $25,000 check clutched in her hand and three suddenly hopeful, wide-eyed children hugging their mother excitedly.

"Rafer, I sure hope you meant what you said about our being partners, because after agreeing to your good deed, I am flat broke."

"That's all right, baby. I think you've got other, equally as valuable and coveted assets to bring to our merger." His voice, while teasing, nevertheless held a note she'd come to recognize. And when she opened her eyes, it was to see that his own glittered with desire as he slowly appraised the "assets" to which he'd referred. Remembering how he'd inventoried them at quite some length last night, she blushed.

"Harper-Starr, Incorporated. I like the sound of that," she drawled impudently.

"Shooting Starr, Incorporated," he corrected just as insolently.

"Starr-Harper?" she ventured, ignoring the sound of her father's voice in her head, telling her that Shooting Star, Incorporated was an established, respected name, one he'd have been proud and glad to have put on their own agency's letterhead if he'd thought he could have got Rafer Starr to join them that way. *Good for business, and good for you, Hayley. Go for it, puddin'!*

"Shooting Starr," Rafer repeated stubbornly, his voice firm.

"Well, I don't think that's fair at all!" Hayley snapped tartly in protest, sitting up and beginning to bristle defiantly, despite how happy she knew that her father would have been for her, how he'd not only wholeheartedly approved of Rafer, but also had thought him the man for her. "Wyoming's the Equality State—and what's equal about that?"

"A moot point, since we're leaving this state."

"We are?" Her eyebrows lifted faintly with surprise. "Where are we going?"

"Nevada."

"Why? Oh, of course...the new Wanted posters we picked up in the sheriff's office. Well, who's in Nevada?"

"Not who...what."

"What? What do you mean...what? Oh, all right, then," she conceded, frowning at the penetrating glance Rafer shot her wryly from beneath his lashes. "*What's* in Nevada?"

"Wedding chapels...lots of wedding chapels."

Hayley sat there dumbly for a moment, her heart starting to jerk erratically in her breast.

"Is this—is this a marriage proposal?" she asked faintly.

"The only one you're gonna get from me," Rafer declared, the hint of a smile now playing about the corners of his mouth.

"Obstinate, arrogant man! Still, I can think of something else I'd rather you do on your knees," she teased provocatively, suddenly filled to bursting with joy.

"Hmm. So can I." His gleaming eyes traveled over her body slowly, significantly. "Reciprocation would be nice, too."

Color flooded Hayley's cheeks again at the images evoked in her mind by their banter.

"What about children?" she inquired hastily—then held her breath as she awaited his response, because, despite her lighthearted tone, she wanted kids.

"Oh, yeah. We'll definitely make some of those, too, while we're at it—at least a couple." Rafer's eyes danced with deviltry. "I hear you have to work at that day and night to ensure success—and personally, I never have liked the thought of failure."

"But—but...what would we do with them...our children? I mean...how would we take care of them after we got them, being on the road all the time and all? I'm not going to have to give up being a bounty hunter, am I?" Hayley queried suspiciously, thinking that somehow, this sounded be too good to be true.

"Nope. After all, we *do* own an RV—and we could always buy a bigger one. We could hire a nanny, too, even a tutor, if need be. There are lots of options nowadays. Somehow, we'll work things out together—I promise you that." All touch of humor was suddenly gone from Rafer's face and tone. Earnestly he continued. "Look—I know that we're two strong-minded, independent people, Hayley. There'll be times when we'll be bound to argue, times when one of us will have to give. But I'm not afraid of commitment or compromise, either one. And no matter what, I'll never let you down as Logan did, but do everything in my power to make you happy. Is that enough for you?''

"Almost." Even though she smiled, Hayley was fighting back tears born of the love that welled in her heart for him, knowing that those last words hadn't come easily, but that he'd meant every single one of them.

"What do you mean ... almost?" Anxiety at the thought that he'd laid himself emotionally bare before her, only to be rejected and hurt flickered briefly in Rafer's uncertain eyes until he saw the smile that trembled on Hayley's lips, the poignant tears she dashed away. She would sit there and sob through every heartbreaking movie they were ever going to watch together in the RV, he knew. But that was all right. Still, he was without a doubt going to burn that nightshirt of hers, the one that read *Hard-hearted Woman,* buy her something small and black and lacy....

"Just what I said," she responded to his question, oblivious of the current direction of his thoughts. "Almost ... because I still have two more questions," she announced with feigned loftiness, recovering her composure.

"Fire away, then. Fire away…and fall back." The humor returned to Rafer's voice as he spoke the old military saying.

"Can I at least have Hayley Harper-Starr on our letterhead?"

"Of course. That's one. Now, what's the other?"

"Are you planning to handcuff me to you every single night for the rest of our lives?"

"If that's what it takes to hang on to you forever, baby, then I most certainly am!"

He was just rogue enough to do it, too, Hayley thought, tantalized, despite herself, at the notion. Still, he was *her* rogue, and she loved him. They might not have been right for others, but somehow, they were perfectly right for each other. That was the real bounty, all that counted—and besides, she'd grown rather fond of those handcuffs, actually!

"Hayley, I've answered all your questions, but you've yet to do the same for my one and only one." Rafer reminded her of his marriage proposal, a trifle impatiently, nudging her from her reverie—although the smug, arrogant note in his voice told her that he was already sure of her reply. "Well, damn it, woman!" he growled when—from pure orneriness, because he was so certain—she didn't respond, drawing out the suspense a little while longer and doing her best to restrain the laughter that bubbled in her throat at the expression on his face. "Hayley, so help me, I'm gonna cuff you to the bed in our honeymoon suite for days if you keep on! Now, answer me or else! Am I on the right road or not?"

Still taking her own sweet time, Hayley glanced deliberately, pointedly, at the passing road sign that indicated Interstate Highway 80, which she knew led to Nevada, to Reno—and to all those wedding chapels. Then at last, relenting, she looked back at Rafer, and the smile she gave him made his heart turn over, his pulse race. A teddy... he would buy her a small black lace teddy; she could wear it on their wedding night—for a few minutes, at least!

"Yes, you are definitely on the right road," she confirmed.

They had the radio on and tuned to an oldies station. Now, as though on cue, the opening strains of the Temptations' "My Girl" filled the cab. Flashing her a wicked, insolent, I-*knew*-I-was-right grin, Rafer cranked up the volume and put the pedal to the metal.

* * * * *

Dear Reader,

When my editor called me about writing
a novella for this collection, I was thrilled because this
would be my first contemporary work, and so a real
challenge for me. How would I take all those
characteristics that had always made my historical
heroes so dangerous and exciting, and put them into
today's man? Obviously, I wasn't going to do a story
about the boy next door! So I started thinking about
some of my own less-than-tame hobbies, such as,
karate and target shooting, and that led me to consider
all the action-adventure movies I've enjoyed over the
years. Then I knew I had to have a wild, seductive
hero that somebody like Mel Gibson, Steven Seagal or
Jean-Claude Van Damme might play on film. So,
thanks to those guys for Martin Riggs, Casey Ryback,
Chance Boudreaux—and for my own Rafer Starr.
Thanks, too, to my friend investigator Mauro Corvasce
for his tale about the female bounty hunter with whom
he once worked—and who, despite her skirt, "got her
man" with a flying tackle. I hope you enjoyed how my
own heroine, Hayley Harper, got Dolan Pike and her
hero, Rafer Starr, each in her own special fashion!

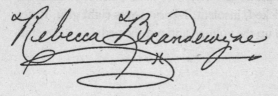

♥ SILHOUETTE
Desire

COMING NEXT MONTH

JUSTIN Diana Palmer

Texan Lovers

Shelby Jacobs had never stopped loving dark, intense Justin Ballenger, despite the fact she'd broken their engagement. She was sure he despised her, but she knew he needed to hear the truth about the past. Shelby knew she was risking everything, but Justin was more than worth it.

PEACHY'S PROPOSAL Carole Buck

Wedding Belles

Pam "Peachy" Keene was determined to lose her virginity, and she knew of only one man for the job—sexy Luc Devereaux. But Luc didn't want to help Peachy become 'experienced'. He *was* attracted to her, yet he knew she'd regret not waiting for the man she loved. How could he convince Peachy to change her mind?

LUCAS: THE LONER Cindy Gerard

Sons and Lovers

Lucas Caldwell knew Kelsey Gates was trouble! The rugged cowboy sensed the big-city reporter had discovered his lifelong secret, but Kelsey claimed she wanted only one thing: *him*. Lucas was sure she was lying, but how could he turn down such a tempting offer?

WOLFE WEDDING Joan Hohl

Big Bad Wolfe

Although wedding fever had hit his family, getting hitched was the last thing on Cameron Wolfe's mind. Sharing a cozy cabin with sexy Sandra Bradley seemed a great idea and things went well…so well that Sandra realized there was a little Wolfe on the way. She knew exactly what *she* wanted, but would the biggest, baddest Wolfe say "I do"?

COWBOY'S BRIDE Barbara McMahon

Kalli Bonotelli had dreamed of owning a ranch with Mr Right. Now she had the ranch, all she needed was the husband…so she set her sights on handsome Trace Longford. Trouble was, he didn't want her hand—he wanted her land!

MY HOUSE OR YOURS? Lass Small

Josephine Morris hadn't seen her ex-husband in almost four years when they were suddenly stranded in the last hotel room in Dallas—together. Chad Wilkins always had been a master in the bedroom, and now he was intent on wooing Josephine back into his life. She knew she should be strong, but how could she resist a veritable force of nature?

▼ SILHOUETTE

Sensation

COMING NEXT MONTH

THE MORNING SIDE OF DAWN Justine Davis

A brief moment and Cassie Cameron was hooked. She'd been unable to forget Dar Cordell, though months had passed. She was surrounded by handsome, glamorous men every day and yet Dar stood out even before she discovered his secret.

But someone else had their eye on Cassie. Would her one moment of passion with Dar have to last her a lifetime?

LOVING EVANGELINE Linda Howard

Heartbreakers

There was no doubt that the woman who called herself Evie Shaw was the key to the conspiracy threatening Robert Cannon's company—and he meant to take her down *personally*. But during that long hot Southern summer he found himself face-to-face with a breathtaking passion for a woman who *had* to be as guilty as sin…

IAIN ROSS'S WOMAN Emilie Richards

The Men of Midnight

Before Iain Ross quite knew what was happening, the earthy, irrepressible—and utterly irresistible—Billie Harper had turned his tradition-bound world upside down. But no matter how he ached for her, the curse upon his house doomed them to be enemies—and must keep them forever apart…

ANGEL AND THE BAD MAN Dallas Schulze

Travis Morgan was reputed to be bad to the bone, silent and deadly. Angie was warned, but in a desperate hour Travis came to her rescue. In a flash he branded her soul. Something hot and exciting sizzled between them…and Angie was powerless to resist it. For the first time in her life, temptation was real and it had a name—Travis.

▼ SILHOUETTE

> SPECIAL EDITION <

COMING NEXT MONTH

JUST MARRIED Debbie Macomber

Zane Ackerman's hard heart had been waiting for someone to melt it.
Lesley Walker fitted the bill so perfectly, he asked her to marry him.
But when he needed to right one final wrong, would he have to
choose between his past and a future of wedded bliss?

NO KIDS OR DOGS ALLOWED Jane Gentry

Cara Fairchild thought her mother needed a man. And since
Elizabeth was so young and beautiful, Cara knew that any man would
be happy to have her. So why had her mother settled on Steve Riker,
father of Melody, Cara's archenemy?

THE BODYGUARD AND MS JONES Susan Mallery

Mike Blackburne's life as a bodyguard had put him in exciting,
dangerous situations. Single mum Cindy Jones was raising two
children and had never left the suburbs. The only thing they agreed
on was that they were totally wrong for each other—so how come
they were falling completely and totally in love?

MORGAN'S MARRIAGE Lindsay McKenna

Morgan's Mercenaries
After a daring rescue, amnesia robbed Morgan Trayhern of any
recollections of his loved ones. Laura Trayhern had to put aside the
needs of her own wounded soul to help her husband. Could she
return Morgan to love...and reawaken the passion of their vows?

BABY ON THE DOORSTEP Cathy Gillen Thacker

Too Many Dads
When a baby was left on his front porch, Alec Roman searched like
crazy for the infant's mother. Playboy Alec was all thumbs when it
came to baby bottles and nappies, so when he found the supposed
mum's sister, he wasn't about to let her go—not even when Jade
Kincaid began to steal his bachelor heart!

CODY'S FIANCÉE Gina Ferris Wilkins

Needing to prove she'd been a good guardian to her little brother,
Dana Preston had no choice but to turn to Cody Carson for help. But
what started as a marriage of convenience turned into something
neither one of them had bargained for...

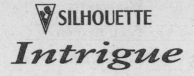

▼ SILHOUETTE
Intrigue

COMING NEXT MONTH

DARK STAR Sheryl Lynn

Mirror Images

Twenty-five years ago, Star Jones's parents had vanished. With no real evidence and no family to help her, she had to turn to private eye Austin Tack. Austin took her to more than an old, forgotten murder scene; they went on an emotional journey to discover her past. Because until Star found her past, how could she and Austin have a future?

UNDYING LAUGHTER Kelsey Roberts

Shadows and Spice

Destiny Talbott had more admirers than she could handle. Wesley Porter was intent on wooing her, but a second suitor was also vying for her attention...and his intentions seemed much more sinister.

Wesley was determined to protect his lover from this dark stalker. He wanted the last date with Destiny!

FATAL CHARM Aimée Thurlo

Dangerous Men

He was tall, dark and dangerous... Not exactly the kind of man Amanda Vila was looking for as a father for her child. He was a renegade, thrown out of law enforcement because he was prepared to use any method to locate his kidnapped daughter.

But no other man had ever made her melt with desire—not like Tony Ramos.

WHAT CHILD IS THIS? Rebecca York

43 Light Street

Armed with nothing more than some vague memories and a grainy old photo, Travis Stone sought his parents. But first he found Erin Morgan. Once they had shared a love—a that love was now forbidden. For everywhere Travis searched he found dead ends—and dead men...

Travis had placed Erin in danger. He couldn't rest until he'd made her safe again.

THE MEN OF MIDNIGHT

Three men born at the stroke of twelve and destined for love beyond their wildest dreams.

Award-winning author Emilie Richards launches her new mini-series, **The Men of Midnight**, in May 1996 with *Duncan's Lady*.

Single father Duncan Sinclair believed in hard facts and cold reality, not mist and magic. But Mara MacTavish challenged his masculinity and his hard-line beliefs. Her warmth and charm captivated both Duncan and his young daughter.

The Men of Midnight traces the friendship between Duncan, Iain and Andrew. Don't miss *Iain Ross's Woman* in June and *MacDougall's Darling* concluding the trilogy in July.

The baby is adorable...
but which man is the father?

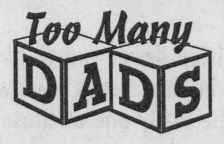

Three bachelors find their lives turned upside down when a baby is left on their doorstep.

Which one of them is the father?

Cathy Gillen Thacker asks that all-important question in her heart-warming new trilogy—
Too Many Dads

June 1996:
Baby On The Doorstep

July 1996:
Daddy To The Rescue

August 1996:
Too Many Mums

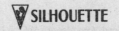

SILHOUETTE

SPECIAL EDITION